Art Town

CHRIS DIETZ

HNS Publishing | Bisbee, Arizona

All quotations from James Joyce's *Ulysses* are from the 1946 Random House edition.

Art Town

ISBN: 978-1-7335729-2-7

Cover images and all images throughout appeared in William B. Scott's 1913, *A History of Land Mammals in the Western Hemisphere*. Digitized and made available to the Public Domain by the Biodiversity Heritage Library.
Book Design: Bill Dietz

HNS Publishing
Bisbee, Arizona

For all the suicides, and the murdered

Part 1

"You know, it's a funny thing to realize you're living entirely inside yourself," which is why Dik Dik Perkins didn't. The glorious June morning fattened up inside his small, wiry frame, until it blasted from his lips and tongue, baptizing the goddess' rose bud, in the fiery world they'd made. This was the fire pose, spark of Nighttown, goddess in t-shirt in her studio in Main, on a cobbed bar stool, so only a few square inches of her lower back and upper pelvis supported her. She almost flew, or levitated, it didn't matter, this very moment one thing mattered: the perfect cum with her wings outstretched, fingers splayed, and her legs lit open, tensed feet arced. The tall studio windows dabbled prisms on her slowly twining limbs. While all Dik Dik had to do was lean in. He would have gotten down on his knees. It was their sweet. Once a week. Her place. No questions asked. She said he was the best. He loved Ava like he loved life itself. Everything slowed, kaput, nada, zilch, then bliss in the monumental erection of mouth and pussy – how fine a woman tasted, scented immersion, the great loosening, the fabulous full rapture. No hold backs. It started the buildup of his own cum. One of these days: he was eighty. 'Spry,' the yanks teased.

His duty now, resplendent worship, surrender. Kiss it! Sting it! And her response – O transfixed body cum! She's gorged immaculate, flower emergent, the big cum with the little squirt at the end. And this will I take with me, he groaned, woman satisfied, me satisfied, gamahunching in June, forever and forever – *'coming musk-rose, full of dewy wine'.*

Carlos Sanchez Arts Collective, which everybody called Main, was the former public school, Main Elementary, of Coltrane, Arizona, erected during Coltrane's mining heyday. A hundred years ago, these hallways and classrooms had resounded with raucous kids picking their noses and cheating on quizzes. Their vibrations spread across the galaxy. In the sixties, district consolidation was all the rage, and Main was abandoned. The school sat vacant. At the same time, copper prices were plummeting, and the big mining companies were relocating to South America. Coltrane, the mining district, was done for. In the late seventies, a group of local artists, many newcomers, finagled a deal to take on Main, in which upkeep was exchanged for a dollar a year to the school district. The town elders saw the wisdom of this, as art could very well, eventually, mean tourism. Dueling, drooling, caterwauling, besmirching, evolving, in fits and starts, over many years, Coltrane became an art town.

No one knew what an art town was. There were a few historic examples, like Taos and Santa Fe. There was no instruction manual. When did the mystique set in? How many ghosts were required? Tourism and art needed some razzmatazz to get sizzling – Main Elementary's building plan was the archetype repeated across the nation, two floors with a full basement. Heavy, thick, stern walls. And the kids had filled them with their cries. Basement bathrooms, next to the furnace and plumbing vortex, still startled with Cthuhlu thuds.

Dik Dik knew an even more somber education edifice, Escher prison of the mind, in the dead rowhouse suburbs, optical illusion neighborhoods, outside of London, houses of mirrors, houses of despair, where he'd grown up.

Carlos Sanchez Arts Collective, because Sanchez had been one of the founders, a key player in the 'collective', before skedaddling back to Miami. His specialty had been shaman counseling, conflating ecdysis, anisette, and psychotropic plants. He had a wonderful deep voice and loved to recite Nicholas Guillen. Memories from the early years scored a standard for freakout, how far it could go. Boldness. Risk. Misfire. Middle of the night tutorials, howling examinations of Philip's gigantic, pointillist murals framed across entire walls. Excavation by flashlight! Like spelunkers. Classrooms made fabulous studios but you weren't supposed to live there.

Now Dik Dik was down, exiting the hollow, hallowed, echoing space of Main, out its front door to its fenced in parking lot – invaluable real estate in Coltrane. Two things mattered in Coltrane: parking and dogs. He slipped his dentures back in, adjusted his wire-rimmed glasses. He hadn't seen a soul. Thank the goddess! He'd managed to vacate the premises without encountering a single artist. Coltrane Commandments Numbers 1 and 2: 1) Beware the Coltrane hug; 2) Beware the Coltrane snub. No hugs or snubs today. He might have run in to one of his readers for tomorrow. He didn't want to force a 'reminder', be a mother hen yob and hex the whole operation.

"Life is about creating yourself," wheezed from Dik Dik's pie hole. For a split second, he didn't know whether he'd actually uttered the line or thought it. Pay attention! He was reluctant to give up the luxurious human delectation he and Ava had engendered. He could still taste her. Fricking aglow in power, he knew humans gave pleasure, humans accepted pleasure, with joyful abandon. All humans could. This united us. Made us part of humanity's army of cum. Pay attention! *Ah, here I am, Coltrane.* To be is dooby! In the far future, in the far past. This was his time. This was his place.

Now, chores, like an ol' *Hausfrau.* Head to the Gulch. Check on those kids for the mic and amp. Phone call the city to remind them of his park permit. He hated phones. He hated phone booths in the rain in Spain. Luckily, they were on their way out. He hated smart phones that looked like a stack of credit cards glued together and painted black. Credit cards and a sewing machine on a dissecting table. Then he had to end up at the library to see about his materials.

Bloomsday tomorrow, June 16, dawn to dusk. He had readers lined up – maybe ten. He was keeper of the list. Instigator and catalyst. And he'd just been injected with life, so was infected now, to spread the joyous disease through Coltrane. Dublin in the desert, O raucous experiment, O dreamy stage – he'd step on through. He'd open a door in the real and walk on in. He would see it through and make it happen. The surrealist's job was to bung the alternative.

Dik Dik had a couple ways he could proceed now on his errands. He could follow the narrow bendy roads back to Main Street, then go around to the Gulch. Longer. The other way was through the alley, then down wide steps with leaking pipes, past a sad wall of rubble. Sad because a kid's bicycle frame stuck out of a cement hard caliche mound. Neighborhood of collapsed shacks. Bike fossil. No one could get it out, and it had been there a long time. Debris everywhere in Coltrane, great piles of art in the flux. Duchamps on every block.

But first: marching up the road toward him, before he could decide, a parade in searing morning light. Young looking men and woman, with bodies contorted, faces too, in plain clothing, and leading the parade, the Queen of Coltrane, her goddess herself, Lise Tattersgill. She was dressed in scraps of color, the fugitive harlequin, with a crown of clover her charges had made for her, and she brandished a wand, or slim walking stick, hard to tell if it was for conjures or brainings. She said it was the rib of a saguaro. She was the finest artist Dik Dik had ever known. She existed in a constant state of alteration. She ate art. She shit art. Now she came striding over to Dik Dik, her left hand raised high to let her commandoes know to halt.

"I'm eating nothing but almonds today," she whispered, bending in, leaning over to get close to Dik Dik's ear. "My cunt will sweat almond milk."

"Ah so, the great and the grand," said Dik Dik. She smelled like garlic.

"You reek of pussy," she added, pulling back.

She returned to her charges – it was a part time gig, got in place, moved them out. Her kindness kept them in line. They adored her, because she believed in them in ways they needed someone to believe. They had Goya heads full of lucidity for their Queen. A town bird, one of those Apache thrashers with orange eyes, that lived in the in between brush bits of parking lot and yard, squelched out an interrogatory. The Queen sang back, a simple tea pot medley, whose rhymes made the parade happy, marching out towards the alley. Dik Dik chose alley way. He gave them a head start. He noticed the bird still singing, asking questions. How its song blended with the Queen's! He didn't want to answer, but he had to. He huffed out a gasp. The bird rasped. This was the beat of the heart of Coltrane and its faces rapt with cum.

Right this second, how many buildings or shacks, or

stairwells or hidey holes, and rat holes, and bamboo nests, how many sheltered seekers ascendant? How many were off the grid of the real, pulsing with a taste of further? Isn't that what anarchy finally meant, a life without boundaries? They had come to this town for its emptiness, miners gone or leaving, haunted steep streets that led nowhere, great Satanic piles of mining mess, jagged pits in the Earth. They had discovered a Victorian town corroding to skeletons. This discovery, its pure innocence and terror, was held in sacred trust. They were the first to see, to realize, to understand, its multiplicity. Everywhere you walked in town, the soft tinkle of bubbling bong water could be heard, the soft cries of men and women begging climaxes.

Down wet, capriciously sized steps, Dik Dik drove on, like some kind of pea pod giant, down the sneaky sweeping flanks of the canyon that gave on to the Gulch. The whole of Coltrane, a system of canyons, two main ones making a big L in the reddish cliffs, speckled with enough quartz flakes to sparkle. This part of the L, the short side, the Gulch, headed north in to the Apache Mountains. The long part of the L was Apache Canyon, which headed west to the divide and tunnel. Canyon walls, layered in houses, were connected by complicated stairs and pathways. At one time the canyons had been covered in trees. The trees went to the smelters. The border town here, now, was all about scrub – brush.

Dik Dik passed a bulge of rubble with a bike stuck in it. Frank Zappa played a bike like a musical instrument on TV. Now Dik Dik did a clang and a skitter with a stick. Distraction was polite nostalgia. Dik Dik had no time for sentimentality. He was an urban lad, a books and theater lad, and this place had smothered him in outside, completing his whereabouts. He knew these paths like ribbons of his own gut, overlaying the canyons' body, splitting into fine threads, each ending in a site where something significant had happened. He'd been up and down every stairway. He knew every alley. His was a desert village where Caliban bloomed boom.

Tripping rotters blundered right into thorns like daggers of a Saturday night. Tourists rushed to horse pistol to have pokes dug out of their arses. Desert meant cactus and agave and mesquite. Desert birds, with pale feathers, skittered through the rocks in the sun. There were Martian ocotillo, where the goddess had plunged space squid, head first, into the white sandy ground, waving tentacles up top. The great monolithic rock formations were always grinding in their own subtle, settling, slipping, chafing, background resonance. Uncanny music. Dik Dik recalled better ears. For some reason he pictured Australia, where he'd lived outside of Sydney, and Harry was yelling, 'Nature? Fuck nature!'

Now he was surrounded by ornamental trees he knew like old comrades. Bugger! He'd be hugging trees before the day was out. *Ah, the fungible feast!* Trees were only like trees, and humans were like tree thieves. This quince would grow heavy with fruit hanging over the fence for easy picking. And here: pomegranates – O, biblical fruit! Their flowers fleshed red-orange, with complicated petals. So quince, pomegranate. Then chinaberry, right now, late spring, early summer, the change in time a crack in time, full flower fragrance. These lush newcomers like visitors from another planet. Like Dik Dik hisself. Water me! Watch me grow! Sweet balloons of upness wafted high as circling swallows. Dik Dik knew they were swallows, because outside got in, and he had memorized that shape and flight in France, where he'd liked their French name, *hirondelle*.

Dik Dik nested in the Gulch, about a quarter mile up the canyon, in a handmade, or re-made, shack, known by the locals as the *surrealist house*. No caps. He didn't like 'surrealist's house' because that implied what he was when he wasn't. But working on it. Surrealism was a process, in enactment. He got this place. He knew this was his last place. The process was his creation. High in the cum moment, Dik Dik heard the waves of the sea. The stately blue agave bucked up, plump with tequila spigots. Dik Dik knew where the minotaurs lived. Caliban hisself. Fleeting creatures always out of the corner of one's eye in Coltrane.

The Gulch now. Those stairs over there, Tanya gave him a blowjob. She sat, he stood. He'd seen stars. That alley across the way by the brick building was where he'd smoked crack with Grandpa Filigree. More stars. The Gulch was lined with shops, bars – Elmo's the most famous, then cafes and galleries. They appeared and disappeared quick as the money got shuttled. And Dik Dik had performed in nearly every single place. The world was his venue!

Every available surface on the Gulch – walls, telephone poles, sides of buildings, was plastered with posters. Coltrane's legacy throbbed through the peeling palimpsest. Artists, miners, cowboys, Indians – they were all here at once, perked up by the big cum. Bright upon us!

Folks were out, zombie-ing about, floaty floaty, stony, drunk, regaled. He knew that guy, who deliberately turned away to avoid eye contact. Coltrane snub! In progress. Did blokes think no one noticed? Dik Dik got a few hello's, and he practiced self-restraint and met their eyeballs with his eyeballs.

Matewan Tower rang the hour. The top of the Gulch had its own exclamation point, a Victorian bell tower rising from a three story building that now rented office space. The belfry was grand enough, curly cued, to curate a Victorian time slip when visitors stepped into the Gulch. The belfry had no bells anymore. Now it was a recording hustled through amps and speakers. People complained, and the city made them turn off the top of the hour ringing after 9 PM every day.

A pretty young girl, with long brown hair in a ponytail, came up fast to Dik Dik when she saw him. Sidewalk suspense. Her expectant smile, as she put away her device, shoving it into her back pocket, seemed...greedy? She wore work shirt and jeans, sneakers. What did she expect? Transference: she wanted what he had. Coltrane Commandment Number 4: Beware the Coltrane psychic vampire. She was a teenager, he knew her parents, who were part of the art crowd, hustling their riffs as best they could to survive. He thought they had a gallery? Daphne. That was her name. She'd been to one of his forums. No classes! He was an anarchist. A forum where everyone was equal and participated. She was a poect. She wanted talent, confidence, adoration.

She declaimed, "Studebaker baby maker / Fiesta siesta / Nine months later." She waited, watching him. "Get it? What I did there? A whole story in three lines!"

Dik Dik smirked and his hands came up, palms showing. He was agreeable, welcoming, advocating. Finally, he went, "Fiesta defenestre."

Daphne turned red and tried to turn him in to a toad. She pressed the spell tight with her pinky fingers, all her might, but no go. Art was tricky to her. But she knew she was special. She was too obvious for wit. She rushed. She needed qual.

. Before she bolted, she cried, "Babylon, man! It's all Babylon."

Dik Dik called out after her fleeing figure: "Metaphor be with you, my child."

Ain't it jus'? A message from the universe, Dik Dik thought. Keep watching the skies! Youth was extravagant with youths. Old people denied that. He continued up the Gulch. Here, his favorite antique shop of the 20th Century. Then, seances. Tattoos. One bar reeked of patchouli. One bar reeked of urinal. A few blocks of a canyon near the border was all it was, where fools set in...where funk set in. The Gulch was an opening to an historical overlap where Dik Dik could estivate. The whole town was like a forgotten back pocket of the universe. A linty place of seclusion and desperation. A multivalent reality show. In the parking area, Homeless Ralphy made breakfast in the trunk of his battered, red car, small Coleman stove atop his spare, frying his bacon. His dog, Rusty, sat beside him, sitting up, alert, but patient.

Coltrane was a place to stop. Coltrane was a place to grow thorns – or feathers. Coltrane was a place to eat pussy.

Daphne'd done the whole voice thing, too: 'bob-a-lon'. Who the hell she think she was? What year was this? No years any more. This moment prevailed, because it was about time Daphne and Dik Dik got their turns at the omniscient. Why shouldn't they do what they wanted. They couldn't do any worse than anyone else. Humans pretended position. In fact, they riled the birds who were always keeping tabs on them. Save me, Falstaff!

"Dik Dik," called a voice. Coming out of the theater entrance, Douglas. "You're just in time. You gotta see this piece, it comes after yours on the playlist."

Dik Dik had founded *Random Theater on the Gulch* five years before, so only had peripheral participation with them anymore. A small space, with a pitiful stage, it had been perfect for his brand of cabaret – torch singers and strippers, animal acts...some of his best characters had come to life on that crappy stage.

Dik Dik muttered, "What's new at the Rialto?" But it was too late. He was sucked in, even with his cum halo. In to the fantasy he'd fabricated, he fumbled, its dusty air gave way to the smell of over ripe fruit.

Douglas, in his sixties, old gay hippy dood, high school drama teacher for thirty years, wore overalls today. Honest to goshness, *Oshkosh Bygosh*. America loved its poor, the working class, noble laborers, and their smart fashions. As long as they didn't come over for supper.

The assembled players, all male, on stage, wore black baggy pants with fluffy white shirts. Dik Dik thought, they look like gauchos. Straight out of Borges.

Douglas leaned in to Dik Dik's face. He was a tall man, Dik Dik short. "Can we talk later? Just for a minute? I really need to – I'd appreciate it."

"What's it about, love?"

"Yes, it's about love. Just for a minute."

A kid in the wings yelled, "'Closet claustrophobic!' I love that line, Dik Dik!"

Douglas ordered, "Phones off! Let's do this Budinski thing. Let's see it!" He scrambled his bulky bod, long arms like rowing planks, over to the hi-tech device he'd bought for *Random Theater's* shows. He flicked the switch, the f/x came on. Lights, colors, strobes. Americans' idea of the avant garde, Dik Dik blabbed to himself, was pat, disguised as playful but finally just dumb. Idiots! Dik Dik had disliked the f/x right away, from the first time he'd 'experienced' them. Fools!

The players got in ranks, colors and patterns splashing over them. Ranks of psychedelic gauchos. But still. In one voice they called out: "Evil cartel! We are the evil cartel! We do evil! We control the border. Every bag of weed equals a dead campesino."

Dik Dik screamed!

Douglas called, "Cut, cut! What? What?" He hustled to hit the off switch of his special f/x device.

"I thought they were gauchos. They're killers? You bloody bastards, you're glorifying the sods. You can't make evil fun or interesting. Fuck that! There's no wit in this. It's obvious. Banal. Sick-o. Anno domino, sick-o."

Douglas reflected, staring at the floor. He shook himself up. "They'd just got started –" He called, "Take five." Then, quietly, to Dik Dik, "We have to talk."

They went in to the storage closet full of props and costumes. Douglas lit a joint, held it between his lips, as he put a long haired, blonde wig on Dik Dik. "Want some?"

"I've already had breakfast," said Dik Dik, "so maybe a puff like an aperitif. An after dinner burrito as you yanks say."

"You did drag with aplomb. You going to the performance tonight?"

Dik Dik puffed, hooting in acknowledgement. "Can't miss it."

Douglas seemed sad. "Big events, tonight, then tomorrow."

"Now, then, the news that will harrow up my bones and freeze my young blood, that you're dying to get off your chest."

Douglas smiled wanly. He kept nodding as he spieled it out: "I called Moriah a 'dumb bitch.' She'll never forgive me."

"My dear, you should only call Moriah the wind."

"I called her 'dumb bitch.'" He trembled with it, puffed, let the joint go out.

Dik Dik said, "Pushing buttons."

Douglas said, "Coltrane Commandment Number 3: Beware the Coltrane shuffle. It doesn't *justify* philandering."

"Ah, taboos lined up, 'til the next one. You have no choice, but to be an asshole. Read some Levi-Strauss. Do something unexpected."

"I'm melting."

"Cuckold! But not. Right-o. Jolly good. Tell her you want to watch. You want to see some gent's beautiful cock go right up her beauteous twat."

"I could never –"

"Suit yourself. Until tomorrow, then. Don't forget your brogue."

Dik Dik removed the wig, came out of the closet. The young fellow who liked his claustrophobia bit was calling for him. He was on stage with another guy, then two young woman. They were outfitted in t-shirts and jeans, boots and sandals – ragamuffins, thought Dik Dik. A boy and a girl in sandals, blue flip flops, flexed and relaxed their feet nervously. They rose and fell in place, the arches of their feet crowning, then flattening. Working geometries, geared up for what they were called on to do. Ready musculature, sinew, bones – ripeness is all! Finally, they kicked off their flip flops to bare feet.

Dik Dik approached the stage. They had small dirty feet, nubbly toes.

The young man announced: "*First Giraffe!*"

The two males went to one side of the stage. The two females to the other end. The men mimed motions, movements as though they were busy, constructing, building. The women stood close to each other, leaning in to each other, intimate, whispering.

The voices took turns:

Female: "Of course it hurts!"

Male: "Hand tighten only."

Female: "I can't mind my own business."

Male: "Cover exposed area."

Female: "I can't abide moderation."

Male: "Do not expose to sunlight."

Female: "Expect the worst."

Male: "Do not X-ray."

Female: "I can't stop judging people."

Male: "No water after midnight."

Female: "I don't learn from my mistakes."

Male: "Dig trowel deep."

Douglas had joined Dik Dik, standing at his side. He was tense, squinting, then he sighed when he saw it was going well. Douglas grunted with pleasure. Dik Dik and Douglas clapped. Douglas commented, "Nicely done."

The barefoot girl said, "What's a 'trowel', anyway? I think it makes men out to be dopes."

Dik Dik said, "If I tell you a lie, spit in my face, and call me a horse."

The kids on stage laughed and clapped.

Dik Dik left the theater. Didn't offer goodbyes. Kept on going. His piece sounded good with the yutes. The great schlep downtown continued. Posters everywhere, glaring at him with little voudou eyes begging him to peek. Too much to register. Aha! His poster for Bloomsday. He must have put it here. Dusk to dawn, Grassy Park, crisp lettering, with a photo of a man in a suit standing on a step ladder, peering in to a window, the part of him in the window, head and shoulders, disappeared in the window. Multitask that, Hoch! Magritte would fumble out a locomotive in a pastry shop. Right here, in desert city cum! Where else to go, for when he went. Who will remember the cum?

Then up a narrow, cement stair between buildings, quick now, high stepping, vital energy, into the old building on the right. Through its door, inside, more stairs inside, to the second floor. He could smell them, he could hear them before he knocked –

Dik Dik yelled, "Ka-nock, ka-nock!" He didn't touch the door.

"Ka-ka-come in!" crowed a female voice. He could tell it was Tiffany, the young singer he'd talked to at the Yard during their band's break.

The door opened, fell back and away, and there was heraldry made flesh – no, it was a wolf-dog, head big as a washing machine pushing forward, greeting him, checking him out with shiny, yellow eyes. Their eyes met. 'Fuck nature,' iterated in Dik Dik's spine.

"Good doggy," he said.

Tiffany appeared behind the wolf-dog, swathed in veils. Scarves. Her face – her face sweetness all over the beast. Dik Dik took in her prance, as she took care of the animal. Golden sinuosity called Changing Woman around here, Aztec heart hunter, solid Earth goddess climbing pyramids. She went, "Wolf, here boy." She collapsed over the front of the wolf-dog, arms around his neck, no collar, and tugged him back.

"Excuse me, dear boy," said Dik Dik in a cheerful voice as he sidled by the zoology.

He kept going, past the bathroom door, into a big square room, double mattress bed in the center, small table, a few chairs, piles of music equipment all over. Bodies – brown bodies, black bodies, white bodies – strewn about, some with guitars in their laps, some checking devices. In the dim light, bodies in shredded clothes, tears, rips...cactus thorn garb...virtual –

"Ah, my mutant songbird, you have a veritable opium den in your back room. But I have to ask, why the name 'Wolf'?"

The big furry fellow stretched out on the bed, hogging all the pillows, guitar across his lap, said, "Cause his big brother already had the name, 'Dog'."

"Ahh," went Dik Dik.

Tiffany persuaded Wolf to collapse in a pile with Dog, squeezed up against the wall in a bare space.

"So you must be 'Man'?" asked Dik Dik to the furry fellow.

No one's breathing quickened.

Tiffany stood beside Dik Dik. She was in technicolor, invincible. In a black and white, dazed world. She sheeshed: "Don't you get it?" She looked over her comrades, into their nodding faces. "They're too stoned.

Salvia."

"I'm Bear," said the furry dood on the bed.

Tiffany said, "He's my old man. Plays bass. We rent this space together. The band uses it to hang out. You heard us play. I'm glad you liked us."

"I like your name."

"Sweet!" cried a figure curled in the corner, a small black guy, with a guitar across his thin chest.

Tiffany said, "That's Mikey. He's lead. He came up with the name. Credit due. You're the bomb, Mikey!"

She pointed to a fat Anglo dood at the table with drum sticks in his hands. "That's D.O.A., our drummer."

Dik Dik preferred the expression 'Anglo' to 'white'. 'Anglo' sounded so Brit!

Dik Dik said, "Bollocks! I saw drum sticks and assumed he was irrigating his ear drums."

The young woman in tattered black, of uncertain ethnic, sitting by herself on a chair to the side, with major eyebrow arteries across her forehead, said, "I saw what you did there. Wolf, dog, man."

Dik Dik beamed at her, and her light came on. He said, "You're the eyebrowist. You do steampunk jewelry. Metal work. Lydia. I remember you, Lydia. We met."

Now, he could see her silvery chain cobwebs wrapped around her tattooed skin. One had to focus in to demarcate particulars. Her body, her accoutrement, her accessory thing. She was sharp –

"We've seen you perform," said the guy sitting on the corner of the bed. Next to him, skinnied in like an extra slice, it had to be his wife. White people. Health food nuts. Bony and wiry. Young couple. Work with their hands? Performance art of course. Write it up then – a blog. Journal notes – entries. Post cards of their –

The guy on the bed said, "We do art cars. This is Geena. I'm Aubergine."

Geena said, "We were playing a game. Do you want

to play?" Her voice was surprisingly officious, like she was explaining instructions on the life boats. She leaned in over the bed, staring at Dik Dik, avoiding Bear's dirty feets. Her eyes were beads Lydia could string. She had stringy hair, the color of rodent. Maybe she was going for dreads? She looked sculpted scrawny. Cheeks, cliffside rashers. "Do you want to play?"

"Of course," said Dik Dik.

Tiffany said, "I'll get you something to sit on. Hey, here, try this little amp. You can't weigh anything."

Dik Dik ended up on a small amp that was a perfect fit for his sit. He piped up: "Thanks so much, you chaps including me in the flash, but don't forget, my dear, I came to you for a favor, because you said you would oblige."

Tiffany said, "This is Dik Dik, everybody. And he's got a gig tomorrow at Grassy Park and needs a mic and an amp. See, I didn't forget."

Bear said, "He can take the amp he's sitting on. He'll need a couple cords. Tiffy, let him use your old mic. It's fine."

"Splendid! Thanks so," went Dik Dik. "Should I take it with me now, or would you mind bringing it down to City Park at dawn tomorrow?" He figured he might as well ask. Get the yutes involved, cross fertilization, and all that.

"That sounds coolio," said Bear. "We'll bring it over. See if we can help."

"Do you need a mic stand?" asked Tiffany.

"No, no, keep it simple," said Dik Dik.

Mikey called out, "Dope, dood! We just won't go to sleep tonight. We can write songs all night!"

"What kind of help?" the drummer asked.

Everyone laughed.

D.O.A. grumbled, "So what're you doing? What's the gig? You have a band?"

"No, no," said Dik Dik. "Tomorrow is Bloomsday, June 16, the one day that takes place in the novel *Ulysses*. We're reading it from dawn to dusk. I have fifteen readers."

D.O.A. said, "To read a whole book out loud? Can't be done."

"But, my dear fellow, our purpose is not to read it through literally, cover to cover, it's to experience the writing out loud. And to commemorate. Re-invigorate a profound moment of human vision."

"Here, here," said the guy on the bed. Aubergine? "By Jimmy Johns, right?"

Dik Dik didn't dare.

Geena pronounced specifically, "The game –"

Bear pulled out from between his hole-y, jean-clad legs a small glass pipe with a bowl the size of a quarter. He laid the guitar aside.

Geena said, "It's called Poison. Typical little pot pipe, right? We pass it around. We each have a little packet to fill the pipe. One packet has *Salvia*, but no one knows which packet has it. No one knows who'll get it."

"Ah," went Dik Dik. "Like soft-core Russian roulette."

Mikey unbent from the floor to a regular figure, with guitar, to approach the game's bed. He cried, "Let's do this thing! Papa Bear, let it blaze! For Dik Dik. For the band. *News from the Recent Terror*. Stoned immaculate!"

The phone booth was talking to him with a woman's voice. He felt belittled in the enclosure, her voice pressed to his noggin. However, *copacetic* was the word. The official voice from the city verified all was in order. A city worker would be at Grassy Park at dawn to turn on the power for him. Dawn to dusk, the agreement read.

The female voice said, "You're the party who submitted the request, Philip Dick?"

"Exactly."

"Have a great time then. I hope your event goes well."

Oh, don't hex it. Her airiness, her affable tone, her yearning accommodation – what do women want?

Of course, they wanted exactly what everyone wanted – equality, opportunity, self-determination. For thousands of years women had told men exactly what they wanted. In poelms and art, in sculpture, in maths, architecture and literature. Men just didn't listen. They were stuck in a phone booth. Dik Dik got out.

He had to get to the library. His shoes had wheels now, so he had to slip slide about gravity. Balloon walking – he contained miles in his giant footsteps like giant gulps. Wheels' speed, cum moment push!

Everything was going so well, so means of transport inconsequential.

Old crusty libraries had a formal dignity they probably didn't deserve, still there was something delicious about a library. Didn't have these in the UK, Dik Dik smirked, when I was a tot. His library intoxication came from years spent in US libraries. Librarians made him horny. Always. Didn't matter if she was plump, old, sad, young. Even the boys were cute.

Lots of nods now, as Dik Dik pushed through the heavy doors at the top of the steps he had taken two at a time. Library was upstairs, above the post office. Nods were good. Compared to hugs. Nodding nomenclature: 'you are there, I see you'. Librarians embraced the cum moment of books by default, always reading, sentencing their own climaxes. He glanced around for his contact. 'New Books' shouted out to him, contact immediately, a red book in particular, he sensed implicitly – John Le Carré.

He picked it up, took it over to the table by the magazine rack and sat. A quick scan? A glance, thought Dik Dik. Ah, not an autobiography. True-life adventures arranged chronologically. Pigeon tunnels to nowhere. Dik Dik read. Marvelous writing. Le Carré in the Great Game, or at least a peripheral peeker. Meetings with the great and the grand. Always a bit aghast, Le Carré stayed...almost playful, too. Le Carré wanted to see if he could extract meaningfulness from this life.

Magic moments came along so rarely but in the long run they didn't amount to a hill of beans. Is that what he meant? Dik Dik pondered. He muttered to himself. He gasped with the experience he'd had reading. Deep reading –

He would have to focus and ask for help. But the librarian came to his rescue. It was his contact, Ms. Louise, taking him behind the checkout desk to point proudly at the goods. A sturdy brown sack with handles. Cloth? Textile turnstile. Inside the sack: the twenty selections from *Ulysses* Dik Dik had made. Each roughly one hour reading time. Plus two copies of the text. With his, he now had three texts, plus the copied selections. Should be plenty.

He thanked his helper. He hustled down the steps to Main Street with his sack. No boner. But the moment was read. One step closer to Bloomsday! To his right, at the end of the block, a tall, cadaverous creature reporting on death, life after death, death on the installment plan. Too late, Giacometti spotted Dik Dik and waved him over.

It was Ed Norminton, a retired military clerk, civilian contractor thirty years. Dik Dik joined him, and they sauntered over to the bulletin board in front of the post office. It was so thick with pamphlets, posters, handbills that it was a veritable, all encompassing art project.

Cacophony collage! At Ed's counsel, they adjourned at his leisurely death rattle roll over to the side of the bulletin board where there were benches. They had to step up to the elevated level the bench was on. They got comfortable. Dik Dik placed his sack between Ed and himself.

"What's the story, morning glory?" mused Dik Dik.

Ed held a small white head at the top of his bone skyscraper. He always wore a suit, a tie. They looked ragged now, thin at the elbows.

"Lemuria," moaned Ed. He squinted down at Dik Dik. "The antediluvian culture –"

He said 'culture' as 'kul-cha'.

He went on, "Lemuria. Read this fascinating piece by Ray Palmer about his comrade Richard Shaver, and their preposterous declarations. Civilization and its incontinence."

"So preposterous they must be true?"

"Exactly!"

Dik Dik thought of Al Capp's *shmoo* or was it R. Crumb's *Whiteman*?

Luckily, it was the time of day when the *gente* were going by to check their PO boxes, so lots of faces and greetings and practical protocols. Places everyone, thought Dik Dik. *Babylon!* 'Act Penultimate, Scene Forever,' he would cry. Or at least squelch, 'Watch your marks!'

Here came a hairy dood out of the crowd. He took the step up, found his place on the bench next to Ed. He had a glow. He let go. Ed and Dik Dik pulled back, but knew he was harmless. It was more of a 'whatever you're on we'd just as soon it didn't brush off on us.' Coltrane Commandment Number 5: Beware the Coltrane contact high. Everyone knew Hippy Henry, professional Deadhead until Jerry died, but a long time parking lot impresario. He looked exactly as anyone would expect of a person called Hippy Henry.

He went, "Heard you mention, *lemur.* That's Latin for ghost. Yeah? Don't look surprised. Hippy Henry knows his shit. Ghosts. Ghost ships. You know what I'm talking about. I know doods who seen Cleopatra's barge going down the San Pete. Right here! Just out of town, a week ago. See what I'm saying? How come they find Roman artifacts around here?"

"Easy, cowboy," said Dik Dik. The sun moved directly overhead to singe.

"Micro-dosing," said Hippy Henry fast. "I've been trying it out. It's the bomb. *Grateful Dead* break up and there goes the LSD, but the urban shamans are getting it going again. See what I'm saying? So you take just enough. Twenty-five or thirty mikes. Take off the edge? Put on the edge? Who knows? Follow the *dark star* is all I know."

Ed came in here, "Dik Dik, we'll continue our conversation later. We can examine the evidence. Back to the archives." He stood: he would have to step down. He negotiated.

Hippy Henry said, going to a whispery voice, "I can get you sloth dung."

"'Sloth dung?'" said Dik Dik.

"Spanish conquistadors killed the last of the giant ground sloths. I know where the den was. It's on the San Pete. Worth a ton." He came in close, looking deep in Dik Dik's eyes. "You can smoke it."

"On that dreadful note," went Ed, "I bid you adieu." He stepped down.

People swung by for a quick 'hey'. Nudging, pointing, pinching. Noon muster! Dik Dik saw what was going to happy. Chaos theater. Non-objective theater. A regular lovefest based on his scent. Scent song of cum. Bloomsday was set. Nothing could interfere.

Across the way, his errant eyes couldn't help but wonder, at the gazebo and its professional derelicts swinging about there. Right across the way from the post office where he was sitting, across the intersection like the crux of the canyon L, a view of Grassy Park, its outrageous metal gazebo, like an orgone accumulator. It kept the monsters at bay. But Dik Dik was looking at who was there.

Ed Norminton had shuddered away. Hippy Henry was hummering to himself. Twelve o'clock high tolled over the Gulch from Matewan Tower. And out of the park, endlessly yapping, Lorna with her boys. She notched him right away. Like a vulture that's keen on joy, not carrion. She stalked in –

Her boys were easy to keep track of: one had blue hair; one had red hair; one had no hair; one had white hair. Put them together: the flag of Zenda! Their names were their colors: Blue, Red, Baldy, Whitey.

She came in, keeping her head low, avoiding his eyes. She slowed as she got closer, her boys fanning out behind her, as she'd taught them. Then, maybe ten feet in front of Dik Dik, still on the bench, she went into slow motion pantomime like an opioid spider. She used her hands in space, or handled snakes. She'd had no luck with drawing or sculpture. She and her hands turned sideways, advancing like a crab. She wore chitinous white boots, golden tight pants, sparkly, and a shimmering top, metallic, with scarves tied around an arm and a leg – they looked like bandages.

She wouldn't look at him. He looked away. He heard her strong, feminine palette, which worked so well in poetry, go, "Going to the show tonight?" Slinky intonation to a beheading.

Dik Dik said, "Ah, yes, the performance at the Yard. Coney Shaman in all his witless glory. Should be a hoot. He's got all the great and grand involved."

Said she: "I can't go." She giggled. Her hand hurried to cover her mouth. "Banned. I *am* banned. We all were. For our piece. We were trying to do our piece. It was too much. It hurt me here." She clutched her throat.

"What are you working on?"

Her energy subsumed. She could've been a black hole. He saw her shoulders come down. The body drooped. She sighed, cleared her throat potently. She stepped up to the bench level, planted herself next to Dik Dik. She got out her *Salems* from her pants, knocked one out, used a lighter on it.

Hippy Henry went, "All right, all right, all right," acting it out with a lot of gooey inferences.

"No right, no right, no right," said Lorna, exhaling slowly. Smoke, mist, ether flowed from her mouth. She stared in to infinity. She had the most intense face, as though always squinting or straining, ready for the bull fight charge. Wrinkly for her age, too. She might have been beautiful once. Now, pain screwed in to every wrinkle. "Working on a lot of things. Maybe poultry is stand up. Switch it around. It's all in the timing. Open mic. Throw a show. Tell some jokes. Rubber chickens, plastic vomit. People want to see humiliation."

"What's the project? What are you working on? You and your boys?"

"Of course. A play: *Mind Rape – Assault by Pepper.*" Her head went up – proud. She murmured, "You like it? Two acts. Three scenes each. Like you taught me."

They sat quietly for a while.

Then.

She blubbered softly: "What happened, Dik Dik? I was the Mexican princess, the punk Frida, that all the Coltrane artists adored. They made me one of them. Now they won't talk to me." Her eyes extruded tears in robust drops. A steady drizzle that fell, not down her cheeks, but, as though projected, flew towards Earth, stopping midway to change to small dark beetles that fizzled away.

"Lorna –"

"What? Tell me."

"We've had this talk before. You have a different way of seeing things that have happened from the way others see them."

"That is such bullshit."

All at once, her boys converged around their queen. They implored, cajoled, reached out for quick hand squeezes. Late teens, early twenties, scraggly, cute, they were street artists. Buskers. Street art: life is art. That's what she taught them. That's what she had learned from Modernism, Post-Modernism, and Conceptual Art. She'd had a lot of mentors in Coltrane.

Dik Dik dove for it. He grabbed his sack and hit the sidewalk high stepping out of there. He dashed around the corner of the post office so out of sight. He didn't dare look back. He had to lay low, get under cover. She was out, trolling for trolls.

She liked to stir things up, get on stage and break down to sobbing confessions. To the artists in town, she seemed primal. She was uncontaminated by education's baggage. She was a local girl, a bad girl, who'd been a drug addict and alcoholic from age ten. But she'd gotten cleaned up for her kids, the fam. Addiction work led her to art therapy. And lo! and behold, she'd grown up in an art town and didn't even know it. From group, it was easy to pull together rants and call them poems that the artists found raw...Bukowski-ish.

For a few years she'd been a rising star. She'd taken creative writing classes at the local community college. She'd mentored under performance artists and visual artists. She picked up the lingo, the 'tude, the tone. She diligently studied her goddesses, Karen Finley and Kathy Acker. She'd found her calling.

Coltrane Commandment Number 6: Beware the Coltrane hierarchy.

Then, a dark period. Maybe it was a low cycle for the

entire town. Anyway, it had her only coming out at night. Very late sightings were reported. She became estranged from her family. Her husband worried she was using. She continued to perform a couple times a year. The performances became obsessed with mutilation. Blood. Wounds. The rot of the flesh stank. She manipulated roadkill. She cut herself on stage.

Nothing must interfere played through Dik Dik's head, as he ducked in to the Tavern, the last and only bar left on Main street. At one time, Coltrane had had a hundred bars. The Tavern was the last of the originals, besides Elmo's on the Gulch. He made it! Away and clear. Into the temple of atavism and mining daze. Dim. Greenish light from the painted front windows, green on top and bottom, middle part clear to see out. A long wooden bar, a row of booths opposite. In the back, an open area to the restrooms, with an old pool table, coasters stacked under each corner leg to level it. A few chairs around the pool table. Some Mexican guys back there drinking beer, playing pool, smoking cigarettes. Cozy as hell. Smelled of holy vinegar. The usual sun dog, an older Mexican guy, sat on a stool at the bar. Ed Norminton there, nearby, on his own stool, at the bar already, slamming down a shot, clear stuff, so gin or vodka, then bringing down the glass hard. He reached for his glass of beer adjacent, ready to go. Chugged. No devices in the bar. It's not like they were forbidden. But right now no one was using. No cell phones. No pads. No dingleberries. Dim.

Dik Dik sauntered over to the bar. Ed must have seen him, or else the booze was kicking in, but his body spasmed. He started shaking. He relaxed. His eyes were squished shut. Dik Dik came in close, raised his arm, hand to Ed's shoulder. He said, "Don't get wobbly on us, young man. I bet you need something to eat, and a proper sit down on a proper chair. Let's go across the street to El Zarape, and I'll get you a nice cup o' tea." He placed the sack on the bar. Ed shrugged his hand away.

Dik Dik razzed him. Ed kept his eyes closed.

The bartender, Ruiz, a short round man, with a big head, smiley, came up to them. He stared at Ed with a look, said, "He's been doing this every day for the past week. Comes in, a shot, a beer, trembles. Scares the hell out of my clientele. *Es verdad, amigo?*" he asked the old man sitting a few stools down.

The old man nodded, said, "Duendes."

Ruiz said, "Like little ghosts."

"Ed," Dik Dik snorted, "ghosts're after you. Let's go, mate!"

Ed turned on his stool so slowly he revived and opened his eyes. "You're not my mother. Give me a minute to catch my breath."

Dik Dik was positioned so that he was facing towards the back of the bar. Now, a couple heads swiveled around to peek from the back booth. Hairy, big heads.

Coney Shaman called out, "Right there, across the street, El Zarop, right there your all American chimichanga got invented. Tell the story, Ruiz."

Ruiz said, "You're making fun."

The hairy head next to his was Tilman, the marble sculptor with thick eye glasses, who called, "'Fun'? That's our middle name. Tonight, we prove it!" He fussed with his head hair, making sure the long, crusty comb over was in place. Then his hands descended to his beard to pluck and pull.

Ed said distinctively, "I'm going to regurgitate."

Ruiz said, "Don't say it like that. That word alone makes me wanna puke. Ricardo, get him to the head."

"Off to the loo!" cried Dik Dik.

Ed solemnly followed his lead, hand on Dik Dik's arm. A few steps farther and Ed said, "I'm fine." He pulled away. "Go away." He continued on fairly sturdy.

Dik Dik's eyes left Ed to notice in the booth adjacent Coney Shaman and Tilman's, a doubled up stiff. Another one of those ageless hippy doods forever at the moment of cum, now at the cusp of elderliness. This one looked post-ripe. Maybe he was in a coma. It was Captain America.

Dik Dik said to no one in particular, "He all right?"

"Who you asking?" asked Tilman.

"Coney Shaman."

Coney Shaman said, "Don't call me that. Ever again. I mean it. I understand your trickster porn-o-rama cosplay, but I am called *Tri-une* now."

Tilman groveled, "Blessed be his name."

Dik Dik said, "I am not calling you *Tri-goon*. What's going to happen tonight?"

Ruiz slapped a shot of the house brandy on the bar near Dik Dik. He said, "Here, on the house, you're gonna need it blabbing with these turds."

Tilman said to Ruiz, "Thank you very much, from the morning rush king who puts menudo on your table."

Ruiz said, "I don't like menudo."

Dik Dik floated over to his shot.

A guy from the back, the oldest one playing pool, maybe in his thirties, came up to the bar with his empty beer glass. He said to Ruiz, "Tell the story. About the chimi."

Ruiz grinned, walked over. "Story goes, right across the street there, at El Zarape, there was a new guy, name of Eduardo, and story goes, he was just learning, and it was a really, really busy lunch rush, and Eduardo – I knew his nana, Eduardo accidentally dropped some bean burros into the French fryer. The rest is history." Ruiz took the man's glass to the tap. "Art. Right, Ricardo?

Chimichanga's a work of art."

Dik Dik said, "If everything's art, then nothing's art." He downed the shot of cheap brandy. "It's all shite."

The pool player at the bar with his refilled glass stared at Dik Dik. He looked like he couldn't quite place him. "Where you from?" he asked.

"New York City!" spat Dik Dik.

The pool player sipped his beer, nodded. "Reason I ask, you guys show up in Coltrane over the last ten years – artists! You're all artists, right? Anyway, gente just wondering, what's it about, is there money in it?"

Dik Dik pointed to the booths of artists.

Ruiz said, "Don't lie to him, Ricardo. Anybody a mile away could tell where you're from, from that accent. He's from Benson. Ask anyone."

Coney Shaman and Tilman laughed and clapped like this was the show.

Dik Dik came back with: "Harry Partch was from Benson."

The young guy went back to his pool game, commenting, "I have no idea who that is."

Captain America surfaced, flickering upright, table as a brace. He moaned, yawned. "What'd I miss?"

Dik Dik saw his chance. He quickly inserted: "You're MI-5. Cointelpro. The Great Game, Philby, Maclean, all those rotters?"

Captain America looked concerned, then perplexed. He wiped his mouth with the back of his hand. He had been Shuman, a Human. Now it was unclear what. He emerged from his stupor. He said, "Dik Dik, I was a weatherman in the Aleutians avoiding Viet Nam. I've told you and told you and told you and told you –"

Dik Dik said to no one in particular, as Ed came out of the back, "What's happening tonight? Tell."

Tilman announced, "In this corner, the cream of Coltrane elite, Simon himself, and the great M.K. Table.

And in this corner, the immortal mysteries of Triune. Who will win? Who will vanish from this plane of existence?"

Coney Shaman said, "Tell them who else."

"Reefer Madness, aka Reefer Mayan, aka Mad, street canine extraordinaire, will vanish along with the elite. After all, Mad's upper echelon in the hierarchy. No tricks. No sleights. The real deal! This way to the omphalos."

Upfront, the door opened. Everybody turned to look.

Coney Shaman sputtered, "Aha, look what the dog dragged in. Speak of the devil."

In a puff of crisp afternoon air, laced with patchouli and dog smell, Tim Asparagus, the Jackal, and *Wunderhund*, Mad, big as a pony, came lurching in. Lurching because Mad got excited to see his friends in the bar, and his huge feet had a hard time negotiating the slick floor, claws clicking, leash whipping, big sloppy head drooling. Maybe some Great Dane in there. Maybe a little man in a dog outfit. Hard to tell –

Mad was a happy monster! He made it to the back booth to slobber over the guys. Coney Shaman gave him a *Slim Jim.*

The Jackal rasped out: "Gives him gas!"

Tilman let loose a chunky fart.

Ed, who'd been navigating past the pool table and its players, muttered loud enough for everybody to make out: "Good heavens. Holy Eschaton. It's Baal."

Dik Dik said to Ruiz, "You allow beasts in here?"

"I allow you, don't I?" said Ruiz, then: "It's one of those companion animals, a caregiver."

Mad ended up in Captain America's lap.

Tim called out, "Tonight's the night!"

Tilman clawed at his throat. He stopped, pushed up his coke bottle glasses, tugged at his beard. Maybe he was trolling for crumbs. He prepared his words carefully.

Ruiz poured Tim a shot of the house brandy. Tim met Ruiz' eyes and nodded, stepped over to retrieve it.

Ruiz said, "You gotta get that dog outta here."

Tim downed his shot, said, "Don't tell me."

Ed reached Dik Dik and said, "I am not going to El Zarape. Mexican food – looks like it's already been eaten."

Dismayed spectators made noises and blurts.

Ed added, "I'm going to vomit." But didn't.

Tim spoke up: "If you guys pull this off tonight, it'll be great. And the thing is, when you go to bring them back after you disappear them, don't."

Dik Dik said, "It's a magic bit? A vanishing act?"

Tilman stood up, faced everybody. "Some may think it's art because it has a name on it. Celebrity is not art. Art is a portal. And there are a lot of portals outside of New York City."

Tim went, "*New York City*," with a terrible accent like a TV ad. Tim said, "Don't bring them back. They're such hosers. Cheaters. Emperor's new clothes all over again."

Snorts and snarky laughter were his reply. The pool players were checking out Mad in Captain America's lap, a booth pretzel of limbs and torsos.

The young man who'd asked Ruiz for the chimi story said, "Big dog." He made a soft whistle. Everybody nodded.

Captain America said, "I showed in New York City."

Mad went, "Woof!"

Tilman said, "Does Megadeath let you bring that thing to bed?"

Captain America jumped, startling Mad. "A pox on whoever started calling her that. She hates it."

The Jackal, whom most called Red-Black, her chosen name, said, "Sounds like a bunch of sour grapes to me." She wore her customary black leather vest over a thin, spaghetti strapped, blood-red t-shirt. Her boots were sleek, black, leather. She was on –

Tim said, "You worked for M.K. You told me what a grabber he was."

She said, "Yes, but that doesn't mean he's not a great artist."

Tim raised his voice: "Oh, come on. That's a Donald Trump all over the place."

Coney Shaman stood, stepped away from the booth. He prayed: "Magic is performance, performance is magic. Everything will be revealed. All debts will be paid. All expectations shall be obliterated."

Captain America churned out baby sounds around: "You're not going to hurt our widdle widdle boy, are you? No sirree – he's the star of the show."

The young man from the pool table said, "You guys are weird."

Dik Dik said, "Ed, the game's afoot. Let's to the co op. Spot o' tea."

Ed grunted. Coney Shaman's white t-shirt was riding up his gourded belly. Tilman had his mouth hanging open like a carp. Captain America and Mad had their heads pressed together – mammals. The pool players stared. Ruiz grunted. The old man at the bar grunted. Tim fluttered out a quick 'see ya'. The Jackal, aka Red-Black, met Dik Dik's eyes and flashed. He knew what could be said but remained quiet, as did she. Dik Dik picked up his sack on the way out.

Her cum he knew so well – 'just rub it'. She wasn't into penetration. She liked her Mons rubbed hard until she splattered. It was one of the great cums of all time.

When Dik Dik and Ed were almost out, before reaching for the door knob, the Jackal pronounced to the atmosphere: "Old Lady Beckett Twister's looking for you. She saw something in your chart. Maybe about tomorrow."

Everybody knew she was talking to Dik Dik.

Coltrane Commandment Number 8: Beware the Coltrane advice.

Red-Black had shown up in town a handful of years

ago, a runaway from Tucson. With a voice. She had the most dramatic voice. A natural. She offered the audience the gift of her presence – in your face, like a challenge to not appreciate her pain. Extra credit for teenage orcs! First, the kid blossomed with natural vigor. Everybody wanted her in their band. She tried community college. Then, suddenly (at least that's what it seemed to the old people), she grew up and she hated everything except big dogs. She wasn't sure about cats. She'd learned Coltrane Commandment Number 7: Beware the Coltrane favor. Now, she modeled for Tim. Ten bucks an hour. She hustled tables at Rico's sometimes, cleaned houses sometimes.

Tim was a very physical sculptor. He worked long and drastically on his plaster forms before ever thinking about going to the foundry. Red-Black was an exquisite model. He loved her flawless imperfections, the angle, bend, swell of her accuracy. He knew the way her curvature ended at her hip, at the pocket in front, a tender concavity, where her hip plied her pelvis, swinging around front to the pubis and tiara of Aphrodite. Tim was a perfectionist, so it was a slow process, plus he had to work. Tim was always broke. He'd weaseled a gig, making the plaster molds for a rich sculptor's work. The sculptor was too busy, too important to make them himself. Tim had worked his entire life, never got kept by a working woman. Tim thought modern art a crock. He believed in good ol' talent. The gift!

Red-Black knew she could learn from him, and when she asked him 'how to draw', he shrugged and said watch. The way his hand and pencil caressed the paper, then tense, hard shadings, she knew he was making love to her. But he never made a move beyond the paper. She knew her body, too. She had a thing called beauty. She hadn't earned it. Her genes. She knew what she did to men, so it was interesting to see Tim transform her physicality.

What the fuck. She didn't sing much anymore. She thought Dik Dik was a phony.

Ed Norminton declaimed, "I think I'm going to drown in my own vomit. It's become an obsession. I'm terrified. Obsession becomes phobia. Phobia becomes syndrome. Fear eats tooth enamel. I like pie."

"We're heading for Lady Death, my dear boy. One day more. That's all we need. See the gamble? What will the universe throw at us next?"

"Has it always been like this?"

"Yes."

"Then what –"

"You're reading tomorrow. Don't be late."

They'd crossed the street, were making their way past a store and a gallery, then there was the co op. Dik Dik opened the old glass and wood door, let Ed go first. The building had been the Goldwater-Castaneda grocery store, scene of the Coltrane Massacre of 1898. Now when you went in, you didn't think massacre as much as concentration camp...so many of the collective's members seemed gaunt, gray, smuggling out potato peels to the resistance. To the right, as they entered, the checkout counter, complete with bulletin board layered in years' worth of offers and announcements. Then, a cash register with a golden man, long blonde locks gracing his shoulders with glee. Oh, how he yearned for eye contact! Greetings! To the left, shelving, hand rigged boards in rough layers for bins filled with grains, seeds, flours. Dusty air with hints of cinnamon, highlights of spoiled organics. Up front, in the center, a tiny table, a couple chairs. Dik Dik deposited his sack on the table.

Dik Dik said to the golden cashier, whose name was Witt, "What kind of soup today?"

"Veggies – all the way," said Witt. "With corn bread, it's super yummy. The corn bread tastes like cack."

Ed went, "'Cack'."

Witt went, "Cack. You know, like corn cack."

Ed hovered, figuring it out. Dik Dik's eyes went up and down the young man's bodily magnificence. Witt wore blue jean cut offs. He was a 3-D muscle manual of beaming white man. Hippy Adonis! He wanted to help...to make a difference. Dik Dik saw a piece: *The Jealous Jailer*, studly youth and his ostrich rodeo. No, radio. Ostrich radio. Beauty is terror.

Dik Dik had Ed sit, continued to the back, past the coolers on his right, then a kitchen area with a counter. Jack Ramp was volunteering behind the counter, slicing a great white brick of cheese. A small man with an unnatural pallor, his head was sharp, like it made a point. He took the inch thick slices he cut and put them in individual plastic bags. Then he weighed the bags on a small scale. The weight must have been off, because he had to shave off edge pieces to correct. These pieces he gobbled. Dik Dik knew Jack as the author of two experimental novels, both published by Black Cat Press. He was from New York City, a talented weasel with a forked tongue that could sting:

Jack said around a mouthful of cheese, "Dood's from the Jersey shore." He shrugged, shoulders motioning to the front.

Dik Dik said, "He can't help it."

"Soup's on!" cried Jack.

"Broth," said Dik Dik. "A cup o' tea and a cup of broth, *bitte schön*. No 'cack'. English Breakfast Tea if you've got it."

"*Igualamente.*" Jack made it sound like there was an iguana in there. He got busy.

Dik Dik checked out the produce section in the back, where a tall, skinny woman in an over-sized apron, jeans and Birkenstocks, poked around the ugly fruits and vegetables. Dik Dik leaned forward over the counter, caught Jack's eye, flicked his eyes over to the woman.

Jack's eyes went wary. He brought over the tea and soup in two paper cups the same size. He found a plastic spoon and a napkin. "Don't ask. Murikkkins are spiritual retards."

Dik Dik took the two cups and noticed how the woman seemed to be talking to herself, so he walked over to listen. She was pale.

"Xerophytes, xerophytes," she repeated.

"Good day," Dik Dik said. "How are you this fine June day?"

She stared at him with soft brown eyes, caressing some withering beet greens. "So sad," she said, "everything dries up." She shook her head. "This place is sun, voices of the sun, and we have to listen. We have to become sustainable. Grow that which grows here. See what I'm saying?"

"Bloody brilliant," said Dik Dik. "I'm Richard Perkins. You're new to our forsaken little burg?"

She shuddered. "I've been in town twenty-seven days. This is my first day at the co-op. My name is...Cynthia."

"Good day to you, Cynthia, my dear." Dik Dik headed back to the cashier.

His head chortled with Coltrane Commandment Number 9: Beware the Coltrane busybody. Why can't we leave each other alone?

Ed sat at the little table, on a little chair. Big boy Ichabod at the kids' table. Dik Dik placed the cups in front of Ed. Ed grunted, got to work with spoon. Dik Dik sat, finished his tea. He retrieved his sack, hefted it. It wasn't getting any lighter.

Dik Dik said, "You can get home okay."

Slurp.

Dik Dik said, "I have to go." He paid Witt, who smiled too much, and left the co op, lugging the sack of copies.

He cut across Main by the post office, skipped through the park, alert for Lorna or her minions, then headed to the Gulch. The sack was too heavy to swing. The Gulch opened before him. And there was Tim sitting on the bottom steps of stairs that went up and up, nowhere fast. He was smoking a cigarette.

Tim called, "I know you. What's going on?"

"Tonight's big show, tomorrow Bloomsday."

Tim stood, dropped his butt, smashed it with his cowboy-booted foot. "Yeah, the whole art thing, everybody's an expert. You know? Who gets to decide? Authority is money. None of us have any money."

"What's going on?" Dik Dik lowered his sack to the ground, exhaled, flexed his fingers.

"You mean right now in town or just for me?" He laughed, strutted in place. "Ben's sword making outfit is getting together. You should see the way they pound their iron. Turning out these great, misshapen cleavers."

"Sa-words."

"Right-o. Isn't that what you folks say? Man, you gotta follow the posters. You gotta learn to read 'em. They're in layers."

Tim looked like a gray Jerry Garcia. Dik Dik wondered if he and the Jackal were fucking. Tim was a 'good guy'. That's the way everybody said it. A decent artist. Was Jackal a 'good guy'? 'Guy' no longer had a gender. Jackal was too cunning.

Tim said, "Sufis at the noodle shop."

"No! They're meeting over miso? And the Episcopagans? Where are they worshipping? Onward enclaves!"

"Psychic readings at the old Woolworth building. Auras fluffed. Wands. Lodestones."

"Goddess help me! They know not what they do!"

"I like to know what's going on, I stop by for a visit. I say I'm curious, just wanna see what's what. They're glad to have new blood. Maybe one of the women will want to mentor me. I love mentors. I love mentoring. I've learned a lot." Tim laughed a thick laugh, sarcastic and/or bitter. "You know what a MILF is? No way, I'm too old."

"Heaven's no, you're not too old." Commandment Number 9 again!

"I learned about Buddha. This guy Gerd-jeff. Know who I mean? Went to his semin-ar. Ha! Flash writing at the library on Tuesday. No, Wednesday. No, Wednesday, Old lady Becket Twister has Tai Chi classes. You know, float like a butterfly?" Tim demonstrated, slowly moving his arms in circles, raising his legs.

"Very nice! Very comely. Positively enlightened. I had no idea you were taken by the esoteric."

"I didn't go to college. I drove a truck."

"I know your art, not your mind."

"Good one." He smiled, slapped a hand to Dik Dik's shoulder. "You gotta keep watching posters, or you'll miss something."

"Posters in layers, juxtaposed. Gurus, gimmicks, gew gaws. Distractions."

"Don't start! They're invitations. I never understand your poultry."

"Palimpsests."

"*Gesundheit*! Probably see you later. It's going to be wild in the ol' town tonight. Which way you going now?"

"Up the Gulch, gotta get back to my digs, prepare."

"Ha." Tim leaned in, whispered to Dik Dik, "We could always go over to the Dungeon?"

"Will I be sorry if you fill me in?"

"This dood we both know, in our age bracket, went over to the Dungeon, and this masked woman beat his balls with a spatula."

"How very –" Dik Dik picked up his sack, ready to zoom.

"No, that's what he wanted. You have to clean up after yourself. Antiseptic. It's not a brothel. It's a place where folks can share equipment."

"No one's in my age bracket."

"I'll go if you go. Cover charge, we're in."

"The equipment is fine, thanks."

'Staples and pins, push pins they call them, armature armor for telephone pole palimpsests.' Stearns would roll over in his grave at Westminster, lolled Dik Dik, as he made his way in a swaying tempo, arms swinging, up the sidewalk of the Gulch. It was warm, it was dry. Bright. No one around. Dry gulch Gulch. The sack dragged on his arm, so he switched arms – his glorious treasures! Dik Dik passed the same shops, bars, galleries he'd passed earlier. The posters on telephone poles and boards hadn't changed.

Now it was town's turn to talk. He queried. He listened. Town annotated structure – buildings and fire hydrants and stairs and walls fulfilled their duties. Then, echoes of before structures with their own posters. Punctuated town with merely reminders where buildings wanted them. In the slots between structures. De Chirico forever! Familiarity was good for an old man. Gulch empty. Must be siesta time. Parking lot with seven vehicles. Three looked forlorn, four were earnest. A little white dog examined a fire hydrant with a poster taped to it. Would the little white dog go? Learn about Gerd? It was just as well, thought Dik Dik. He needed a nap.

The Gulch narrowed, canyon walls steeper. Layers of

houses joined by stairs went up and up, four, then five layers. All sorts of houses, mining shacks with saggy roofs, refurbished cottages with fake adobe, then modern designs with solar panels. Impossible parking here. A bend in the canyon, and the walls opened up, backed off, and there was a store, Mimosa Market, motto: 'Everything you might need most of the time.' The little grocery was run by a couple of elves. They had to be. Coltrannies were never that helpful. The store had a small parking area, then, set back, houses resumed their climb up through the layers. The bottom layer had Dik Dik's house. Sixty-four steps to his front door which was installed upside down.

Approaching his place, the way it jutted out from the canyon wall, it looked like the do-it-yourself enchanted hut from a dark desert fairy tale. On the outside, wooden slats had been obsessively nailed over crumbling walls. Slate in patterns, slats lined up straight, floor to roof. The new front window he'd put in was so wide that, from the street below, it looked like a display case, or even an aquarium, maybe full of electric eels. Corrugated tin roof probably a hundred years old. Leaks aplenty. He unlocked his upside down door, but before he went in, like he did each time, he glanced at the apricot tree in his tiny front yard.

It had grown tall and full. He recalled wonderful fruit... jams...chutneys. Now he examined the growth of its tumors. Just for a moment. He didn't want to overdo it. Like to like! All that rubbish. Dik Dik had noticed the tumors' appearance last spring. So a year now. Mainly in the top branches, woody growths golf ball to baseball-sized. They were spreading. They didn't look like Christmas ornaments or regular fruit. They were covered in bark the same color and texture as the branches, smooth for the most part with a few bumpy patches. He'd left his ladder beside the cancerous tree, since he'd first climbed up for a closer examination. Ladder and tree, now, made a Magritte post card. True life readymade! He had to bring the ladder in before someone stole it. He thought that every time he saluted the tumor tree.

He went on in, slung his sack of copies and books atop a work table. His work room: table saw, work benches. Stacks of lumber. His tools and supplies nearly put away. He had another key for the inner glass door to his home. Home sweet! One big room: a Great Room, like the inside of his noggin, like to like. A cabin...rustic was too kind...with more slats up and down these walls too. The walls didn't press in, they played with the eyes seeking patterns. Plus, he had secreted in to the walls various alcoves, niches of different sizes to allow dioramas or displays. To the right, an elevated area, carpeted – step up...two steps. Elevated area, like a mini-loft, with pillows, book shelf, lamp, small table...his Comfort Zone. Across from there, kitchen area, ancient gas stove, funky mid-sized refrigerator with thick black paint proclaiming 'FUCK!" across the front. A handmade credenza astride the kitchen area looked like a fancy ironing board. Ah, it was a tombstone? The photographs on the wall were mainly his, black and white, framed, crisp in their blur, or repeated images in what might have been a bee hive. Mainly of people, studies of parts and faces.

He went to the cabinets built on to the wall with scraps of wood, put together like Kandinsky explosions. He got out a can of sardines, put the kettle on to heat, and settled on his bar stool behind the credenza, the helm of his ship...heaving through the canyons, defying gravity by human will. He found some WASA toast, a plate, a fork, opened the sardines. He shook the sardines out of the can while trying to hold back the oil. He could have used his fork but that would have been cheating. He overheard himself humming.

Of all the nights – why tonight? Interference! Nothing must interfere with tomorrow.

That's when he realized he'd lost his cum glow. Sardines! Fuck sakes – the jealous flavor aroma of sardines had taken over his sensory. Kettle began to chirp. He kept up his hum, while stepping over to the stove. Opposite, after the cabinets, a woody alcove, one of his favorites. Inset: a silvery wire man in a standing, pushing position, up against a boulder.

Dik Dik ate. He sipped. He sighed. He got up and walked past his second favorite niche with the wooden Shinto figure from Nagasaki. He'd found it in the rubble just weeks after the blast.

He had to have a piss.

The bathroom wall was right up against the solid rock wall of the mountain, barely a crawl space between them. He made ready to pee. The growth on his penis was exactly like the growths on the tree. But no bark. It was too much to bare. He finished his piss, took out his teeth to soak, headed for his bed and mosquito netting.

He'd added the bedroom on...roughly, like he'd added on the bathroom. One wall of the bedroom was shelving of multiple sizes, holding a mass of reel to reels, canisters, VHS tapes, then boxes of sleeves for photographs. Then stacks of manuscripts, notebooks, scripts. A celluloid, cellulose coral reef. The bookshelf by his bed held his favorites, Camus, Celine, Philip K. Dick. His bed was covered by mosquito netting to keep out kissing bugs which he was deadly allergic to. Right now was nappy time.

He got comfortable. Joyce was ready. *Exile, loneliness, cunning.* Long time coming. Behold! Art! Fricking diva – oy! His juggle was levels/layers of existence never resolved. They would be ignored for the span of one June nap. Even perception was a perception. *Nature is a tumor.* What made an artist prefer celebrity over a big bowl of steaming reality? Art and life had to merge, so they could emerge. Consistency might meet market filters. The only thing that ever mattered was the cum moment's joy. Potentiality. Eventuality. Every second counted – so many seconds! As though time kept track? Now is later. Tomorrow is yesterday. 'So in the future, the sister of the past, I may see myself as I sit here now but by reflection from that which then I shall be.'

PART II

Silky Grand Guignol at the Stock Yard! The creepy glare tangled customers' puppet strings. Night in the Gulch: the night glared. Reflections treacly. Plus, peeps on Coltrane time – so no time but this time. No passage or chronology, everything at once. Narration outside of time was called *stoy*. Coltrane Commandment Number 10: Beware the Coltrane time. No one knew when things might get started so they got started.

The Yard launched tonight! The red-bricked edifice was a three storied galleon. First floor at street level – used to be a Chinese restaurant. Second floor, the bar, so above the Gulch. A covered promenade wrapped around the second floor, where the smokers and the fried hung out. The third story, top deck, held apartments for the rich and needy.

The bar entrance at the prow overflowed with voices begging to agglutinate. Voices executed with high pitched bleats, then dialogs, monologs, rebuttals, all of it, high range, low range, in and out of timbre. Maybe some music, too, maybe a tune suddenly the filigree on top. Every once in a while, a trumpet blasted. A guitar lick shouted out.

Stoners approached thinking this was the Lusitania and there were no life boats. A scrawny brown dog dashed from the entrance pursued by a biker in leathers who was vaping as he ran, or else he was on fire. A throb foghorned off the ship. Concerns vanished. Pulsars imploded. The crescendo skirmish ice berg angst depended on how stoned you were. White water consciousness.

Dik Dik worked his way in. He wound through the people on the stairs to the entrance. He plunged. 'Hallo,' 'hallo,' bounced around him. Solid people, from the entrance to the back where the stage was. Pool table and bowling table dribbled with bodies. Tables pushed to the side. Seats taken. Nowhere to sit. He wanted a gin and tonic. The noise became a *bee* stuck in his ear tube. He had to get to the bar, place his order. 'Excuse me, excuse me,' he repeated out loud, so he pushed his way through. There wasn't a cum around: this was all fetish work.

Old Lady Beckett Twister (from here on referred to as OLBT) had staked out a secret corner of the bar. Her extensive iconoclasm endowed her with a margin of space not intruded on. People didn't want to get too close to her. Anyone's intuition would note a nest of weavings bound around an old lady neutron star, and step aside. Dik Dik stepped right up.

Too noisy to talk, they looked into each other's eyes. Dik Dik nodded very slowly, very dramatically. Finally, she reached in to the weavings about her bosom and pulled out a pen and pad. She slapped them to the bar top.

Dik Dik got in close to her, pronounced, "I want to order."

She nodded.

Four bartenders boing-boinged behind the bar, pulling beers, setting out shots. It looked impossible to get an order in. Of the four women working the bar, three were young, slim, athletic tough. One was hefty, older, and street tough. She was the one who caught OLBT's look and came over.

"What'll it be?" she mouthed.

Dik Dik shouted, "Gin and tonic!"

OLBT tapped her shot glass, so the bartender would know to bring her another one. Dik Dik caught the bartender's tender glance at OLBT and wondered at intentionality. The bartender blasted away. Discernment was the key.

OLBT wrote on the pad, "Mercury," drawing its alchemical symbol next to it, the one that looked like the female symbol with a hat.

Dik Dik took the offered pen and pad, and drew in some exclamation points.

OLBT took back her pad, turned to the next blank page, and wrote, "Who did the Mona Lisa?"

He wrote underneath the question, "Nat King Cole."

She took back her pad and pen and wrote, "Let's stabilize this jimmy. Bunch of addicts. New classification in psychohistory: the 'philosophical zombie'. Coltrane Commandment Number 11: Beware the ides of Joyce."

At his turn, Dik Dik wrote, "Is it official?"

She shouted, "Official?" looking up at him.

He wrote back, "A new Coltrane Commandment?"

She wrote, "Just made it up. Art can be terrible."

Dik Dik wrote, "Art can be deliberate."

The bartender splashed down their drinks. OLBT waved her away, she'd take care of the bill later. Dik Dik picked up his glass, had a sip, then leaned in one more time to the mountain that breathed, drank, drew, read, and thought...that was his comrade, for a hug.

She whispered in his ear, "I love you. I'll see you tomorrow."

He whispered-shouted back, "I love you because you smell like a lion."

As he pulled away, stepping back to the fracas, she

shouted, "Stabilize!"

She had the most amazing head. No neck. But a baby doll, bulgy head of big brains. She was too smart, and it too often came out in prissy private code that few could fathom. Everybody made a sound. We got used to each other's sounds. Her sound cackled. This was what big brains ended up doing when they didn't slave at the think tank. Independent scholarship invented new sounds. She relished her crone status. Some claimed they'd seen those beacon eyes of hers turn totally black. Could she 'stabilize?' Maybe if he helped? Let the magic begin –

Dik Dik navigated toward the stage. He wanted to be close to the debacle, to feel its full rampage. Faces, elbows, knees, trunks. Dik Dik said in to the melee, "Those aren't the lines you were thinking of." People looked. He smiled, waved to people he knew. All kinds of humans: young artists, old artists, old hippies, wannabes, druggies, dealers, bikers, street kids. Then the fellow travelers with real jobs who could be picked out by their clothes – new and clean. Devices were held up, pictures taken, flashes rampant. A young man and a young woman were filming the crowd with tiny palm held devices. A poet must have picked up on Dik Dik's one-liner he'd continued to repeat, as the burly fellow stretched to his full height and bellowed:

"The sweet pink
Of her hot meat
In the citrus of sighs!"

Applause erupted, hooting. Whelps of glory! Then something odd: things stabilized. After the applause and hoots died down, the music cut – Dik Dik couldn't identify what the music had been, then the lights dimmed. The decibel level did a phase transfer. People by the door headed out to the patio for one more cigarette. Bodies inside rearranged themselves more gracefully. Dik Dik held his 'stabilize' juju intact, as he gained the stage.

It was a decent stage he'd played many times. Not too big, not too small. Wooden, raised about a foot above the floor, it was built right up against the building's back wall. Three windows in that wall, rectangular windows, inset, tall. Sound equipment at the sides of the stage. One mic on a mic stand to the side as well. Because center stage was commanded by three doors. They looked like regular wooden doors, with regular knobs and hinges. The doors were mounted in wooden frames that made a box around each door, that went back behind the door a couple feet. All three doors were closed.

Stabilize! Dik Dick began to turn to check on his gente. He'd almost forgotten the crowd was there, so transfixed was he by the strange doors. But Lise was beside him, studying the doors as he had.

She recited to him and he could hear her plainly: "I found a turtle digging in the desert. I brought her cantaloupe the next day. She was still digging. 'Where are you going?' I asked. 'All the way down,' she replied."

Finally, she moved her eyes from the stage and its doors to see Dik Dik. She said, "You're *doing* it."

Dik Dik cried, "The game's afoot!" Laughing, he took a pull from his drink, snorted.

Two men swooped in on Lise and started sniffing and prowling, trying to get in close to her. They were like hummingbirds, and she was the flower.

Dik Dik completed his turn to the crowd. Lydia and the Jackal were jostling to the front, bending and swaying to the bodies to inch forward. He saw their flush, didn't have to see their eyes. Then he saw Ava, her height and beauty signaling 'hello' straight at him. She was with her beau, a big dood dressed cowboy. There was that art car woman, no boyfriend, looking subdued, droopy...but she seemed alive. Douglas and Moriah were there, dressed in going-out-of-an- evening attire. Tiffany in life! No Bear or Dog. Tim Asparagus by himself, in a funny hat. Faces!

Faces ready for the show. Faces leaky, beaky, weepy, salty.
Now why had he come up here? Ah, yes, to pay his
respects –

In front of the stage, three tables with chairs for stars
and their entourages. The two smaller tables held the
players of the evening's rout. Simon's was the smallest,
but he had the smaller entourage, two middle-aged
women in hippy skirts and peasant blouses.

M.K. Table's table hosted Mad, who legend had it was
raised in the desert by M.K. in his feral period. Now the
beast was stretched out across two chairs. He looked
pretty comfortable. M.K.'s two female assistants were
young. He had a professional agent in a monkey suit.
Captain America and Megadeath completed his grouping.

The biggest table was Agatha's. The Stock Yard was
her place. Dik Dik beamed over to her. She was the owner.
This was her show, her boat, her stage. She smiled at Dik
Dik and reached out for his hand. Her cowboy-booted feet
were up on the table. She was pure goddess, lolling with
power.

He took her hand, came in close to say, "I heard they
spotted Cleopatra's barge on the river, and I knew it was
you."

Her eyes bristled with intense contentment. She said,
"You're such a cutie." She bent forward to peck his cheek.

Dik Dik released her hand, straightened, backed away.

Agatha was of indeterminate age. She told stories about
riding behind Robert Mitchum on his motorcycle. She'd
been, as they say, around, with all the exuberant and scary
implications that might entail. Dik Dik and her had
enjoyed talking about Hong Kong, where they'd both
lived at one time. Either she had especially good drugs, or
she was a *radiant* entrepreneur. Her entourage was all
men, young men, and each dressed in a theme, so one
cowboy, one Wild West gambler, one artsy hipster with a
goatee and little hat, and one maker – her mound of

muscle sycophant named Oscar. They all had drinks in front of them, and a waitress made sure to keep them full.

Dik Dik nodded to Oscar, stepped over to M.K.'s table, taking a long pull on his gin and tonic. He spluttered a bit, before he got it out: "New John Le Carré at the library."

M.K. looked ragged and gray, gaunt. He was all scrunched up in his chair, knees to chin. So hard to follow his spiels of celebrity when he looked like a homeless guy. What was wrong with him? How old was he? How many teeth did he have? He had sold a bunch of paintings over the years, and he had shown many times in New York City.

M.K. turned slightly to acknowledge Dik Dik. His head angled to see right through him, as he said, "Who is that Brit spy novelist I always say is my favorite? Can't think of his name. First? Furst?"

Megadeath, a slight thing with bad feet, said, "I'm reading Schiller."

M.K. snapped, "No one's impressed. Remember when I turned everyone on to Magic Realism in the eighties?"

Dik Dik slid, levitated, wheeled over to Simon's table. Simon nodded to him solemnly. Simon wore no shoes. He was dressed in sack cloth. The two women with him were knitting.

Dik Dik said, "So, mate, going into the great beyond, are ya?"

Simon had an Arizona desert cliffside of a face. He could be a pinnacle, a needle of rock. His wrinkles had wrinkles. Of wisdom. Of implosion. Of lousy moisturizing.

Simon said, "I'm reading nothing but Terence Mckenna."

One of the women (Dik Dik didn't know the women) said, "You said you were reading *M. Butterfly*."

Simon said, "Counting. I've been counting. Do you count, Richard?"

"Very nice," said Dik Dik. "Yes, I count."

Simon explained, "I've been counting pills. Counting pills is counting ills. I've been seeing if big pharma tells the truth. What do you think? Count the pills. County, count. Bought a case of aspirin. Hundred counts. I counted them. That's what it says. Hundred count. I counted them. I graphed my work. They varied from ninety to a hundred."

The woman said, "He promised to take us through the portal to Earth." Her head elongated. Was she a question mark?

The other woman jumped in: "Then he started counting, counting, counting."

Simon said, "I realized my abstracts, my Southwest horizons were really Mars."

The first woman who had spoken, said, "This isn't Earth. It's a space where half-ass talent makes more money than genius. That's a crime! Count that, master! Money whores. All they want is celebrity."

The other woman added, "Even when they've been counted."

"Hush, now," went Simon.

Dik Dik wondered if he should make a dash for the loo, the hallway to the restrooms was right here, this end of the bar. There went Daphne flitting up to M.K.'s table. Oh, sure, he was a butterfly collector! Behind her, in the jam, Dik Dik caught a red-headed flash. The red was unmistakable, glowy red, chemical red in trickster light. *Her* boys were afoot! He took the short hall, turned in to the men's room. One guy at a urinal, urinals separated by side panels.

The guy said, "I met you at the Tavern. How ya doing?"

"I remember your voice. Everybody has a sound."

"That's just the sound of pee, *jefe*." He laughed. No, I know what you mean, that's true," said the guy at the urinal, and finished, so passed behind Dik Dik to the sink to wash his hands. Dik Dik joined him a few seconds later.

After they'd washed and dried their hands, the pool player from the afternoon stuck out his hand. Dik Dik took it, shook.

"Johnny," the pool player said.

Dik Dik said, 'Dik."

They nodded at each other, walked out together. They paused at the end of the hallway before the bar.

Johnny said, "Funny night, funny people. All mixed up."

"How do you mean?"

"All the shit going down, all sorts of shit, everybody's got their angle."

"Ha! Isn't it always like that?"

Johnny shrugged. "I don't know. Look at that couple," he said, his eyes fastening on Captain America and Megadeath. "We call them the Joads. Like from that book we had to read in high school. That guy over there, who was at the Tavern? Jerry Garcia. The big deal artist, sitting there...what's his name? We call him *Zopilote*. What is his name?"

Moriah mused over, probably heading for the restrooms. She wore a dress, a blue dress. Women in Coltrane didn't wear dresses often. She looked good, her hair up. She glared at Dik Dik. Johnny nodded to him and took off.

Moriah said, "What you said. What you said – is it real?"

Dik Dik hurried: "Surely, Douglas told you the context of my remarks. There was no hint of tautology."

"Don't be an ass." She stopped, looked at him, looked away. "I'm drawing. Personal work. Very personal. I found these pencils, Rickendorfs they're called, and they are the real dealio, okay? Pencils from my deep bones."

"Glad you're working. We should all be so lucky."

"And fucking. I'm fucking, too. People think middle-aged women don't like to fuck. You know what? They do.

They like all sorts of things. And you know what? You know what really riles is when a man spurns you? Doesn't even see you. Even when he's a ghoul."

Dik Dik cluttered away in a two step, right in to the arms of Tiffany. She was radiant tonight, too.

Dik Dik said, "You look sublime."

Tiffany said, "What's a 'tautology'?"

"Eavesdropping! The Great Game overheard!"

She pulled back.

He said, "Where's the band?"

"No gigs. We're broke."

"Lack of money is the root of all evil."

"Amen, brother."

They looked over the crowd, but stayed close, almost touching, standing at the wall. Everybody was patient. It had to be soon. Now Dik Dik saw Daphne up at the bar with a rough looking character, a big guy. They were having an intense exchange, when the man reached into his pocket and pulled out a shiny metal tube –

He pressed the tube to Daphne, who put it away, made it disappear – out of sight, out of mind. Coltrane Commandment Number 11: Beware the Coltrane deal. Then Dik Dik recalled Number 9 which made him snort.

It was all in the timing. Everybody's drugs and liquor quotient was peaking.

Tiffany said, "Ethyl chloride."

Dik Dik came closer: "Say again."

"That tube."

"You know Daphne."

"Everybody knows everybody, and it doesn't help."

The big guy melted in to the crowd, making for the door. A couple biker doods, pressed in at the opposite side of the bar, gave him the eye, following his getaway. Dik Dik considered Johnny's comment, so much shit going on, going down, going round, everybody involved in some shit, and that shit got in the way of doing your own shit.

Nothing must get in the way of tomorrow!

Tiffany and Dik Dik kept scanning the room. That band guy, the guitar player, Mikey, was talking to Daphne now. Then, here came the kid from the theater who liked his claustrophobia bit, right up to Mikey. They conferred, they decided, they zoomed, pulsing through the bodies, in and out, around and under, towards the door.

Tiffany said, "Something's rotten in De-troit."

Dik Dik roared with laughter. Johnny showed up beside him. "What's so funny?" he asked.

Dik Dik winced, with a mewling, mutiny sound.

Johnny said, "Aren't you going to introduce me to this lovely young lady?"

There was a metallic screech and rip, as Coney Shaman, who must have snuck on to the stage, tested the mic. Lights blinked, went out. Stage lights came on. A big cheer with applause began with gusto then cut off fast.

Coney Shaman's top hat, tux, and gloves made everybody ID him a child molester. Like. Parody perversion required participation. Coney Shaman's bulk beefed up this posture, gaining altitude for the hairy melon, plopping from the hat. This was his scarecrow, pumpkinhead, Obadiah moment of limerence and liminance. Auticulture. Stage lights spotted his warpath. Theremin music offered a sound sculpture background, from the gossipy insides of an electric storm, what it sounded like inside distant *brujos* with asthma.

Oh, fuck, special f/x.

Presence, contact, negotiations – Coney Shaman used the mic.

"Some say God is the Word made flesh. Each time we

make a word, we create. God kins, god kins. Utterance. Speech is art, and art is magic. Abracadabra. Implicit impeccable. God kins, god kins. We begin tonight's transmutation. We are already on our way. You felt it. I felt it. This is what we do. This is what we like. Tonight, we declare. Tonight, we embrace."

Suddenly, Dik Dik could hear Coney Shaman's sweat glands. Shiny skin patches, between hairiness, pinched out pus.

"Adam taught Man alchemy. Adam invented the alphabet. Kircher was the first to decipher the hieroglyphs, understanding they were Adam's primordial language. And the alchemists called on blessed Enoch, the one who walked with God, who ascended into heaven directly, for guidance. And Enoch transformed in heaven: Enoch became Metatron, angel most high. And Hermes Trismegestus became –"

Dik Dik popped off: "Begat! Begat! Get on with it!"

Laughter! More word pops jumped out from the crowd, but guffaws popped out, too, with question marks.

"Let him finish!" from Tilman up front, to the side of the stage, ready to assist, in his own regalia.

Coney Shaman came back more emphatic, more gesturing. The height of his hands increasing –

"No pictures! No recording! Please!

"Abracadabra. Words, air, birds, love. Change becomes charge. One letter, one sound, or cult of the tongue, and everything – " He paused. Everybody could tell it was his idea of dramatic effect. "Everything is everything and someone else's dream. Change, charge. Shaman is showman. Alzheimer's is old timer's.

"Tonight, tonight
How many worlds tonight
How many worlds will we plunder of copper
Gleaming, gleaming, gleaming
Over the night!"

Tilman squawked. The crowd muttered. Theremin ambulance now.

"Like to like. As above, so below. Regale us – we accept, we give back. By the sacred triangle, phi, pi, and cleft, set forth by Paracelsus, ashes to ashes, life to life – live, damnit! Power upon us! Power is with us!"

Mild applause. More guffaws. A great shuffling.

He got to it: "Now, I'm going to call up on stage our three players for the evening. I'll call their names one by one. First, world class artist, auteur, raconteur, saboteur, M.K. Table. Please come up."

M.K. stood at his table, rolled his measly shoulders, did a quick glance over the folks with a little wave. Proceeded to the stage. He ascended. Coney Shaman placed him in front of the door at stage right, which the audience perceived as on the left. This was the side where the mic stood. M.K. straightened by his door, holding his hands together loosely in front of himself. His right hand was holding his left hand's thumb.

The polite applause was hushed by Coney Shaman who warned, "Not now, not now." He returned to the mic.

"Our second lucky contestant –" He laughed nervously, but played it out: "Just kidding. Our second volunteer, Simon! Simon, please. Barefoot seer of the ley lines, wonder artist, time traveler, please step up."

Simon rose like a craggy, brown gopher coming straight out of its hole. He looked around with a dazed concern, lips moving, twisting. Gum? Glossolalia. Simon prayed to the entities not mentioned by Coney Shaman. Simon stepped to the stage, ascended. Simon joined Coney Shaman by the second, or middle, door. Coney Shaman aligned him, hands to his shoulders, squarely in front of his door. Coney Shaman went back to the mic.

"And last, but not least, you know him, you love him, Slim Jims give him gas, you've seen his feces in a thousand installations – Mad! *Wunderhund!*"

Mad jumped, fell out of his chairs, assembled himself, woofed, glanced about to see who was running this show. Megadeath came to his side, hand to his collar, and guided him to the stage. They negotiated their way. Coney Shaman waited at the end of the stage, at the last door. Megadeath patted the stage floor by him. Mad hefted himself up, front legs first, a balance, a bound, he was on stage in front of the third door. Megadeath stayed where she was. Coney Shaman rubbed Mad's ears, made polite promises he couldn't keep, repeating seamlessly, "Sit, sit, stay, stay. Sit, sit, stay, stay." Mad complied.

Coney Shaman went to the mic, notably fluttering. He had the heebie-jeebies. Every time he was to perform, or present in public, right before he was to go on, he would have a moment of panic and want to run. Use it! Bleed it! Make it work for him – raw!

"These three, these brave volunteers! Now I think it's time to examine the doors. A little help, please! Deacon Tilman, would you mind to be so kind?"

Tilman got up on stage. He said, "Of course, Triune. Happy to is –"

Coney Shaman stepped away from the mic. He went to Simon in the middle, taking his shirt sleeve, and said, "A tad over, just for a sec, while we examine the doors. Stand by M.K."

That was too much for Simon who blurted gustily, "I stand by no –"

Theremin came in all space naughtiness, whistling tunicates, the winds of Titania. The electro f/x stopped.

Tilman and Coney Shaman took opposite sides of the middle door and brought it forward to the edge of the stage. It wasn't apparent whether they lifted it, or if it slid or wheeled. They turned it all the way around. Coney Shaman made a show of walking around the door, rapping on each of its sides. Tilman had stepped aside with folded arms.

Coney Shaman said, "Deacon, do you see any escape hatches? Secret compartments? Cubicles? Carbuncles? Kryptonite? Hidden releases? Please, make your own examination."

Tilman walked around the door knocking on each side. He closely examined seams, joints, knocking at several spots. He opened the door, looked in, felt about, closed it. He announced, 'I'm satisfied! Oh, Triune! No escape hatches, no secret releases. Only way in or out is through the front door. Stable. Stable, all the way."

He and Coney Shaman pushed the door back to its proper place.

"Thank you, Deacon," said Coney Shaman and waved him away. Tilman walked to the edge of stage left. He had his arms folded in front of himself. He seemed to be hard pressed, or holding in a dangerous fart.

"Now, Simon, please return to your position. Very good. Are we ready? Mad?"

Megadeath said, "I can help."

Coney Shaman ignored her, and, with a flourish made his way to M.K. Went straight to his door, took the knob and opened it. He said, "M.K." And M.K. stepped into the doorway, turned to face out. He fit fine. Not too snug at all. M.K. smiled confidently but with tight lips.

A few coffin jokes rose irresistibly from the crowd.

Coney Shaman said, "Comfortable?"

M.K. said, "I'm fine."

"Now I will close the door," and Coney Shaman did.

He went to the middle door and opened it. "Are you ready, Simon of the Desert?"

Simon said, "Every door is a portal," and he stepped in to the doorway, back to its back. He was taller so a little scrunch on top.

Coney Shaman closed the door. He walked over to the last door, Mad sitting there, on his haunches, watching the whole thing.

"Good dog," said Coney Shaman. "We've been practicing, haven't we?"

People laughed with concern or doubt. 'No way', nervously chuckled through.

Fast, Coney Shaman said, "He'll be fine. He fits. Let's show 'em, Mad Dog."

He opened the door and Mad went in, but he was so wide and long, no way he could do it. He kept circling, eager to please, trying to squeeze in.

Megadeath went, "Oh!"

Tilman hurried over. He and Coney Shaman took up positions on either side of the dog and Tilman patted his hand up at the upper right corner of the inner door, and Mad gangly up sidewise, so his head and forearms were crammed in to that corner. The rest of him fit.

A couple boos groaned over the palpitations.

Coney Shaman closed the door, nodding frantically, Tilman exiting. Coney Shaman went back to the mic. He had to act fast. "Abracadabra! Are you ready?"

M.K.'s dulled voice came out: "Are you asking us or the audience?"

Simon made some muffled roars. Mad whimpered. You could hear it. It was killing Megadeath.

It was Coney Shaman's moment, what he'd been waiting for. His punctum! What he'd been planning a long time. Coney Shaman concentrated everything he had –

Tim Asparagus shouted out, "Don't bring them back!"

The lights went out.

The mic thud was deep and solid. Power outage! Everything stopped. The universe inhaled its navel and spit out a pit. Then a tremendous barrage on stage! Shuffling sounds, weighty and guttural. Pure dark took over. It didn't sound magical: sounded rough. Then it was quiet.

People had their phone lights on. A buzz took over the crowd: 'what's going on?' 'is this part of the show?'

Coney Shaman yelled, "Razzamatazz!" No mic, so simply a shout.

Nothing happened.

He yelled it again: "Razzamatazz!" Again: "Razzamatazz!"

Megadeath cried out in a high voice, "Too long for Mad. Too long for Mad."

By the bluish glare of the strobing phone lights, Dik Dik saw Agatha step forward. Tiffany took his hand. Everybody could feel it. Something wasn't right. Agatha looked tense, stern, hands at hips, elbows out.

Coney Shaman screeched, "Somebody, turn on the lights! Turn on the lights! This is not part of the show! Not what's supposed to happen. I think there's been a power outage. Sorry, everybody. Just chill for a sec. Get the lights! Somebody, check on the lights! No one is in any danger. There's no danger."

Megadeath insisted now: "Let out Mad! Let out Mad!" She scrambled, trying to get up on stage, going, "Here, Mad! Here, Mad!" Her sneaky, pleading voice in the dark with LED lightning bugs.

Dik Dik and Tiffany stepped closer to the stage.

Coney Shaman exploded, "All right!" No one could see his face, but imagined what a vampire pumpkin looked like. He walked forward, fumbly, stumbly, right in to the middle door, knocking himself to the floor.

"Get the lights on!" someone shouted. "What was that?"

Megadeath and Tilman managed to get over to Coney Shaman who was hauling himself to his feet. Coney Shaman yelled, "Open the doors!" Megadeath screamed.

Tilman threw open the first door. Phone lights cast blue radiance at emptiness. Indigo void called for stalagmites. Or a hallway? Coney Shaman opened the middle door. It, too, empty.

Megadeath followed them to the third door. The last

door. Coney Shaman opened it. Megadeath squawked.

Now the peeps surged. Everybody talked at once. An exit line formed at the entrance. Mind the gap! Shouts tested their nerves. A couple cackles, a few wails, but no real panic, as at least half the people that remained thought this was part of the happening, this *was* the performance. The other half was too blitzed to care. It was all performance in Coltrane, and a Coltrane Commandment waiting in the wings for consensus suggested: Beware the Coltrane performance.

Tiffany and Dik Dik stayed, watching in the phone lights. The entourage tables had skittish players up on their feet, conferring, speculating. A grand milling began in the dark, the great human grab bag of clinkers and miscues, where all concerned fought for the inside scoop. Who knew what was going on? Did he know? Did she know? *Who was in the know?* Dik Dik giggled. Tiffany glanced at him a smirk he missed in the dark. Dik Dik was remembering the early days of art town, how it became a joke when new people met, wondering, *does he know, does she know, how far have they gone.* Dik Dik puzzled the crews, Simon's table, his women knitting, Oscar stood behind Agatha, M.K.'s peeps flustered. Coney Shaman, pacing on stage, hissed and begged and spat and 'splained, refusing answers, denying charges, eking out pathos.

"What's going on?" asked a voice behind Dik Dik.

He turned, releasing Tiffany's hand, and face to face with Lorna. Not enough light to see her eyes. Her face had a black brick across its eyes.

"We haven't a clue."

"But something not right. You can feel it."

"Artists feel too much."

"Do I need to be punished, Dik Dik? Is that it? Would you like to spank me? Ah, you would! You would like that."

"Dunno, dunno. Oh, my, I've misplaced my drink."

Tiffany spun around: "You put it down."

Lorna said, "You still haven't answered me."

Dik Dik said, "I've never been one for incorporeal punishment."

The lights went on.

Dik Dik and Tiffany acted fast, moving to the stage. A cheer went up. Voices called out, 'where are they? 'where's the dog?' 'what happened?' 'is this the show?' Dik Dik glanced behind. Lorna was gone.

Coney Shaman and Tilman scrambled around stage, pulling aside curtains or hangings. Agatha got up on stage to confer with them. Oscar went with her. Agatha sent a couple of her boys running. Others got on their phones.

Megadeath squealed, "Where's Mad?"

Captain America appeared by the stage. He needed a drink, so he was going to the bar the long way, by the stage, see if he could do anything for –

Coney Shaman hustled forward to confront Megadeath. "I don't know. I don't know! Okay? This was not the show. This was not what was supposed to happen. I assume it's a prank. But right now I haven't a clue where Mad, or M.K., or Simon, are."

M.K.'s jubilant publicist said, "Should we call the police?"

Agatha took over. "What for? I agree with Triune. It's a prank. A Coltrane double whammy on the performance artist. What is real – all that jazz. Beware the Coltrane prank."

Coney Shaman said, "We gotta figure this out."

Agatha said, "We are. We're on it. After all, a joke's only as good as its punchline. You gotta complete the prestige."

Bartenders were crazy busy selling drinks again. People were leaving. People were coming in. Chairs and tables were pulled out, rearranged. People got comfortable. Was the show still going on? Did you win a prize if you held out the longest, or did you just feel like an ass?

Tiffany said to Dik Dik, "You know Lorna?"

Dik Dik nodded. Tiffany's eyes widened. "Everybody wants to fuck you."

"Do you?"

"Not really. But I like you. I'm glad we're friends. We're friends even if don't fuck, right?"

"What do you think?"

There was more commotion on stage. Swear words bubbled aloft, floating around like contagions. Tim Asparagus made his way to the stage, at the other end from where Tiffany and Dik Dik stood. He talked to some folks.

Tiffany said, "Something's happening."

Dik Dik said, "Nothing must interfere with Bloomsday. Tomorrow."

"It's gotta be a prank?"

"Maybe."

Tim came over to stand by them. They exchanged greetings. Tim had a big smile across his face. "I guess I jinxed 'em," he said.

"What?" went Tiffany.

Johnny came over from somewhere, stood by Dik Dik. "What's going on?" he asked.

Tim said, "Nobody knows. Looks like they really disappeared."

"It's a joke, right?" asked Tiffany.

Lise was there, in front of them, before the stage, watching, listening.

Finally, it was revealed: up on stage, Tilman pulled back the carpet in the rear corner. There was a trap door underneath the carpet. Agatha told him to open it. Dik Dik and his cronies got closer to see.

Agatha explained, "It's to the run off tunnels from the old days. Flood control. They say it was used by pirates. Who knows? But I keep knowledge of it on the down low."

Johnny murmured to Dik Dik, "Doper tunnels. Everybody knows about 'em."

Tilman said, "Well, I don't see how or why they'd use this "

Agatha said, "We have to check. This could be an emergency."

Megadeath crowed, "Why? Why? Where *are* they?"

"Hush," went Agatha. "We don't know yet."

Tilman had the trap door open and was peering down with a flashlight. "It goes beneath the stage to the floor, the original opening. Nothing I can see. Can't imagine Mad –"

Coney Shaman said, "Where does it go? We should send someone down to where it goes. The opposite end."

"We already did," said Agatha.

Dik Dik said, "Maybe if we knew what you had been planning – what the show was supposed to be, maybe then we could figure –"

Agatha nodded. "Good idea. Triune?"

Coney Shaman mumbled, then got it out: "I'm not – I'm not supposed to tell."

The Jackal appeared at the stage, stepping out of the crowd. She said, "The timing was off."

Dik Dik said, "How would you know?"

Coney Shaman said, "Don't make me do this!"

"Stop it," said Agatha.

Coney shaman recited, "It'd go fast. The whole thing in minutes. I'd say the magic words, the lights would go out. We had each sequence down to a minute plus. Maybe a minute and a half. It'd be very smooth. It had to be. We practiced and practiced.

"In the first sequence, after the lights go out, boom, then back on, I open the first two doors, and Simon and M.K. are switched. In each other's doors. I wouldn't check the third one. Mad was already gone. Safe. Then I say the magic words and close the doors, and the lights go off. A minute jibber jabber. Then lights on, and I check the doors. All three this time. They're empty. All three of them. The lights go out. Minute. Minute. Lights! They're back."

Tim spluttered, "How in the world would you get that dog back in its door, after all the trouble you had getting him in in the first place?"

Johnny laughed. "All this hassle for a twenty minute show."

Coney shaman said, "You don't understand. Doors are portals. Doors! Like to like. Opening doors."

Everybody was looking at Coney Shaman. He felt pierced. He felt naked and afraid, so he grinned, went into nervous giggles. He pivoted, came around fussy: "I'm not – I'm not up for this, okay?"

The Jackal said, "It's not your fault. I wasn't even in position."

Agatha said, "So Simon and M.K., and Mad, decided to wreck your whole show by not coming back? They must have planned this."

Coney Shaman said, "Power went off!"

Lise said, "Or they really vanished."

Dik Dik said, "Or there's a third party involved, who took matters into their own hands." The Jackal met his eyes. They were thinking the same thing.

One of Agatha's boys blasted through the bar's entrance. He hurried through the tables and to the stage. It was the guy who went as Wild West gambler. He announced, "Tunnel's clear. No way they could have gone through before we got there."

"How do you know?" asked Dik Dik.

"The tunnels are funky. Tight. The only way out is at the end where we were. The filth hadn't been disturbed. You could tell. The muck in the tunnels wasn't messed up at all. No prints. Footprints."

"Good, Colin," said Agatha.

The Jackal said, "So if they didn't go in to the tunnels...there's no other way." She clattered about in her boots, pacing, a rough staccato.

Coney Shaman exclaimed, "This is no prank! I can't deal with this –"

Tim said, "They're probably in Naco by now, having *carne asada* and *Tecates* at the Blue Moon."

Undercurrents, bad vibes, hysterical bolts, scythed through the ponderers.

The Jackal stomped her black boots, enunciated, "The windows! It's the only way."

Agatha shook her head. Got pesky: "They're locked. Can't be opened."

Oscar added, "Besides, it's twenty feet to the ground. They'd need ladders. All sorts of help."

Voices from all sides yapped it up in response.

Oscar said, "Come on, people, we're growing donkey ears here. Over thinking it. It's gotta be a joke. Right, Agatha?"

Agatha grinned, glanced around. "You guys, run over to Simon and M.K.'s places. See if they're there."

Simon's knitters had come forward. One said, "He's not there." She held up a key.

Agatha said, "Double check. Meanwhile, I'm gonna make some phone calls."

Agatha got busy with her devices. All around her people got on their phones and started plugging in.

Dik Dik said, "Let's go sit down like civilized Sherlocks. Have a drink, talk of the death of kings."

One of Agatha's boys, the hipster from Brooklyn, said, "Don't say that!"

Dik Dik sauntered to Agatha's big table and sat in her chair. Tim came and sat next to him. Tiffany and Lise pulled up chairs. The Jackal sat, writhing in to her chair, vest flapping. She couldn't hold still. Ants in the pants!

Day on fire! Johnny strode over, stood there. Dik Dik motioned him to take a seat.

"I seem to have lost my drink," said Dik Dik.

The big lady who'd taken Dik Dik's order before zoomed to the table. "What'll it be?" she said.

Dik Dik said, "Beckett still over there?"

"Sure," said the bartender, "she's enjoying the fun. What a performance!"

"Quite," said Dik Dik. "Tiffany, what do you want? Drink's on me."

The bartender said, "Let me get your order, you guys figure out how to pay."

They gave their order, which was easy: five beers and a gin and tonic. The bartender took off.

The Jackal said, "Nothing to do but wait."

"For our order?" said Johnny.

Tim and Lise laughed.

"Who the fuck are you?" said the Jackal.

Lise sang, "*Who the fuck are you?*" to no one in particular.

Johnny said, "I'm Johnny."

Dik Dik said, "We were all there when it happened. We saw it. We heard it. Anyone's guess –" He shrugged. "All we have is guesses. If guesses were yeses. But we have to have a time table. Hear me out! Let me explain. Tomorrow is Bloomsday. Some of you know I've been planning a dawn to dusk celebration of Bloomsday for some time. Maybe it's my last chance. Bollocks! Here's the whammy: we have to solve this double whammy prank before dawn tomorrow. What time is it?"

No one had a watch or thought to check their devices. It was that kind of moment, keyed up, blistering, all eyes on Dik Dik. The bartender approached with a packed tray. She said, "It's after ten." She distributed drinks. Money was brought out. Dik Dik put a Jackson in the kitty.

Dik Dik tasted his gin and tonic. Fine. He raised his

glass and toasted, "Prestidigitation!"

Tim went, "What he said!"

Everybody raised a glass and took a swallow.

Dik Dik went on: "So we have – what? Eight hours until dawn? If this whole farce isn't cleared up by then, Bloomsday will be threatened. You know it's true."

Lise said, "A time table usually refers to re-creating a murderer's actions leading up to the crime." She puffed her lips, blew out. "I read mysteries."

The Jackal said, "That's crazy. Don't worst-case-scenario this."

"A time table," Dik Dik clarified, "for what *we* do, the avenues *we* will traverse to solve the conniption."

OLBT rumbled forward, stomping to their table. Lise squealed, "Twister!"

"I'll titty twist you, you skinny little thing!"

"Ow!" cried Lise.

OLBT got to the table, looked at their faces, glanced up to scan the stage. "Wasn't I right, Dik Dik? Addicts! Keystone Kops! I can feel Brownian Motion in my vitreous."

Dik Dik said, "It's a prank. An enigma angina. A bit of spoiled potato. We can solve –"

"No, you can't," cackled OLBT. She rumbled to the stage. Dik Dik sighed. OLBT started raising hell with the stage crew.

Tim said, "She's like a fucking mummy, wrapped up like that."

"Mummy dust," chortled the Jackal, slapping her hands.

Tiffany said, "What do you want us to do? Agatha's already got people checking on Simon and M.K.'s places."

Dik Dik said, "There's a little gumbo limbo time here. A window of opportunity, as they say. We all have friends and acquaintances. We know everybody."

Lise jumped in, "We know everything."

Dik Dik frowned. "Let them take care of the obvious,

we'll check out every other hidey hole. Say an hour? We meet back here in an hour? That should be enough time to get things percolating."

Tim said, "Where should I go?"

Dik Dik said, "Check out the Tavern, Elmo's. See if anyone's talking about anything. Feel it out."

Tim said, "What does 'talking about anything' sound like?"

Lise said, "You've got it!"

Tim said, "I know what you mean."

"Tiffany, go check on your band," said Dik Dik. "See if they've heard anything. Then, the rest of us check the co-op, galleries. Is anything going on at Main tonight?"

The Jackal said, "We each have our own peeps. We'll be scouts. Meet back here in an hour. Drink up!"

Lise said, "Co op's closed. Most of the galleries are too. But maybe not. I'll check the noodle shop. They usually stay open late."

The Jackal said, "Also, full disclosure: part of my 'anything': I was supposed to help out tonight, with the act. But it never happened."

Tim said, "You know any more than we do?"

The Jackal hissed. "Not really."

Tim splurged: "Drink up!"

Drink up they did.

They headed out. The second floor porch had lotza people. Shabby smokers, shabby drinkers, shabby blabbers. A dog barked close by. Every one of the spelunkers looked for the dog, then they addled off in their own directions.

Tim called, "Giddy up!"

Dik Dik mumbled, "Bash Street itself. Any time now, Plug, hisself, gonna come jolly gagging down the Gulch."

Johnny was next to him. He shook his head, smirked in alarm. "Dood," he said, "what is that? You like quoting Shakespeare all the time? What's this deal tomorrow?"

Dik Dik snorted. "I'll fill you in."

They wove their way down the steps to the Gulch. Buildings had funny lights, like blotto Christmas lights, like building make-up. Town talking back again. De Chirico mannequins in every stairway. The place looked like a cheesy used car lot, tawdry but rapacious. It was a warm night but not comfortable. Washed out sky. A motorcycle roared. Another dog yelped. Up and down the streets, balls of light, the street lights randomly showing how the Gulch was really a bowl. A big bowl. Enough light to avoid blundering into telephone poles, but not enough to discern. Smells of yeast and oil.

A girl covered in tattoos, in shorts and a t-shirt, flip flops, meandered over to Johnny and Dik Dik. She held a small Styrofoam cup in front of her with both hands. She pushed the cup towards them, offering –

Johnny peered in the cup. "Little white ones with blue heads."

Dik Dik took a look: "Champignons!"

The girl said, "Tonight's the night."

Johnny took a few, put them into his mouth. Dik Dik took one, ate it.

The girl smiled barely, went looking for the next candidates.

Dik Dik said, "At first I thought you were talking about maggots."

"Man, nighttime weirdness. Nights get that way. During the day, you gotta work, hustle." He chewed his chaw of 'shrooms.

If everybody on the Gulch was tripping, then maybe secrets had no compunction.

Dik Dik worked this over, tossed it as measly distraction.

Johnny said, "Don't want to 'worst-case-scenario' this, dood, but those tunnels...they could be connected to bad hombres."

"What are you saying?"

"I don't know." He made a gulping swallow, breathed. "I'm saying, if a load was moving, and their guys ran into your guys. I don't know."

Death came for Dik Dik. It wasn't ugly. He wasn't afraid of death. He made a face. He didn't know what to make of what Johnny said. Those Coltrane goofs, and the dog, imperiled? It made no sense. It was too sudden. Not estimated. Everything was going along so fine, fine, super fine, tomorrow the day, then this night came barging in.

Smell of good bud wafted in – skunky.

Johnny said, "I'm gonna go check out some stuff. No big, probably nothing. Meet you back at the Yard in an hour."

"Good, thanks," said Dik Dik.

Dik Dik wandered through the Gulch, up some steps, down the sidewalk, in the middle of the road, through parked cars. It wasn't a puzzle. He knew where he was going. Still, he puzzled the overlap of images and thoughts that rained in a cascade through storm fonts in his noggin. No inventory necessary, no notes. Conflagration! The before time had come crashing down, no matter where the missing were, and tomorrow was endangered. The vibe was scared to preoccupation. Egad! That was how it went for old men, brooding on fate. Good thing Dik Dik didn't know any fate. Besides, he refused to carry a notebook: all the writers in town carried notebooks, their ceaseless, obsessive note taking. Anything worth writing down would get written down. He organized his bitter walk, saw where he was going. In a transposed, quick glance at a cheap set of bad posters on a wall, he flashed on the covers of A. Merritt and Allan Quartermain books he'd known as a child. The lurid illustrations in his head were private tattoos – or Christmas lights. Pareidolia. Smothered by awareness. Those books, reading them, then re-reading them, had been essential moments of his crisis. When he experienced such glorious pleasure, he knew the issue of life was not what to do, but how far to go.

Lise made her way over to the noodle shop, whose proper name she couldn't pronounce. No one in town could. She'd tried to get Li to teach her, but her throat and mouth wouldn't make the dips and rises in pitch that were required. Li's place only had ten tables, but it was very popular. She worked very hard. Lise stood at the door of the small café with the 'closed' sign showing. Li was in the back cleaning up. A tall, thin Asian woman, she must have picked up Lise's eye beams on her, for she turned and smiled to Lise, waved her in.

"Ola, Lise!"

Lise smiled back, stepping in to the small café. The door was unlocked.

Li called, "I'm just finishing up. What are you doing? Want to go get a drink?"

"No, that's okay. I saw you through the window –"

They let an agreeable silence register for a few moments.

Li said, "Busy – good night. But weird too. Even for Coltrane. The energy?"

Lise said, "I don't know what that means anymore?"

"Tell me about it! Everything...topsy turvy. Love that word. Or is that two words?"

"We call them double mints."

"You do not."

"What happened at the Yard?"

"I know, it's gotta be a joke. Fools. The egos!"

"What have you heard?"

"There was panic. Then Agatha found one of her protégés, one of the local girls, having sex in the bathroom with that red-haired boy."

Lise pulled out a chair at one of the tables, sat. "Is it okay?"

Li said, "Of course. Sit. Let me finish up. We can talk. I was just putting away the leftover miso. How about a cup? Please."

"I'd love some."

Tim always thought that walking around Coltrane at night was like one of those *Twilight Zone* episodes when the characters at the end learn they are in a little girl's toy town of doll houses. Coltrane, the old downtown, was small enough to put in your pocket. Everybody'd been up all the steps, learned the best views, pledged to the goddess their undying adoration, because they'd made it, they'd discovered this place. This toy Hollywood set they could play in. This L-shaped downtown was all façade. 'Bunch of phonies,' thought Tim. 'Why do people put on airs? It's like fucking high school,' brooded Tim, coming on the Tavern.

When he pushed open the door, his eyes locked on Ruiz', behind the bar, and Tim popped, "Give a guy a chance."

Tim could tell Ruiz was pissed. Tim hustled to the bar, leaned in. "What's going on?" he asked.

Ruiz said, "Those dip shits are in the bathroom. Get 'em

outta of there for me."

"I ain't your bouncer."

"Tim. I'll pour you a shot and a beer."

Tim moseyed back along the bar. Most of the bar stools were filled with older Mexican men. He nodded. They gave him dirty looks. None of the booths were occupied. No one played pool.

Tim thought, 'What if something bad had happened to M.K. and Simon? What if it was a gag, but a guy found where they were hiding, and put the kibosh on certain numb skulls? There was a "window of opportunity."'

The restroom was locked. He knocked, wailed, "Gotta go, gotta go!"

"Hold on," said a voice.

"I'm gonna puke! I'm gonna puke!"

The door flew open. Captain America glared, softened. He chirped, "Get in here!"

Tight fit: a Mexican dood with one foot up on the toilet, then some young guy Tim didn't know, and Captain America. They were doing lines across the side of the sink.

Captain America sucked him in for a touchdown: "Go, brother! Take the hit! Let it percolate. Isn't that what Dik Dik said?"

Tim was thinking crazy stuff. He rammed in and took the bump.

Tim said, rising, rising, rising: "This isn't cool. Let's get outta here."

"All right, all right," said Captain America. "We are done here I believe. Everybody's happy." His big eyes went from person to person. His *compadres* muttered goofy. Out the door, they stalked like flightless colugos.

Tim angled Captain America to the side by the pool table.

Captain America groaned, sniffled, managed: "Never played pool. Don't know a thing about sports of any kind.

Not even the basic rules. Don't know anything about games, or cards, or magic."

Tim said, "I don't wanna play pool. You hear anything?"

"'Anything'? Sure: my wife is hysterical, her beast is gone."

"What happened? You know?"

"Oh, yeah, that's right! You are *so* stoned! I didn't do anything. She can't blame me. I didn't know what they were planning. I mean, other than in a vague way. We all knew in a vague way, right? Magic act. Performance. I didn't know anything more. What it was supposed to be. Or supposed to not be. See how that works? How com-pil-a-ca-ted it gets. Layers upon layers. Levels upon levels."

"Dood, chill. It's just – I can't believe it's all a joke."

"No clue, man."

"Who knows?"

"Agatha knows all."

"It's a prank."

"Who knows? Triune gave quite a speech tonight. Before things went south...*ape shit* is the preferred expression, I believe. Before things went ape shit, yeah. Who knows? Who cares? Maybe he cracked open the world for a second. Long enough for us to lose our brethren."

Ruiz signaled Tim from the bar, pointing to his shot and beer.

Tim said to Captain America, "Cap, take it easy. It's a weird night, and I know we say that every night, but tonight –" He shook his head, shrugged. "Something big."

"Oh, yes, that's right! You are *so* stoned! What're you proposing? Teleportation? Teledildonics? Time travel? You're percolating!"

Tim joined Ruiz at the bar, did his shot, went for his beer.

Ruiz said, "Wipe your nose, dumb fuck."

Tiffany knew it was late enough they'd be out on the prowl. Their little place had its walls closing in by now, until no one could take it. Or someone needed ciggies. Or their last BIC fluttered out. Who was with them? Had they picked up strays? Was D.O.A. hanging with them? They'd be moving in pairs, or loosely grouped, calling out flashes, always aware of each other, where each other was. They'd glide the alleys to the t-bone cul-de-sac only they knew, then hunker down behind wretched wrecks of buildings, under a collapsing roof, in a tiny atom spot, maybe with some flowery volunteers and a Twinkie wrapper. That was the best place to snag a smoke, to live it proper. There was a song there, Tiffany knew. She worked it out of the trash and holes. Lyric, rhyme, pitch, melody – she hummed with it.

Every town had hidey holes only kids and dopers knew. Living in the ruins their whole lives, in the interstices, the kids had a talent for scatter, a talent like any other, specific to certain things like skulking. They were great at skulking. Annihilation, what their lives were all about. They began at the end. Tiffany imagined the band crisscrossing songs, spinning erratic patterns that were quick to derange. They were a bunker band set free at Ground Zero. Their atoms didn't belong to their parents, to their parents' times. Their atoms were eking out their own vibrations, in tune with this post-post-post *remoderniana* world. Was there such a word? Tiffany knew a detonation was coming, so enthralling that everything and everybody would be so freaked they'd have no choice but to live. Tiffany knew there was no point in re-inventing the wheel. She was glad to read and learn from her predecessors. But since the cat was out of the bag – *it was total corruption and misery from the git go* – things like history seemed an abstraction, like stamp collecting. Total human extent, total human corruption – totes rigged, totes' ultimatum. But the poets – yes, good material to steal from. Dik Dik was her dip stick. She wished she had Arthur Rimbaud in her band. On drums. But D.O.A. would have to do. And Bear and Mikey were real, and hard. When they went ballistic playing together, those precious moments thrust their surge to the cosmos, with a unity of vibe, a unity of fierce, a unity of desire. The boys'd be set by now. Ready to dig. She'd find them...

...at City Park: Bear and Mikey sat on the edge of the clamshell stage, dangling their legs, kicking them. She ran to them.

Mikey went, "Bear says Old Lady Beckam, whatever, is your fairy godmother."

"Of course she is," cried Tiffany.

"You look jacked," said Bear. "Come here and give me some sugar."

Tiffany got between his jeans-covered and cowboy-booted stems, wiggled in close for kisses. She said in to his beard, "Where's the beasts?"

"At home. They're fine. I'll go back for them. We just needed to get out a sec. Stretch our legs. You heard what happened at the Yard? You look nice."

They heard laughter and voices from the side of the park with the ramada. The way the lights were arranged at the park, it was dark on that side under the ramada, with its blobby picnic tables. Tiffany made out a bigger blob, maybe sitting at a picnic table.

She said quietly, "Who's over there?"

Mikey snorted.

Bear said, "Potter. You know Potter."

"I know Potter. Who's he with?"

"Guess."

Tiffany stepped out of Bear's arms and legs, came around, called, "Potter? Potter, is Daphne with you?"

Giggling and fast talking came from the ramada. The blob bifurcated, and Potter wandered over, too dark to make out what kind of sheep, hands in pockets, super cool but wary. He said, "It's a beautiful stage. I want to perform on this stage one day. I'm in the theater on the Gulch." He backed to the stage, arms at his sides on the stage, hefted himself up easily, to sit by the other young men.

Tiffany said, "We know. You told us."

Bear said, "Don't be a busybody, Tiff, the girl likes to suck dick. It's none of your bees wax."

"It is!" said Tiffany. She pushed in close to Bear's face and huskily whispered, "She's not all there. You know that. Don't act like you don't."

She practically ran away from him then, over to the ramada. She made out Daphne in the shadows. "Come on. Come with me."

Daphne said, "Where we going?"

Tiffany said, "For a walk."

"I like walks," said Daphne.

They headed out of the park from its upper gate, swung around to the left on a narrow road that zigzagged up the mountain. They got off, walked on a smaller trail, through an alley, towards Main. Main's fenced in parking area had a high curb around the outside. They sat.

"Daph –" began Tiffany.

"I know what you're going to say. I was upset. It makes me feel better. I like it. Lorna says it's nutritious. Good for you."

"Don't make me sick! That's just gross. You're gonna get some nasty disease. Come on, you'll find someone. You're young."

"Like you and Bear?"

"Bear's okay. The band's great."

"Not the same thing."

"Don't listen to anything that woman says."

"Lorna? She's crazy. But her boys – well, I was upset because...because Agatha found me in the lady's room with that red-haired boy. He's the one that told me about Lorna's theories. He said she sucked them off once or twice a day. But Agatha was really mad. She's been helping me out –"

"When things cool down, you can talk to her."

"Things may never cool down now."

"Come on –"

"Red knew something, or had seen something. I don't know. But I've never seen a dick so hard. Not like a regular boner. It was like a piece of iron. Know what I mean?"

"What happened that turned him on so much?"

"My sweet young ass, wadda ya thunk? I don't know. I don't want to know. It's all Babylon."

Johnny ran over to this place he knew on the Gulch, where these guys hung out. They nodded and slapped at his hand as he slapped at their hands. Welcome! They stood around their black SUV's, in a dirt drive way, by one of their mom's houses, shooting the shit, sipping their brews, vaping, snorting, farting, spitting. Real men! They were way too chill to have come from slaughter. It was a quiet night on the Gulch, and all was right with the world. In between loads. Maybe later – bidness. Right now, peace holding. Everybody cool. Smell of benzene.

When out of the quiet coils of the Gulch, the dark tunnel road that came from the secret depths up higher in the canyon, here came a pickup, not too old, white with colored side panels, moving way too slow, so cautious as to raise a flag and shout, 'look at me'. Johnny and the boys shut up to watch it creep past. Two up front, one in the back. Female riding shotgun, bald guy driving. They could see that.

Death was a joke on cue. No punchline yet. Red Black wouldn't kill anybody, even if he paid her to beat his nut sack with a spatula. She didn't know anything about death. Except to avoid its practitioners. She knew how to play death. Get all black and Morticia, serve the boys, save the boys. Art was madness. Performance was all. She could do this. Fuck 'em.

Red Black was finding a voice in this skin. Not so much pain, like cuts, as this skin in this air welcomed her. She mustn't crush it. She had to work it. She had to figure what she could do. What she had to say. Images, ideas came so fast, then suddenly they were gone. And she'd be back to worrying over how much she worried. Day to day, dusk to dawn, hustle took all her shitty time. Kept her from the work. *Distractions*. Dik Dik's word. But it fit. Turn off the fucking phone! First, the artist must choose her media. Then, the artist must choose her punch to that media. Voice-song, until her whole body tingled, giving her all in a performance! But Tiffany was better. Tiffany was a natural, too. Just like Red Black was proclaimed...at first.

Red Black had a dream about how ugly beauty was. This was a drawing in her head of silvery sutures, like Lydia's cobweb jewelry sewn across faces. Red Black couldn't do jewelry, all those little knots and wires made her itch. But this drawing exploited her seething presence joy cum. She had to get it out.

She would draw it. Cruel beauty. Terrifying beauty. Scarred beauty! She would make it her own. She'd find time without distraction. She would conjure skill. But tomorrow, after that Joyce stuff, she had to go to Sour Town for her shot. Fuck.

Now she turned to the duty at hand: caves, portals, accidental overhangs, hang outs. Out to the bunkers, where the Trogs clustered. They had many names: Ewoks, Wooks, reprobates (Dik Dik's word), the homeless. She had to check out the bat cave. The night was filled with flying insects. There was enough food for everybody.

The guy lived in a mine shaft with his dog. They were always arguing. He cooked his last can of beans to share with her. She had no flashlight, but she could make out with her skin eyes the movement of the small, black, writhing bodies around his camp: scorpions, cockroaches, vinegaroons. She recalled his lecture on beneficial poisons. He'd been experimenting, stinging himself over and over again with scorpions. She hadn't noticed him adding any surprise ingredient to the can of beans. She choked down her share. She wondered what he knew, what he had seen. Lost souls living in the dirt saw a lot more than civilians.

He burped. "Vehicular truck baleen."

The cave people were mainly men. And men were disgusting, so why did she check on them, and even bring them food? Distraction or Serotonin overload? Old Lady Beckett Twister told her men were failed woman. That's why they brutalized women. They knew what they were missing.

The smallest bar in Arizona was located on the second floor of the Silver Queen. The old wooden building had a heaviness about it, like the timbers had given up, sagging in geriatric defeat. It was a bulbous wooden cube of a place. The Silver Queen had been a boarding house for miners, now, besides a tiny bar, it held small apartments for the pious. Everybody in Coltrane assumed they were special. There should be a Commandment about it. Regular people thought they were regular. Coltrane people thought they were getting extra credit. Everybody else – it was rumored there was a world outside of Coltrane – had other things on his or her mind.

This tiny bar had a tiny, wooden wraparound bar, polished to a honey gloss, in a room not much bigger than a closet. Two bar stools. One tiny table with two chairs. Mainly locals congregated. But the smallest bar in Arizona was a thing, repeated on blog and zine, reported on public broadcasting, so tourists did wander in.

When Dik Dik walked in to the smallest bar in Arizona, his head was pinging with potions, curses, threats, and book covers. Yet, the troops were mustered. The game was afoot! He had an hour – less than an hour. He needed something to wash down the ague.

At the small table sat a pair of cute tourists. They were very white, very clean. He was positively ruddy handsome, polo shirt, chinos, sandals. She was blonde with flips at the ends of her do, pretty, pale with red lips. She wore a silky button down blouse and white pants, golden sandals. Perfect pedicured white feet, sculpted by Rodin. At the edge of the bar – literally – just inches from the tourists was some homeless guy hunched in, on full harangue. He held on to the bar top for dear life. He was dressed in layers. It was difficult to see where one garment began or cut off, as though they had grown together. He had a flat head with big, outspoken ears. A rubbery face. He was a shave needing a face, in the sultry bar light.

The bartender was a stout woman whom Dik Dik

knew slightly. He couldn't think of her name. She'd been around for a while, tending bar at most of the joints in town. She and Dik Dik conferred at the other end of the bar.

"Brandy," said Dik Dik.

"The good stuff?"

"Why not."

She plucked a snifter from the rack of glasses. She found the bottle of the good stuff and poured Dik Dik a generous shot plus. He paid her, remained standing, keeping the empty bar stool between himself and the haranguer. He didn't want to listen. He sipped.

Fire!

The bartender moved over so she could hear, too. She pretended to be wiping down the bar top. The couple at the table drank their beers, watched the guy, listened. Then they glanced at each other. Then they looked back at their interlocutor. They weren't alarmed. They were genuinely captivated, like anthropologists at Olduvai. .

O Shabby One explained, "What I been doing is following ghost tours. But at a distance. Never get close. Never touch! Never touched a soul. I can't help myself. When the tour people get close to real ghosts, I have to shout out, 'leave the ghosts alone!' Is that wrong? Was I wrong to do that? That's what got me in trouble. Tour guides started calling the cops. Can you believe that shit? I been arrested in three Wild West towns for 'ghost tour disruption'."

Dik Dik placed the stray man. This guy had been coming to town for years, usually in the winter. Maybe forty, fifty? One of those wanderers that blew through town that would periodically grow agitated. Dik Dik realized his own ineptitude: he'd never helped out the poor sot. This guy leaned in, his left hand cradling his can of Bud Light. He was listing.

The cute tourist woman said, "How could you tell

when they were getting close to a real ghost?"

The homeless man took a long slug of his beer. "Didn't you hear what I was saying? All across the west, all these tourist towns, they've all got ghost tours now. It's a racket. They put out ghost traps for the connoisseurs who pay extra for them. The tours are a con. Cover up! It's my job to spring those traps and make people leave the ghosts alone."

The cute dood said, "He's a ghost whisperer, like that show on TV."

The woman said quick, "You just like that girl with the big butt on that show."

"Point taken," said the guy.

The homeless haranguer knew he'd lost them: this audience wouldn't spare a shekel.

Dik Dik intervened: "My dear fellow, what do these 'connoisseurs' do with the ghosts?"

The bartender said, "Good question." She got closer.

The ghost whisperer said, "They snort 'em."

"Nice," said the guy at the table.

Dik Dik drank a big snort of his flaming blood drink, and knew there had to be a plot to the night's shenanigans. If it wasn't a Coney Shaman screw up, and it didn't seem likely to be a prank of M.K. and Simon, who despised each other, then it had to have been the surprise entrance of an antagonist that had thrust a battering ram in to the script. It could be ghosts. Ghosts with a plan! It would have taken a lot of muscular ghosts –

The homeless guy at the bar shook his beer can. It was empty. He sighed dramatically. "Night, love," he said to the bartender, who smiled and nodded to him. He didn't even glance at the tourists.

But he came around before he left to face Dik Dik. He said, "Ditch."

"Aha!" went Dik Dik.

The ghost whisperer was out the door. Pretty soon they

could hear the clatter of his steps going down the stairs.

The tourist guy at the table said, "We went to the performance tonight. Just down from here, the next place over."

The bartender said, "The Yard?"

"That's it," said the woman.

The guy continued, "It was wacked! Like some kind of hippy dippy gong show. Do you remember *Firesign Theater*? My parents had those records. LPs."

"Lots of stoners," said the bartender.

The guy nodded enthusiastically. "You could get high just being in that room. Their bodies exuded THC –"

"And who knows what else?" added the woman.

"What happened?" asked Dik Dik.

"Who knows? We sure don't," said the man.

The woman said, "I think they were too stoned. They messed up. I don't think it was supposed to happen that way. Unless it *was* supposed to happen that way. Like, you know, art."

The man raised his head, tilting it high. He put his hands on the table in front of himself. His head came down. He announced, "This place is like a bubble out of time. No terrorism. No Wall Street. No traffic jams or long commutes."

"It's like *Brigadoon*," said the woman.

Dik Dik, out on the Gulch again, overheard some bombast:

"I hope to find God, senor," said a burly fellow, walking away from some doods by Elmo's entrance. The big guy must have gotten to his car, as he leaned over the driver's side door, his hands and forearms on the top of the car. The vehicle was straight out of *Mad Max*, a battered husk, ready to pilot a shark squad. He said to his buds who'd followed behind uncomfortably, "I gave that fucker thirty beans." The voice was connected to some girth, and that thickness had a leg like a ball peen hammer, which started kicking the old beater's door. He was kicking in his own car's door! Perfectly spaced thumps. Thump! Thump!

Maybe he was the minotaur. Not hairy enough –

O, blue night, I sing of arms and kicks and temper tantrums!

Huge motorcycles, big as dinosaurs, ready to rumble, in front of Elmo's. Guys in alley ways, flailing whiskers and suction cups, growled into the pavement. Leather men around the tattoo parlor, squeaky, dusty. A few women in dead cowboy attire smoked cigarettes nearby. Smell of wax. Smell of shatter. Smell of dub. F/X green strobe lights from the tattoo parlor seized the pupils out on the sidewalk. A dark palette crept up onlookers' spines.

Dik Dik made his way to the Yard. *Gravitas: what have we done*' But he didn't know if it was a projection or the end of a story. There were themes in the night in the Gulch that repeated across the planet. This was his planet. *Get used to it!* Pointless and pathetic humans, yet humans danced together, loved together. They knew the real cum. Humans were contrary, contradictory, so to have 'answers', or easy ways out – ha! Not by a long shot. Rather, humans knew kinetics: resiliency. Balance. We're all jugglers! This was where art came in. This was where humanity raised its voice, *yes, I am here!* More than other monkeys. Survival with benefits – exultation. Dik Dik had a great idea that he promptly forgot: *art was always the latest way humans expressed their resiliency.*

The Yard's lights were on, but the peeps had thinned. The structure's broadcast was completely alien from earlier. No galleons. Two Coltrane police cars parked out

front. Neither had their lights on. No yellow crime scene
tape decorated the Yard. Bystanders were kept to the side
by two Coltrane police officers, a man and a woman. They
were official acting. Dik Dik, scanning the set up, grunted,
marched right in, figuring he'd look like he owned the
place.

At the stairs to the entrance, the police woman stopped
him: "Where you going?"

Dik Dik said, "I was there. Umm – been out looking for
our friends, make sure they're all right. I need to report
back."

"Well, if you know something, you should talk to the
captain. Go on up."

"Thank you," said Dik Dik.

Bright bars at night always looked like trouble. This
one looked like lockdown recess, with its small
sequestered groups at tables, then in the front by the
stage, the cops. People lined up along the back wall by the
door, too. Standing in a row, a regular line up, a cross
section of Coltrane, *strata Americana*, humanity's fault
line: Dik Dik, a bartender, then OLBT, Oscar, Johnny, the
Jackal. Full on psychopixel coruscant! Tigers had stopped
over to weigh on the back row's shoulders. They were lit.
They were digging it! Dik Dik went all prosaic. Where
was the emergency?

Finally, Dik Dik uttered, "Bloody hell! Like a frigging
noir film, tis. Bollocks! The frigging usual suspects."

Johnny said, "Does anyone ever know what he's
talking about?"

OLBT bellowed, "Blustery –"

A voice called out, "Quiet down back there." Had to be

a cop.

The bright bar didn't have the buzz of a crime scene. There was no heavy gallows treatment. No *gravitas.*

The Jackal whispered like a shy werewolf, "So lit in here, you could do surgery."

Dik Dik came in slow, heading for the stage, so he could see the blocking needed. Like with a pool table, or a pin ball machine, if he knew where things began, he knew where they'd end up...if he went this way, he'd flip over there next. The sequence gratified –

The stage had a chunky Mexican policeman walking around with a measuring tape. Middle-aged guy plumped in to his blue uniform. The three doors were present, occupying, pressing out, and all of them were open...like mouths on their side, tongues sticking out. No. Like sprung monoliths, menhirs laid bare...Tardis Carnac chaos. Coney Shaman and Tilman sat in a corner cubby between bar and stage, defeated, silent, pale in the bright. In front of the stage, a cleared space, tables and chairs pushed back, except one table and a couple chairs. Two police officers, both standing, in front of the young woman in a chair – one of the bartenders. The younger policeman held out his phone before the woman. He said, "Say, *queso.*"

The closest table by Dik Dik was held by Agatha and a couple of her minions. The others must still be out. Next table over, by herself, had Megadeath. Then, a table with Simon's two female comrades, knitting, knitting, clicking needles...knitting. Needles. Needles. Who will find the answer? Tick tock, tick tock...in time?

Did Dik did not agree to fate, cycles, reflexes, coincidences, or accidents. There was no repetition: there was only re-invention. Always allow the new in. Dik Dik swooned in to a chair by Simon's friends. "I'm afraid I don't know your names. After all we've been through."

They smiled graciously. Never slowed their knitting.

One had a plump face with brown hair. The other was leaner, older, like a hawk maybe or a question mark. The softer one said, "I'm Matilda. Simon calls me Til."

"Til," said Dik Dik.

"Tilde," said the sharp one. "Catch it? Catch it? The cross hatch hat – it's a hat!...tenacious –"

They breathed separately. The tension released. The plump one went, "That's a grapheme."

"You've had a long night," said Dik Dik. He rose and scuttled over by Megadeath. He said, "Brave, love."

She said, "You don't care. He was just a dog to you. To me, he was my little boy in a dog suit. I know! I know how it sounds. You don't care!"

"I take it there's no news."

Megadeath rose from her chair. She was Dik Dik's height. She stabbed, "It's a madhouse." It came out not gently. She said it with acceptance and walked away.

Next, he said hello to Agatha. She had changed in to a scramble suit so it was difficult to focus. Her energy was like a hive of triggers. Before he could pop a second sound, thank the goddess, the cops finished with the bartender, and the young woman hurried over to confer with Agatha. One of Agatha's young men was next, the hipster. His name was Belo, the cowboy. The cops were taking names.

Dik Dik meandered closer.

The younger policeman said to Belo, "Take a seat. I'm gonna take your picture. No big deal. Just to have a record, you know. Part of our process. So we can sorta have a list of who was here."

Dik Dik said to the young policeman "Don't tell him to say 'cheese', that doesn't work. Tell him to say *money*. That always works. Try it."

The policeman was tall and lean, a good looking young man. He said, "Money?"

"Try it."

"What the fuck –" went the other policeman, who was older, stouter, with white hair sticking out from under his cap. As he spoke, he stepped fully forward to face Dik Dik.

"Richard Perkins," said Dik Dik, immediately extending his hand towards the hulk. They shook hands.

"Captain Rodriguez. You have any idea what's going on here?"

"What do you know?"

"Don't play games with me. Agatha's upset. Apparently, somebody yelled don't bring them back when they disappeared them. And they didn't come back. Were you here when it happened?"

"Yes."

"You know the missing?"

Dik Dik nodded.

"Okay, get in line. We're compiling names of who was here. Probably a joke, right."

"We were out looking for them, our friends."

"Unless you found them, save it. We got no sign of a struggle. We got no reports of threats or violence. We'll talk to the guy who yelled. I'm not exactly sure why we're here. Missing persons, you wait at least twenty-four hours before calling in the troops. But Agatha phoned, and she's worried." He shrugged and raised his hands in a question. "I told her we'd come by, let's not make this any harder than it has to be."

"We have to figure out what happened when the lights went out."

"Oh, yeah? You got this figured out, huh?" He shook his head, offering a sourpuss to Dik Dik. "Okay, Mr. Wise Guy, what happened when the lights went out? That's when the magic was supposed to happen? How long were the lights out? Mr. Tri-oon, over there, can't remember. Maybe a couple minutes, he says."

"At least – maybe five or six minutes."

"Did you hear anything? Officer Travis, add that to your question list." He looked bored.

Dik Dik, designated Mr. Wise Guy, preempted: "The lights went out. All the lights in the entire establishment. Dead still. Silent a few seconds. Then commotion. Heavy sounds, like who knows? Objects thrown around? Somebody moving furniture? I don't know. Everybody assumed it was part of the show. But the lights didn't go back on. Finally, Monsieur Triune started cackling, and we knew things weren't right. They opened the doors, and they were gone."

"There's no evidence of a crime. Agatha, says it's probably a prank. I know her, I trust her. I'm just doing her a favor. We both know *probably* ain't worth much." He said slowly, "Might have been an outage. They're pretty common. Agatha's gonna check."

Dik Dik glommed away, bored by the Captain's tropes, flummoxed by objectivity. He scooted to the stage unnoticeably, to watch the police officer with the tape measure. He seemed to be taking a lot of measurements on the doors.

The captain called to Dik Dik: "Don't touch anything. Let my officer do his job." The captain got back to the kid in the hotseat, Belo.

Dik Dik stayed where he was, studying the way the officer made his measures. The officer took the tape and bent it in two, so he had two lengths of tape measure parallel. He had no pen or pencil and pad to make notes.

Dik Dik said, "You're doing calculations."

"An old trick I learned from my grandpa," said the police man.

"No computer necessary."

"Absolutely."

"Measuring the doors?'

"Trying to be precise. Depth. Volume. Neat design, simple trap in the back –"

Tilman scrambled up from his corner. "No one has the right to examine our doors. That's proprietary material. Copyrighted. Registered trade secrets. We protest."

"Thanks," said the policeman.

Tilman sat back down.

Dik Dik said, "Could they get out any time they wanted?"

"Hmm, I don't know. There's no lock."

"Could anybody get in when they wanted?"

"No lock." He shrugged, made a face. "No sign of a struggle though. I mean, if someone had tried to force them out –"

The captain's gruff voice took over, "Sergeant, what is that woman doing on stage?"

Dik Dik turned with the sergeant, to the last door on stage that had been Mad's. Megadeath was on her knees in front of the door, bent over, bent in, burrowing right in –

"Ma'am, don't touch anything," said the sergeant, striding over to her, in a methodical but urgent manner.

Megadeath straightened enough to lean out of the door and cry, "Is this a crime scene?"

"No, ma'am, but just in case –"

"Just in case! Just in case!" She leveraged to her feet, face in fireworks, tongue plugging out, hand extended high, as she declared in a piercing cry: "Look at my hand! Here! Here! Just in case! Just in case! See! See!"

Her hand held high was smudged with red on the fingertips. Anybody could see it in the bright lit bar. It looked like blood.

"Cap, you better come see this," said the sergeant.

The captain trudged over to the door on the end. He was muttering, "This woman thinks she can just –" He stopped, faced Megadeath. "Wadda ya got there, sweetheart?"

"Don't you dare call me 'sweetheart'. This is Madness blood. It was in the corner. I knew it was there. I sensed it.

A molecule of Madness essence was calling out to me goodbye."

"And what is 'Madness blood'?" asked the captain.

"The dog, Captain, that's what they called the dog," said the sergeant.

"Sergeant, did you go over that door?"

"Yes, I did, Captain, but only a scan. I was going back to it for a closer look."

"Well, the lady beat you to it, unless she put it there."

Megadeath screamed.

"Oh, for crying out loud. I was kiddin'. You gotta take it easy. That's the door for the dog, huh. Maybe it cut its foot. We'll get samples, send them to the lab. Maybe it'll help us figure if this is a crime scene or not. If it's just the dog's, we got nothing."

Megadeath cried, "You got nothing! You got nothing!"

"Whoa, whoa, whoa. You're getting all worked up. Now calm down. Sergeant, get me the lady cop up here right away. You, lady, you go wash your hands and take a seat. Make sure one of my officers has your name."

Dik Dik found glory running from the stage, and, to his delight, he discovered the rest of his troops were back. Except for Tim. They clustered by the door. He sauntered over, eyes and eyebrows jumpy, and led his group outside. OLBT and Oscar came along. They found a picnic table they liked. Tiffany, Lise, Johnny, Dik Dik squeezed in on the benches. OLBT gathered at her own picnic table across from theirs, with the Jackal.

Oscar leaned against the wall of the building, arms folded in front of himself. He said, "Dik Dik, you got yourself a posse."

Johnny looked at Dik Dik, lowered his head, came back up, staring at Dik Dik hard, and said, "Far as I can tell, nobody's been in the tunnels. I don't think any of the hombres are involved at all. That's good."

The sergeant took the stairs two at a time buzzing up,

with the female police office behind him. Dik Dik gave him a wave as he flew by but he scowled back.

Oscar said, "Now everybody knows about the tunnels."

Johnny said, "Enough already did."

"Evidently," said Oscar. Then: "Agatha's pretty upset. Now, blood, from Mad's door."

Lise said. "Blood? I had miso. If we're reporting in. Where's Tim?"

Everybody did the quick once over of puzzled faces. *Blood?*

Oscar said, "Coney Shaman doesn't know a thing. I know, what a surprise. But neither does Agatha. Now, they're gonna be thinking the worst. The cops don't like it. You know, dog's blood probably, but they came over because Agatha called the captain."

The Jackal spoke up: "'The worst'? Do tell! Caveman up the Gulch told me he saw a pickup way, way up the Gulch tonight, where the road's for shit, about the same time –"

Lise piffed, "That's what you got?"

The Jackal smirked back on cue, but smiled a tiny one: "Better than miso. All I got."

Lise went, "You know what was supposed to happen."

The Jackal started to get to her feet, but thought better of it. She folded her hands in front of herself. "The two guys were to switch. That was the first part. Tilman was on lights. He'd hit the lights, the guys would switch, quickly, quietly, no big duh. Tilman and I would take care of Mad. I'd hold him off to the side. Nobody went in to the tunnels at all. It was all done with black cloths and hangings on the sides and back."

"Tilman did the lights?" asked Lise.

"No, no, that's the dealio, Rasputin," said the Jackal. "Tilman was set at the light switch when the lights went out. Total blackout! Tilman didn't do it. No cues! My cue was off. Do you get it? Tilman panicked. I didn't know what to do. I should've gone for Mad. You can't do a show without cues. It was so carefully timed, the only way it would work. We practiced so much. Nothing could go wrong. Tilman was so freaked out, but he's always like that."

Lise said, "You were supposed to take care of Mad?"

"Well," groaned the Jackal, "me and Tilman. I'd get Mad out of his door. We'd walk three paces to the black curtain that hung at the side wall. Scrunch in. Behind the blackness. Freeze. Go invisible. We had it down, me and the big dumb dog. There must have been a power outage at that exact moment. Me and Tilman couldn't see anything. It all came apart – it wasn't our show anymore."

OLBT said, "No cues."

Johnny said, "How could you get Mad back in his door?"

"We practiced. Tilman was there to help. Mad likes me."

Dik Dik said, "We have six hours plus. There's blood now. *On ne sais jamais!* Maybe from a cut on Mad's paw when they were getting him into the door. We still don't know where M.K. or Simon are. If it's a prank, why wait so long for the punchline?"

The Jackal shuddered, wiped at her mouth, feeling her bottom lip with her left forefinger. "Impossible! Corpuscles clean up and removal, erasing, obliterating, demolishing, all signs in less than ten minutes."

OLBT said, "Blunt object. Crack their heads. Drag them out fast. Swiffer wipe."

Lise gasped. Tiffany exhaled sharply.

Dik Dik said, "What are you saying? 'Crack their heads?' Dragged to where?" He stopped, realizing the profundity. "It doesn't make sense. Worst case scenarios gone wild. Where are M.K. and Simon? And Mad. Secrets."

Lise said, "Close."

Oscar went, "Secrets? You mean like ghosts?"

The Jackal twisted in her seat, tugged at her vest, slapped her knee and giggled: "I got a shiver. Whew! You mean, like they really, really disappeared?"

Oscar laughed.

Lise said, "We are a glib bunch."

OLBT said, "Method, motive, opportunity. Richard, you don't read enough mystery novels."

Lise said, "We know the opportunity."

Oscar said, "Those guys were oddballs. I know, I know. That's being generous. They were goofs. A lot of people disliked them."

"Motive," said Lise.

Tiffany said, "'What happened when the lights went out' is the question, like Dik said. We know who was there generally. We could come up with names to...think about."

OLBT said, "Persons of interest."

Dik Dik realized he was a clasp. What could they do? He didn't want to lead them. But Bloomsday! But their concerns and worries let out a weird jellyfish vibe, clingy, stingy.

Johnny said, "We know who was there: bikers, artists, dealers –"

The Jackal butted in: "Poseurs, kids, douche bags. We fucked up. I should have got Mad out of there."

Johnny said, "There was a lot going down – it was too fast. But like Dik Dik says, 'like always'."

Tiffany said, "Everybody was there. Like we saw Daphne, then in the crowd we saw Red, that guy who works with Lorna."

Dik Dik said, "We saw Lorna. I saw Red."

Tiffany said, "I guess the police are mainly getting the names of Agatha's people, for now. The bartenders."

Lise said, "It begins: the overlap of synergies. I didn't want to mention Daphne and Red in the same breath."

Tiffany glared.

Johnny said, "I saw that weird pickup tonight. I mean, like your caveman said – hey, what's your name? I don't know your name."

The Jackal said, "Call me Red."

"Two Red's in one night?" went Johnny.

"Then call me Black," said the Jackal. "But don't call me Jack, short for Jackal which some call me. And don't ask why they call me that. Just imagine it means I yip with joy like a jackal when I'm cumming."

"Wow! Talking to you guys is like being in a show or some shit. At least you don't have to raise your hand," said Johnny. "I didn't know jackets zip. I mean, jackal's like a coyote, right?"

Lise said, "What about the truck you saw?"

"I don't know," said Johnny. "Moving so slow so we noticed it. Couple guys, a woman." Johnny stuck out his hand to Lise. "We never got introduced. I'm Johnny."

Lise took his hand but didn't shake it, just held it. "You didn't know them?" asked Lise. "The people in the truck?"

"No. There was no traffic. I mean, at all. That's why it was so noticeable."

Lise said, "I'm Lise." She let go his hand.

Red-Black-Jackal-Jack blurted, "Caveman didn't have details either."

Tiffany said, "What do we do now? I'm gonna get the band. We can help. Keep looking. Talk to some of the others who were there."

Lise said, "Red-Black-Jackal-Jack, let's go see your caveman."

From down in the street below them came a hoot and a holler, and they knew Coyote was on his way. Captain America crowded around and through law enforcement who were busy, and easily distracted. He levitated the steps in no time. People were still out, maybe not a bona fide throng, but for late night, before Bloomsday, popping.

Captain America splurged his way in. "Hey, homies, I can see you got it going on. Y'all are aglow. A real nice, pinky aura." His arms went out to embrace the ether. "This must be the place. The place! This is where it's happening! I am so glad to be part of this noble endeavor."

OLBT said, "You are so fried."

"Twister! Always a pleasure. Saw you earlier. You don't remember? Oh, I see, what's happening here: you think I'm someone else. I'm not who you think I am. You don't see who you think you see. I'm Tim. You all know and love Tim. Me. Tim. Ask me a Tim question? Don't be shy! We're an incestuous bunch in Coltrane. Beware Coltrane Commandment Number 3."

Oscar straightened, sighed. "I'll leave you to Cryptotimbo. I need to see Agatha. Keep communicating. I'm depending on you guys."

As he walked away, Cryptotimbo cried, "Oh, he's such a phony. I wish Triune would make them disappear then not bring them back. Do you remember my prediction? Some of you were there. Oh, yeah, I didn't go to college, but I know what I like –"

Tim was at the foot of the stairs looking up, watching, listening. How much had he heard? Looked like Jerry Garcia's gray beard was vibrating.

Tim called up to his bud: "I'm gonna punch you in the nose and there's nothing you can do about it."

Lise groaned: "Oh, stop it."

OLBT said, "I'm betting on Tim. Cold cock the mofo!"

Captain America said, "I thought you liked me?"

OLBT said, "I do."

As Tim took the steps huskily, out from the bar's entrance came the police captain.

The Jackal lit a cigarette. "Captain Rodriguez." She nodded.

Captain Rodriguez stepped their way. "Wondering

where you all went. What's going on out here?"

The Jackal said, "Smoking cigs."

The captain nodded, smiled, chuckled. "Sure you are, sure you are." He came in a little closer and said, "Now we got blood. If this – what you people call yourselves these days? Beatniks? Hippies? Yippies? No? Pervs? Nudists? Satanists? I remember that old fashioned word from the academy, reprobate. Know what that means? Yeah. Artists. Scum of the Earth. What about ingrates? That's old fashioned, too, but good. What about the old time term, parasites? How does that sound? Ring any bells? I guess they're all good. They capture something of the filth and the fury of Coltrane hangeroutters."

"Nicely done," said OLBT clapping.

"You go home," said the captain. "I want this place cleared out, except for them I need to talk to. Whole new ball game now. Nothing solid yet, but – oh, Mr. Pilgrim, I believe, weren't you supposed to be in line? Didn't I tell you to get in line?"

Dik Dik said, "Perkins. I'm here. Waiting. I had to confer with my *compadres* to give you our latest intel."

"You are fucking with me." Captain Rodriguez went, "Confer this: I'm in no mood to play games –"

His voice rising....

– when Johnny cut in: "He talks like that all the time. Dood thinks he's Shakespeare or some shit."

The captain quoted himself: "Listen to me, citizens. We got a fast evolving situation here. State boys on the way. Forensic team. The works. Plus, plus, plus, it has come to our attention – well, you know how these old Coltrane buildings are, but it seems right back there on the stage is a trap door to the Coltrane rain tunnels. Can you imagine our surprise? Of course, everybody in town's known about the tunnels for years in the transport of contraband by you guessed it, gangbangers."

Johnny said, "See where this is going."

"Come on, Mr. Citizen, let's me and you go have a talk."

Johnny said, "Hanging out with white people is so much fun."

Dik Dik said to him, "We're on this."

Johnny stood, walked over by the captain. "Just go on in," said the captain, "I'm right behind you. Then, Pilgrim, you're next. Rest of you, clear out, go home."

Tiffany mouthed to Dik Dik, "I'll wait for you."

Dik Dik followed Captain Rodriguez and Johnny back in to the Yard. They heard a dog bark. They always heard a dog barking in the distance in Coltrane They smelled gunpowder and cum, which the captain thought was the smell of molten wax.

Conferring went bizarro in this next chunk of time, with Dik Dik and Johnny made to wait up front, sitting side by side, as more and more law enforcement showed up and conferred. Had they decided it was a crime scene after all? Were they gathering for a hootenanny?

Johnny and Dik Dik watched the entire ritual go down. It went like this: first, the newly arrived officers would introduce themselves, then they all shook hands, and went at it, talking in short, clipped, declarative sentences. The yellow tape was brought out. The stage was closed off with yellow tape. The remaining 'bystanders' were now too close to a crime scene and had to back it up. They had to do it again, still too close, until Agatha, preened amid her scramble, trying to keep a handle on the new faces, making for the bar, proclaimed, "Drinks on the house! Everybody!"

The captain's shout was louder: "No way! They can have water. No adult beverages."

Who knew what was happening? Agatha went over to talk to the captain and the other officials. They wouldn't all be there unless things had revved up.

Dik Dik loved it, hated it – if this played havoc with

Bloomsday, he would be SOL: "Do you know who James Joyce is?" he asked Johnny.

Johnny sat hunched over, arms on thighs. He turned his head to Dik Dik. He shook his head.

Dik Dik shrugged. He mumbled, "Where you from? What do you know?"

Johnny grunted. "What do you mean? How can a person answer that?" Dik Dik was silent. Johnny sat up, straightened. "I'm a home boy. Work when I can. Mainly construction." He smiled, coughed. "My grandma has a little place not too far from here. It has a shed in back she lets me stay. She's a sweetheart. I got it fixed up. I come and go as I please. But I don't know nothing. High school's a long, long way from here. I don't get anything. Why shit goes on and on like this. Total chaos and corruption."

"Do you have a device?"

"What? Like a phone?"

Dik Dik nodded. "They'll want to check it."

"Can they do that?"

"Home boy, you know how this plays at the Rialto. But you were with me the whole time, and Tiffany. We're your alibis. We'll get out of here, figure this out, then you can help with Joyce Day tomorrow. Or today, if it's past midnight...which I must assume."

"I been watching you guys for a while."

"What do you mean?"

"You artists dress funny. Like in types. Hippy. Back to the lander. Mystic."

"How do I dress?"

"I think you're what they call a 'dandy'. Is that the right word?"

"A 'dandy'?"

"I wondered what the fuck. Why dress up? Are they like costumes?"

"Why do you dress the way you do?"

"That's just it, I don't have a 'way'. This is how I dress because I don't have a lot of clothes."

"So, it was our clothes?"

"No. I liked art in high school. Okay, that's more'n ten years ago, but still. I never knew an artist."

"So –"

"What? What do I think? I don't know. Artists seem to take themselves very seriously. Everything that happens to them is very special."

"Huh. True."

Dik Dik glanced around. Coney Shaman and Tilman were at the bar. Near them, were Megadeath and Simon's friends. They were huddled at the end of the bar by the entrance. One bartender served them, the older woman. They were all guzzling tall glasses of water. Agatha and Oscar were at the bar, but more in the middle. They were furiously talking at each other, heads bowed together. Agatha broke away, headed back to the stage.

Dik Dik said, "They've forgotten about us."

Johnny could identify Coltrane PD, sheriff's department, *La Migra*, and here came the state police, two male officers in a completely different hue of dark blue than the Coltrane uniform. Captain Rodriguez seemed to have it under control, allowing Agatha into the confab.

A couple more state police officers walked in, and these men carried large metal cases and what might be called a foot locker. They went up to the stage, greeting the others, and got to work. The metal cases were cracked to reveal surgical equipment for monsters. They fussed, rifled through their stuff. They assembled gadgetry, adjusted, shifted, checked the batteries. One of the forensic officers took to the stage with a black light device. The other one opened the foot locker.

Johnny whispered to Dik Dik, "Are you thinking what I'm thinking?"

"Of course."

"Now?"

"It's all in the timing."

"You want to see what they find."

The forensics officer on stage wandered around with his light, going over the doors, then around to the back of them. He brandished the device like it was a weapon. He called out in frustration, "This is a mess!"

"What do you mean?" asked one of the state police.

Captain Rodriguez said, "What now?"

"There's definitely splatter – blood," began the forensics man.

Megadeath screamed.

Captain Rodriguez bellowed, "Get those people out of here!"

The state police officer, who must have been the ranking man, said, "Wadda you got? Is there a trail?"

The man on stage continued examining the doors with his light. "The back of each door. Not a lot. Drips? But it's been wiped, then smudged. That's what I'd guess. Total mess. Not sure how much we can get out of here."

Captain Rodriguez held back from exclaiming – he wouldn't take it out on Sergeant Molina in public, letting civilians on stage. How many had been up there before Agatha called? What a cluster fuck!

The forensics man wandered around the back of the stage now, with his magic light. He said, "I'll have to take my time, go over the entire stage inch by inch. But right now, a quick look, I get a big fat nothing. Nothing back here at all. I'd say it's been wiped. And not with Clorox either. That's what it looks like. Something went down, but –"

Captain Rodriguez let it go: "Here's what we got. Lights go out, multiple perps come in, take the two men and dog fast, quiet, some blood, then they drag 'em out, all in a few minutes. Only possible way, the tunnels. Think about it. They were little old men. Even the dog. No more than a hundred pounds each. The killers clean up as they go. Wiping up. They stuff everything, wipes, the bodies – I don't know – in big garbage bags, so there's hardly any sign. It's the only possible way. It'd take at least two people. Three would be better. We have to go over those tunnels with a fine tooth comb. Guess who knows the tunnels better than anybody?"

The state police knew he was asking rhetorically, and argued to wait until they knew more. Without a body – what could they do? What did he want to do? Start rounding up every Mexican in town who knew about the tunnels? Wait and see what forensics turned up. They said, for now, we know there's something sketchy here. Maybe, a missing persons situation. But don't get ahead of yourself! *La Migra* argued about jurisdiction because the tunnels were also used for human smuggling. Apparently, the tunnels had been under surveillance for years by various agencies. The sheriff deputy wondered whether this could be a kidnapping, so maybe they should get in touch with the FBI.

Captain Rodriguez was writhing. He scanned the bar and saw citizens leaving at the entrance. The Mexican kid and the old Brit sat nearby. His tentacles reddened. He told them to clear out. Police business. He said, "A statement will be issued in one hour."

Tiffany stepped in to the bar. "Can I use the bathroom?"

Dik Dik said, "I gotta use the latrine, too."

The captain waved at them disgustedly.

Tiffany, Johnny, Dik Dik went in to the men's room. They pissed. They took turns washing their faces and hands. Tiffany said, "I had brothers."

They decided to go over to Lorna's.

Tiffany, Johnny, Dik Dik took to the night. They left the Yard, its drastic lights, its deprived people; and night came down and enveloped them. As they drew farther away from the Gulch, night punctuated with smells, shadows, signs. They headed into the heart of Coltrane, straight up against the mountain, where wooden houses were stacked five and six deep to the top. They got away from shine. Gauzy, sultry air of dark, now, breathed their lungs satisfied.

The gente had been breaking up at the Yard, the crowd dissipating. By dawn, everybody would know about the missing artists. Bloomsday was in danger. No one could string the bow. Bloomsday must go on! What was with the sky?

On a steep narrow stretch where the pavement had deep cracks and ruts, Tiffany said, "They're dead." She stopped, panting. "I never knew a dead person. Other than my grandpa."

Johnny said, "It wasn't *los home boys*."

They heard sirens from the Gulch. All over Coltrane peeps in their beds would turn over in flagrante –

Dik Dik said, "Death don't have no mercy." He said it straight out, no drama, no ponder, bigger than a whisper. No shrug. He finished: "Without a corpus, not much anyone can do."

Tiffany said, "You think Lorna kidnapped them?"
Johnny said, "Where we going?"

Tiffany said, "To Lorna's."

They sashayed closer together, shadowy figures to each other, silhouettes they knew now. The sky was hazy – no stars. No stars. No stars.

Johnny said, "Who's Lorna? I thought that was a cookie."

Tiffany said, "You finished? She's a friend. Okay? Lorna's someone we know."

They left the road at a cul-de-sac and got on board an

escalator to the stars, one of the tallest, longest stretches of steps, going straight up, with houses on both sides.

"You know which is hers?" asked Johnny.

Tiffany and Dik Dik both knew the house. It wasn't Lorna's house, or her family's. This was the house of a friend of a friend, who hadn't been in Coltrane in ages. No one knew how Lorna ended up squatting there when she went on sabbatical. Neither Tiffany nor Dik Dik had been up there for a long time.

They climbed up the stairs between chinaberries. Dik Dik remembered these chinaberries. He'd talked to them. They were known for their pungency. Dik Dik didn't believe in anything: no souls, no gods, no spirits, no fairies. No supernatural. Yet, he kept running into sequences beyond the commonplace: chinaberries had a voice. What could you do? Tonight, the chinaberries decided to let it all out. The big cum. The air's sweet scent flamed. They breathed deep. And Dik Dik knew they'd figure it out. And what? Everybody would live happily ever after? The chinaberry scent didn't want to pressure anyone, but it couldn't help it. There was a cinder – a living, burning coal in all this, and when they found it –

Tiffany gasped, then: "This is it."

The place was on the left side, a terraced slope out cropping, so they had to step down to it from the stairs. Never had a house seemed so squat, like it was deflating, or like it was a giant wooden toad, sinking in to the Earth. Perhaps to lay its eggs. They got up next to the house, to the front door.

Quiet, dark toad. No sign of electrics. Windows dark, covered on the inside. Impossible to see in. Dik Dik knocked at the door. They heard the shuffle of bodies, maybe some staggering, but it was hard to tell.

A voice behind the door: "Who is it?" Dik Dik and Tiffany recognized Lorna.

Dik Dik said, "Gente."

She threw open the door. Candle light behind her made an oily aura, her compact form mixing the glow with her own emanations. For her shirt was silvery shiny, her slacks dull gold. She was barefoot. Her eyes were all over them. She said, "Your new team. You're all going steady. But aren't fucking yet."

Dik Dik said, "Nothing ever happened between us. You know that."

"Did I say that? I didn't say that. You *inferred* I meant that. But I didn't *imply* that. What do you want?" Her face – her face contorted, little twinges of squints or strains, with rounded bug eyes and flaring dirty lips.

Tiffany said, "We figured you'd be up, and we saw you at the Yard tonight, wondered what you'd heard. We thought we'd stop by. This is Johnny."

Lorna kept her peepers away from Johnny, keeping them on Dik Dik. "I know your nana. She was a friend of my aunt's, the one that had the restaurant. She's gone now. Come on in."

Lorna stood to the side and they filed past her.

"I like candles," said Lorna.

Tall candles. Short candles. Squat candles. Glow.

The living room's walls were layered in hangings, even over the windows, those hippy paisley fabrics that could look better than cracked, smeared walls. The place was pretty bare, except for a blonde-haired fella and a blue-haired fella stretched across floor and sofa with control modules, playing some game on a massive flatscreen TV. They were naked, and they had buds in their ears. The boys didn't turn from their play.

"We can go back here," said Lorna, "leave them alone. Boys had a big night. Yeah, yeah, me boykins." Lorna led them to the side to a closed door.

The air was so thick...the air was so heavy, it kneaded their lungs like bread. Soggy loaves of lung bread. They couldn't even remember chinaberry smell now. Now, all was kennel. Maybe someone had raised ferrets here. The hangings and flooring must absorb and store funk. Absorbatrons! Never had there been such haphazard flooring, years of carpet scraps piled up, one on top of the other, until it was a lumpy Mongolia of glommed together, freaky dunes. A brand-new ecosystem! New species emerging! Desert critters + human funk = mutant Solpugida. Cross referenced resignation, the melancholia of pious bugs, the absence of conviction an assurance of immediacy.

It was a miner's shack, a living and sleeping area, slim kitchen and bathroom. The door must lead to an addition. Lorna reached for the door knob. "I'll show you what I'm working on."

The small, candlelit room had bare plywood walls like a shed. They could see through its seams. Real live air flowed in! A long, wooden table along one side, covered in stuff. Then, a little bed, more like a cot, on the opposite side, covered in naked bald guy, with a formidable hardon.

Lorna yelled, "Baldy, get out of here! Put that away! Can't you see, I got company?"

Baldy remained where he was, stretched out on his back. He said, "We weren't finished."

Lorna lowered her voice, growled, "Get out! Out!"

Baldy sat up, came around, grabbing for something to wear in the odds and ends of potential garments at his feet. He found gym shorts, snatched them up, shimmied in to them. He stood up in front of the visitors, opened his arms in greeting and farewell, dick head peaking from his shorts, and wandered off. They stepped in to the small room, and Lorna closed the door behind them.

Lorna moved over to the table. Stuff! Craft works. Kindergarten art center. Or else, she used a baby tornado to organize art supplies. She pulled items together, pushed others away. She went to the end of the table. From the floor back there, she raised a big cardboard box to the table.

"Prototypes," she said. She took from the box a gaily painted, paper mache sphere about the size of a basketball, covered with protuberances.

Johnny said, "Wow! Like a psychedelic cow udder piñata."

Dik Dik said, "No, no, it's a dick piñata."

Closer inspection revealed the dicks were infected. Some had boils. Others had sores and ulcers in bright colors.

Lorna said, "It's a prototype. Full size for sale, stuffed with treats. I wanna stuff 'em with shooters, those little liquor bottles."

She lay the dick piñata on the table to the side. She reached in to the box again and brought out a black death mask covered with little red dicks.

"Nice," said Johnny, "definitely not an udder."

Lorna said, "Are you an artist? Cause I'm getting this vibe, seems like you're being all sarcastic. I've stabbed men for less."

Dik Dik tried, "What about tonight? What about the magic show? M.K. and Simon are still missing."

Lorna was fast. "What about tonight?"

Dik Dik made a face. He nodded. "Where's that red-haired boy?"

"You're not my father."

"Lorna, I'm –"

"Asking all these questions! Oh, daddy, it's so big, I can't get it all in my mouth."

Tiffany, positioned farther down the table, picked up a white cloth ring from a pile. "What's this?" she asked.

"Ah," said Lorna. She put the mask back in the box, then the piñata, closed the box, and returned it to its place. "That," said Lorna, "is my muff." She giggled. "No, for reals, feel it! So soft, downy, silky. Totally absorbent! See, when it rains, the worst part is when the rain goes down your neck. But if you have your muff with you, all you gotta do, is –" She took the muff, snapped it open, wound it around her neck, snapping it back together. "See, it's gotta snap. See how it works? Then, in the rain, you will be spared that indignity, rain going down your neck. It's all about dignity. Right, Richard?"

"Curious, calling your piece a 'muff," said Dik Dik.

"I know, right? Muffler? Isn't a muff like a fur wrap ladies of quality put their hands in when it's cold? I don't remember. You do. You remember everything. You remember all the names."

Dik Dik didn't say anything, so she went on: "Oh, I know, you mean 'muff' as in pussy? Right? Muff, pussy, cunt, twat, bush. You know all the names."

Lorna began to sing, not too loudly. They could make out the words:

"'In the white room with black curtains near the station Black roof country, no gold pavements, tired starlings Silver horses ran down moonbeams in your dark eyes –'"

Lorna kept singing and they knew their interview was over. Suddenly, she stopped singing and spouted: "Art – you always said you had to go all the way. You always said you had to put it on the line. But we didn't. We're all losers. None of us good enough. That's what you said. And then we die. That's what you said."

When they got back outside, moving away from the house, stepping up to the stairway, the door closed behind them, and they heard Lorna singing another tune. They adjusted their works, their clothes, then had little shivers. They started down the stairs.

Johnny said, "I recognized her and her boys right away."

Tiffany said, "You've seen them around town?"

Johnny said, "No, tonight. Or yesterday? That truck – the pickup? The bald dood with the big dick was driving. Lorna was on the passenger side, riding shotgun."

"Doesn't mean anything," said Dik Dik. "It's so hazy, can't see –

Tiffany said, "Does she have a truck?"

No one answered, but everyone stared at the blurry sky.

Step. Step. Step. Down. Going down. Step down. Dark retaliated: if they lost their focus, vertigo, impetigo. This should be a Coltrane Commandment. But, oddly, it was never brought up as a possible addition. Maybe to make the steps part of a Coltrane Commandment would draw attention to them, hex them, so there would be accidents.

Back at the cul-de-sac.

Dik Dik groveled: "What now, what now. I suppose we head back to the Yard. Maybe they found them."

Johnny said, "You getting tired? You sound tired all of a sudden?"

Tiffany said, "The sirens have stopped."

Johnny said, "You guys gotta be the coolest cucumbers ever. I mean, that lady – Lorna, and those guys! That was some weird shit. I mean, I mean, come on –"

Tiffany stopped, turned to Johnny, "What? What do you mean?"

Dik Dik said, "The Yard's bright, bright. Look, you can see it! Don't know if I want to go back to the vortex just yet –"

Johnny said, "That lady back there, she's cuckoo."

Tiffany said, "You watch too much TV."

Dik Dik said, "Agreed. We all agree. I agree with both of you. But how this ties in, if it does, aye, there's the rub."

They all did a collective shrug, then moved slightly faster down towards the Gulch. They avoided the Yard, walking up the Gulch's broken sidewalk, heading towards Elmo's, when a black SUV pulled up alongside them. The driver's window slid down. A young Mexican guy, all stony smiles, said, "Hey, bro, what's up? Gotta show you something. Get in. Just for a sec."

Johnny walked up to the driver. "Hey." The AC hit him in the face like a cool cloth.

"Go on, get in."

Johnny turned to the others and said, "I'll catch up with you later."

The backseat window slid down. A big dood with a big head was back there, and he had raised his big hand to show his big gun.

The driver said, "Nah, everybody. Your friends, too. Get in."

The back door opened. The big guy slipped out, gun out of sight, moved over to the side, waving Tiffany and Dik Dik into the back. They crammed in.

The driver said, "Bro, you get up front with me."

Johnny went around the front of the truck, opened the passenger door, got in.

The driver squealed the tires with a sharp thrust forward that shattered Gulch quiet. The passengers were jolted. He powered down, got all responsible, keeping the speed down.

Johnny said, "What's up?"

The driver said, "You guys okay back there? No biggie, *jefe*. Just show you something and talk."

They drove up the Gulch. No light but their headlights, which somehow didn't count. It seemed like a slipstream. Nothing alive any more. Nothing moving. The AC was fierce. The driver turned in to a narrow dirt road – a driveway? They cut through brush, then, beyond the brush, the lane opened to a cleared area with two small buildings set back. They looked like garages. One was lit up, with men busy around a vehicle. The driver stopped, turned the key. Lights out. The men in the garage raised hands to acknowledge them.

"Everybody out," the driver said.

Tiffany, Johnny, Dik Dik stood close together at the side of the SUV. The driver and big guy from the backseat came around to face them. The big guy suddenly struck out, his grisly bludgeon fist right into Johnny's stomach. Tiffany went, "No!" and fell back. Dik Dik caught her, got an arm around her.

Johnny collapsed to the ground, gagging to catch his breath, spitting, gasping, on all fours between them.

The driver crowded up by him. He said, "You're okay. You're okay. Take it slow. Breathe. You'll be okay. See, bro, turns out somebody's got a big mouth and all of a sudden we got law enforcement up the yin yang. Right in the middle of our spring season. No good, bro. They're picking up gente. Something about the tunnels. Something about some gringo artists who might have got wacked tonight. You and your friends know anything about that?"

Johnny got to his feet. "Come on, man, you know me, you know I'm not stupid. I would never say a word about anything. People got crazy tonight because of –"

The big guy stepped back to Johnny, too close.

The driver went over to Johnny, put an arm around his shoulder. "Yeah, I know," he murmured. "Come on, bro, we got badness to conduct. Because why?"

Johnny said, "Because they were so high, and there was this magic act at the Yard. It got crazy. These guys were supposed to disappear and come back, but they didn't come back. Everybody thought it was a joke. But they still haven't shown up. They ended up calling the cops, and the people who run the place had to tell them about the tunnel that connects on stage. That's all we know."

"A co-ink-a-dink?" He shook. "No good, bro. Cause, see, after I seen you earlier, we had some bidness. Right? Everything normal. Our guys go for the pickup. Guess what? Some shit up there. Guess who has to go straighten out this mess? See what I'm saying? You be careful, bro."

The big guy moved away from the two men, stepped to Tiffany, like an ice berg tiptoeing to an elegant schooner. His humongous head was expressive but ugly. He said,

"You stink of vermin." He held out a hand with an extended forefinger and poked her in the stomach.

Tiffany pulled back.

Behind them, a booming voice cried, "*Buenas dias, compadres!*"

Everybody came around to see Oscar hurrying up the driveway between the bushes. "What's happening, mi gente?"

One of the guys in the garage let loose a crazy loud whistle.

Oscar joined them by the SUV, exchanging complicated handshakes with the driver and the big guy with the melon issues. Was the big guy thinking, 'What's with my head? Turn that frown upside down!' No, he was thinking, 'She's built like a dancer. Long limbs. Long toes.'

Oscar said, "Sweet, we all know each other. I need a bag. My old lady's a wreck, and she's got nothing, nada, zilch. I guess you heard what went down tonight?"

The driver said, "We were just talking about it."

"Listen," said Oscar, "you guys hear anything about those artists, you see something, let me know."

"Sure, *jefe.*"

Johnny said, "We were just leaving. You guys finish your business. We'll see you later."

They walked away, down the driveway through the brush, cancer trees and cane and mesquite. They hit the pavement. All of them bucked, swinging around, dancing a jig. They jiggled up the Gulch, got away from that bend in the road.

Quickly, they shriveled. Johnny dropped forward, bent at the waist, hands at his knees, breathing heavily. Tiffany came over to stand by him. Dik Dik said, "You okay?"

Still bent over, Johnny said, "So you got to meet my little brother."

Tiffany said, "He's your *real* brother? I thought you were just – you know – talking, riffing."

"My real brother. Family business. He had to do that. In front of the guys. Show them he wasn't soft. It's what it is."

"What's *vermin*?" asked Tiffany. "Do I smell?"

Dik Dik huffed and said, "To put the chinaberries to shame, my dear."

Tiffany said, "I was scared back there."

Dik Dik said, "I was a fearless panther ready to pounce."

"Shakespeare," went Johnny, "shoot me some of that mojo."

They heard heavy steps approaching fast, made out movement coming up behind them. They still couldn't see in the dark though. It was Oscar, his tall, broad form not even breathing hard. "What the fuck, you guys? What was that about? No, don't tell me."

Tiffany blurted, "Simon and M.K. – anything?"

"Nope," went Oscar. "Should I wonder what that was about?"

Dik Dik said, "No news?"

"For right now, until forensics finishes, until the lab reports come in, they're making this a missing person's thing. Let the local police handle it. All those different agencies are backing off, and they're pissed. They think it's some kind of hippy dippy joke to make fun of police. Captain Rodriguez is pissed."

Tiffany said, "No one's found them. Poor Mad."

"You guys walking back to the Yard?"

They set their stride and got it done.

"What time is it?" asked Dik Dik. He was glancing around wildly, at the new palette to the street lights.

Johnny said, "I hid my phone – you know, what you told me."

"I don't have mine either," said Tiffany. "I leave it at home, I can't afford it, the monthly payments."

Oscar said, "Oh," and checked his watch. "Three-thirty.

In a few hours this will all be over. We'll be sipping brews at the Yard, yucking it up."

"In three hours we'll be deep in *Telemachus'* journey," said Dik Dik.

"Ah," went Oscar, "you got a gig."

Tiffany said, "I should find the band."

Johnny said, "Back to the scene of the crime."

Oscar said, "I'm going in the back way, over here, the side street."

They followed Oscar to the back of the Stock Yard building, behind its edifice. No lights back there. The massive wall of brick, with high windows, showed muscular, and made Dik Dik say, "Kafka lives here. In this alley way. Brick fiend."

Johnny said, "I think I met him?"

Tiffany said, "Oh, Johnny –"

They were beneath the bar, under its windows.

Oscar said, "I go this way. Back door. I gotta get this to Agatha, then I gotta go find her truck."

Tiffany and Johnny and Dik Dik couldn't see each other's expressions too clearly, but they imagined the pop up's and pop out's.

Tiffany stuttered, "Wha – what...a truck?"

Johnny said, "A pickup?"

"Yeah," went Oscar. "Yeah, a pickup. Agatha's. She loaned her pickup to Lorna and her boys for a job they did for Agatha. They never brought the truck back."

Dik Dik said, "They finish the job?"

"Think so," said Oscar. "That was a couple weeks ago. Agatha didn't make a fuss so it must have been adequate."

Johnny said, "Should I ask –"

"It's so random," said Tiffany.

Oscar sounded impatient: "What are you talking about?"

Dik Dik said, "The job – the job they did for Agatha, what was it?"

Oscar pointed up. "The windows. One of those boys is a glazier. Supposedly trained at reform school. He's even got some kind of certificate."

They stared up at the windows, transfixed. They pictured how it would have looked. They imagined how it would have gone down.

Johnny murmured, "They'd need a mattress in the back of the truck."

"What the –" Oscar stepped away, came back. His arms were moving. He slapped his hands together. "No way," he said. He was shaking. "They had our ladder, with the extension." He straightened. He said softly, "Mattress? No way."

No one watched Oscar. They had their eyes on the wall, scanning for sign in the black. Maybe their peepers were sensitized now. But no luck.

Dik Dik said, "We have to check the windows. In and out like the wind. Not a word to Agatha or the coppers. We have to be sure. We have to see. We have to see. Don't tell anybody yet."

Oscar said, "Half hour. Thirty minutes. Meet me at the front door." He made for the back door.

The others walked past the building, adjacent a side street that gave way to a metal staircase up the side of the canyon. It could have been the skeleton of a giant praying mantis. Post-post-modern cliff dwellers descended the staircase into their arms. It was Red and Daphne.

Daphne clasped Tiffany in a bear hug. She pulled away. "We're getting out of here. We're getting away right now."

Tiffany said, "You got a ride?"

"We're gonna hitch," said Daphne. "He'll protect me." She started walking.

Tiffany followed, said, "Red, what's been going on tonight? At the magic show? We saw you there –"

Howling hoots rang out. Everybody looked for the

source. They went to see.

The Jackal said, "We're like a coven." She laughed, coming closer, her eyes going over each face.

Lise joined them, said, "We went to the center of the Earth, and have come back to spin yarns."

"Anything?" asked Dik Dik.

Lise laughed.

Daphne burst: "What the fuck she doing here?" pointing to the Jackal.

The Jackal said, "Blazing up, my dear." She lit a doob with a BIC.

Johnny said, "There's cops all over the place." He accepted the joint, had a hit, passed it to Dik Dik.

Dik Dik toked, said, "Just one hit."

"Then it's out, cross my heart, hope to die," said the Jackal.

Daphne burst again: "You and your Aphrodite's kiss. Scissoring. If I had some scissors, I'd scissor you!"

Daphne and Tiffany pushed at each other with claws. Daphne tried to slap the Jackal but missed. Johnny immediately stepped between them.

A police car zoomed in out of the darkness without its lights on. Then it put its twirly colored lights on. Two Coltrane police officers stepped out of the vehicle, a man and a woman, each with a bold, black-hanked flashlight. The man, who had been driving, stayed by the vehicle, leaning up against the side, nothing serious, arms at his sides, easy. The woman walked over and assessed the group.

She began: "You know there's a curfew."

Lise said, "It's an emergency. We're worried about our friends. You have to understand that. We've been looking all night. I know you understand. I know you do." Lise stared in to her eyes, insuring she understood – and agreed.

The police officer stared back at Lise in the reflected

light. She kept her bludgeon flashlight at her side. It wasn't a test of wills: it was a test of understanding, and it almost worked. Finally, still staring, the police officer said, "I smell reefer." She raised her voice so her partner could hear: "Reefer over here."

"Oh my," said the male police officer.

"They didn't know about the curfew."

"Ignorance of the law – uh-ho, uh-ho," went the policeman, skedaddling off to the far side and other end of the group. He announced: "We got runners!"

Perhaps Johnny and Dik Dik were sidling away, hoping to disappear. Dik Dik had an important appointment. Now the police officer was in their faces, not touching, but close, and pushy, and he said, "Let's go."

Dik Dik and Johnny glanced at each other. They started walking back to join the others, the police officer behind them, who said, "You really named your dog *Reefer Madness*? Is that what you named your dog?"

"Not my dog," said Johnny.

"That is the dumbest name I ever heard."

The female officer said, "Wadda we got?"

"We'll take this one in for questioning. Hands behind your back."

Johnny said, "You gotta be kidding."

"Hands behind your back." The officer handcuffed Johnny.

Lise said, "Those young women were having a fight. It's been a crazy night. Our friends are missing. We keep waiting for word. We've looked everywhere. This young man was simply trying to help. He was the coolest person here. He's not the one you want.

The female police officer almost smiled. "Okay, I hear you."

Lise spieled, "We came to your beautiful town because we could be open here, to new experience. Here's a new experience for all of us. We're in this together. This is our town, too. But it's been a rough night for us. You, too. We're okay now. We appreciate your help."

The female officer moved to her partner, and she stepped around him to Johnny. She opened his handcuffs. "Don't say a word," she said. Nobody was sure who she was talking to. "It *has* been a crazy night. You guys, go on home. No good hanging around downtown waiting for something to happen."

The police officers returned to their vehicle. The man got behind the wheel. He knocked off the colored lights. They backed away slowly, no lights. They weren't even out of sight when Daphne took a swing at the Jackal. The Jackal backed off, ducking the hit.

Lise flashed to Daphne, "Enough."

Daphne said, "We are out of here. Come on, Red."

Tiffany said, "Red, what happened tonight?"

Red came in close to Tiffany. "I know you," he said, "from the band."

"What happened?" asked Tiffany.

Red jerked away, swung around to Daphne. "Don't know what you're talking about." He put his arms around Daphne, squeezed. "Come on," he said. "Let's leave these fools."

Dik Dik said, "Maybe not the best time to go."

Red said, "Yeah, why is that?"

Dik Dik said, "Because there's a lot of cops out. They're all keyed up. How old is Daphne? You and Daphne out there on the road, right out in the open. Besides, maybe they'll need to talk to you and Lorna and the others."

"Oh, yeah?" went Red.

Tiffany said, "We're just saying be careful."

Daphne and Red walked away, not in an angry or paranoid way, but in a piss and vinegar, youthful array. They were asserting their innocence over the horrors they'd witnessed. They started skipping, holding hands, heading for the bypass that connected to the highway.

They both had a backpack. But small ones. What would they take? Daphne and her poems? Red and his art, his poems? Everybody in Coltrane was a poect and had poultry.

Dik Dik said, "What do we know?"

Lise said, "Cave people see in the dark. We adjusted, adapted. We shifted over. We became like blind catfish darting among the rocks with them. The road's rough up there, but a pickup can do it. They saw one get up there tonight. There're these flood control dams built by the WPA up there. Cave people said that's where people dump bodies. Traditionally. Cave people said especially dumb murderers who want to get rid of bodies fast."

Dik Dik said, "Did they see actual bodies?"

Lise said, "I don't know."

The Jackal said, "Why would they tell us that?"

Dik Dik said, "We don't know anything."

Tiffany said, "Simon and M.K. had many foes."

Dik Dik said, "It's coming on dawn."

Johnny said, "When Oscar goes for the truck, maybe he can –"

Tiffany said, "Lise, Red-Black, you think they're up there –"

Dik Dik said, "Let's go find a place to sit, where you can wait. I have an appointment. Shouldn't take long."

They knew the town so well, they pseudopodded over to a convenient wall, let Brownian motion guide them. There was even a mental bench nearby. Everybody got comfortable. Johnny and Dik Dik remained standing. It was a new tourist spot, a pretend park full of gore.

A siren whooped. Maybe a block away. The sound cut. Hardly seemed worth the effort. They heard a car gunning its engine, then it stopped, too. Then a dog started barking.

Hoots! Terribly familiar hoots! There should be a Coltrane Commandment about hoots. Beware! Hoots signified 21st Century lumpen street theater going funkytown, acting all kinds of primitive... spontaneous... letting it out... letting go... war cry, peace cry... cum cry.

A real crowd of doods congealed around the wall and bench. They sought their own places in the mix. The atmosphere changed from basilica to locker room. Smell of Patchouli –

Tim Asparagus honed in to claim a seat next to the Jackal. He said, "Red! There you are. I want so much to work on your piece right now. Let's go right now to my studio. I mean it. I got do-re-mi."

The Jackal stared him into oblivion. He couldn't see her eyes probably. Everything was a blur for him now, but he knew her face was aimed at his. She said softly, "Not now, tiger. Chill."

Captain America sat on the arm of the bench near Lise. He said, "You are so fried. Everyone's awake. The whole town is buzzing. You can feel it. You thought the town was asleep. Uh-uh. It's all out buzz. Red knows what I'm talking about."

The Jackal said, "Redhead porn is the most popular in America."

Captain America said, "There you go."

Coney Shaman and Tilman sat next to each other, off to the side, away from the others, on the cement wall. In the dark their heads were big balls of yarn nattered by kitties.

Coney Shaman said, "We've been looking. Non-stop. Everywhere."

Captain America said, "I see your underwear!"

Tilman popped: "This is serious. No clowning around. No clowning around."

Dik Dik pulled Johnny away, kept his voice down: "Stay here. Okay?"

Lise said, "We should all be home brewing a nice pot of tea. But that's not true either. This time, this moment right now, this is it. We have no choice but to be here. We fit here. This is our place now. We have to do this. Only one imperative: we have to keep looking, we have to find them."

Coney Shaman said, "Zot."

"Do what must be done," said Dik Dik. "Back in a flash!" He tottered off.

Lise went, "Zot!"

The Jackal answered, "Zot!"

Coney Shaman said, "You're absolutely right. Who would have thought we'd be pushed to such awareness by such horrific circumstance? So law of necessity. Zot is from Hasidism. The notion that God is beyond category. God is the thisness of isness of existence."

Lise said, "It's up in the air." She giggled questioningly. "I mean, what happened tonight. Worst case, best case. Maybe you hacked performance to the next level. The time-space continuum had a fart."

"I hate computers," moaned Coney Shaman.

The Jackal said, "Well, who hated M.K. and Simon enough to kill them in some elaborate Edgar Allen Poe mash up?"

"No clowning around," muttered Tilman.

"Everybody's so buzzed," said Captain America, 'you haven't even noticed the sky."

Johnny said, "I get it. You guys think your buzz from partying all night is some kind of cosmic buzz of insight and shit. Like awareness. You guys are fucked up."

OLBT honked over from the alley, clapping her ham hands. They could tell it was her from the eclipsing silhouette. She called out, "Nicely done."

Lise went, "Nephelococygia."

A police car slid into view up the Gulch, but past Elmo's. It's twirling colored lights started up. The police car stopped. No headlights. The colored lights stayed on.

Captain America said, "Light show. 'The sky is full of

pine cones, telephones –'"'

Tiffany got up from her perch. "I'm gonna go find the band."

Johnny wandered over to her, walked with her a few steps. Johnny said quietly, "You're so on all the time. I know I don't have to say be careful, but it's what Dik would want me to."

"Thanks, Johnny."

Oscar met Dik Dik at the entrance to the bar with a small ceramic cup on a saucer, his famous, awesome espresso. "Thought you could use this," he said. He held the yellow police tape up for Dik Dik to scoot under.

Dik Dik said, "How thoughtful. We could use some water too."

"Sure, when we're done here, I'll get some for you."

Dik Dik slurped his espresso in the dark. Oscar had his flashlight off while he drank. Bitter. Bam! He finished it, handed the cup to Oscar, who stepped over to the bar to leave it.

He flashed his light on. Dik Dik followed him to the stage. Oscar offered Dik Dik a hand to high step to the stage. Dik Dik murmured thanks. They skirted the doors, weren't sure why. Dik Dik avoided them out right. Didn't want to touch them. They seemed imperfectly there. Something as random as a door had become unsightly. Dik Dik felt atrocious near them. They moved back to the windows, a few measly steps.

Oscar ran the flashlight across the two large windows. They looked bold, new, high tech. Dik Dik couldn't figure how big they were. Two feet by three feet? Three feet by four feet? But plenty big for the task. He wished the police officer with the tape measure was here. He probably had taken the windows' measurements.

Oscar said, "Looks okay. Looks like they're both locked." Oscar got up close to a window, flicked the lock mechanism at the middle top. He raised the window. A blast of night air came in, hit them in the faces.

Dik Dik said, "No, you were to check if they *were* locked."

"Oh," went Oscar. He let the window down. He flicked the lock mechanism back to the way it had been. He tried the window again. It went right up. He lowered it. Flicked the mechanism. The window went up.

Dik Dik said, "It's a fraud! It's just for show. There's no lock. Check the other window."

This time he checked it first before touching the latch. The window went straight up. He lowered it. He flicked the lock the other way. It went straight up.

Oscar hissed, "She's been planning this for weeks."

"Bloody bastards. Who knows," said Dik Dik, "maybe they thought they'd pop in and borrow a cup of booze."

"Fingerprints! Now I've got it all chingered up with my prints."

Dik Dik stood by a window, looking through it, then he raised it. He bent out of the window, hands holding on at the sides. Oscar did the same at the adjacent window.

Oscar said, "Long way down."

They pictured where the truck would be.

"They'd already be dead," Dik Dik said. "It's the only way."

"Why the mattress?"

Dik Dik wanted to gag with espresso heart burn but managed: "Too noisy, too messy."

Oscar said, "There's hardly ever traffic back here at night."

They were quiet. They stared in to the dark. It welcomed them. A cat meowed too loudly. They couldn't spot it. By a dented dumpster, small movements with tails, or question marks coming out of asses.

"Agatha okay?"

"She's pissed."

Dik Dik said, "They used your ladder from the truck to

get in and out. The three of them. The bodies in garbage bags, tossed down. It'd take just seconds."

"Taking out the garbage. When they drove off, all a person on the street would see is trashy kids hauling trash."

"It was late. Hardly any traffic."

Oscar said, "How would she do it?"

"Blunt object. She probably googled it. Single blow to the skull that kills instantly."

"Why three?"

"One killer, two haulers. They stuffed the bodies in bags and threw them out the window to the back of the truck with the mattress."

"Who's driving?"

"They'd need a fourth. You're right."

Dik Dik added, "Lorna mustn't know we know."

Oscar said, "You think she'll run? Take the truck? I have extra keys. I'll get the truck. Where ever she parked it."

"She could do worse. Don't touch the back."

"Should I tell Agatha?"

"If we can't find the bodies." He left it hanging there. "We've got nothing."

"Let me get you that water."

The night staggered under the post-party groan. The whole bunch groaned when they saw Dik Dik coming towards them, his arms filled with plastic water bottles.

"Give me one of those," claimed Captain America.

Dik Dik gave one to the Jackal, Johnny, Lise, OLBT.

"Oh, it's like that, is it? Team Dik Dik, Team Triune," said Captain America.

"Hold your horses," said Lise. She had a second drink then passed her bottle to Captain America.

OLBT said, "I don't want this. Whose side do you think I'm on?"

Coney Shaman was rolling a cigarette from a package

of *Drum*. OLBT said, "Roll me one, kimosabe."

The Jackal lit one of her own.

Pretty soon, tiny orange tips were drawing constellations and corrections in the night air. It had cooled –

Lise said, "Tell us."

Dik Dik spilled the beans. He was hesitant at first because of Captain America and his gang being big mouths, but then he figured the more that knew, the more that would be looking. Lorna knew they'd figure it out. Dik Dik told about the windows, the rest of it.

The Jackal said, "Dik Dik, what do you call fake clues?"

Lise sputtered, "Flues!"

The Jackal giggled. "What is the *really happen* in this *really happening*? See what I did there? Is bait being dangled? How come we jump to conclusions? We could have a murderer right here with us. Something completely different is always happening. We complete the magic circuit – "

OLBT said, "Fuck off! The real breaks on through. Always! An explanation is necessary, means consequences. They had to get rid of the bodies. It has to be close, because they were seen. Everybody else was still at the Yard freaking out."

"Could be, could be," said Dik Dik. He stared at the night sky. Then: "In answer to your query, *red herrings* is what they're called."

OLBT said, "Obvious. I hate fish."

"So they're dead," said Tim. "It's not a joke. Even the dog. Everybody heard me yell." He shuddered. He plucked. "One of us."

Captain America sizzled: "Mad is dead. I think I'm gonna vomit." He stood to act out gagging motions, then cried, "I wish there was magic. I wish they'd really disappeared to some stinky hell where they'd be raped with pineapples every day. All except Mad, who didn't deserve any of this."

Coney Shaman said, "We take it to Lorna right now. Citizen's arrest."

OLBT said, "Don't be an ass. Shallow graves – I bet they had them prepared. They could be anywhere. Ah, the flakiness of fascism, or the good guys would never win."

Lise said, "We think we know where the bodies are. Close, like you say, close. Up the Gulch. Maybe graves. Maybe just dumped. We need a truck. Get this over with."

The Jackal explained, "It's because people saw a truck going up there. Everybody know that? Right after the 'disappearance', alleged, a truck was seen going up the Gulch, then coming back. Multiple witnesses."

Coney Shaman said, "I got a truck. No, it wasn't me going up there. I was on stage being humiliated. Gets dicey up the Gulch, back in the canyons. I know the way."

Captain America intoned: "Leave no turn unstoned."

Johnny said, "I should go with you guys."

Lise said, "Yes."

The Jackal pushed in: "You and me, girl, we been there and back already, we don't need no boy –"

Coney Shaman said, "We're gonna do this. We're gonna find 'em. I'll get the truck, be back in five. Ten minutes tops. Promise." He took off.

"Is he coming back?" asked Johnny, watching the cupcake bobble away in to town.

Tilman said, "No clowning around. We got this. Proof is evidence. Didn't you hear what he said tonight?"

Johnny said, "You mean before the show?"

Tilman said, "Who are you?"

Tilman came on: "It'll be an expedition. I'm second in command. In search of death. In search of answers. Looking for corpses. Vibing them! We band of ghouls, begging for sensory overload. Can we take it? Can we take it?"

Captain America popped: "No clowning around!"

A voice called from the darkness across the street: "Johnny!" Bobbing towards them, figures – two-legged, four-legged. The voice called, "Johnny."

Tiffany and some guys walked over. Tiffany said, "This is Bear, Mikey. Potter – he's not in the band." She had the dogs sit.

Mikey said, "He's a fricking barnacle."

Bear made the dogs behave.

Tim came to his feet in a burst of lurch, clambered over to Captain America. "Like you," he said. "You're a fucking barnacle, too."

At his garbled excitement, one of the wolf-dogs got to its feet. Tiffany said, "Easy, easy peasey."

Tim, wobbly standing there, crooned, "Who let the zoo out?"

Lise said, "This is exhausting."

Dik Dik said, "Hello, there, *News From the Recent Terror.*"

Tiffany went up to Dik Dik. "How'd it go? What's going on?"

Johnny said, "The short version – give her fifty words or less –"

Dik Dik laid it out fast and measly. Bear whistled. Mikey said, "Those pervs."

Dik Dik said, "What light, from distant sky – the East is the goddess, and the East has changed the world. Bloody rotters, look, look, dark has gone blue. *Azul!* See the blue. Gray-blue. It has begun."

"You have a thing about this goddess, huh?" asked Johnny.

Captain America called out: "We have an embarrassment of riches in our agony."

Bear said, "It's dope, dood. We promised we'd help." He got closer to Tiffany, wrapped himself around her.

Potter said, "I'm not following. What's going on? Tiff told us some."

No one answered. The water bottles were empty and squished. Cigarettes were completed, smashed out.

OLBT gahumphed and gurgled, "It's a scam, a con, a practical joke gone too far. It's a performance that's kept us up all night."

Tilman said, "No, no, it's not like that at all. I wasn't clowning, making fun. It's – I don't know. The omphalos. No way this could have happened on my watch. But it did." Tilman pulsed, "No fun. No fun. We owe it to them."

Johnny said, "It's a set up."

"Pat," said OLBT.

"As though we were supposed to. Step by step," said Lise.

The blue was spreading, swarming, inking, engulfing the gray and black.

"I have to get to my place. Muster the materials," said Dik Dik.

Mikey said, "What do you need us to do?"

Tiffany said, "Go get that mic and amp we were talking about. Bear, take care of the guys. We'll meet up at Grassy Park for the reading."

Bear said, "What're you gonna do?"

"I'll go with Dik Dik, help with his stuff, then we'll meet at the park."

Bear grunted.

Potter went, "I wanna read!"

"Excellent," said Dik Dik. He would not groan or growl. "Tell your friends. Bring them along. We'll get them a part."

OLBT said, "Meet you there, little brother. Don't blow a fuse, and if it's already blown, don't put a penny up your arse to fix it." She started laughing too loudly, called, "Grassy Park. Bloomsday."

Tim said, "You guys be fools, worrying over those goofballs. Fuck 'em! You get what you sew. You sew what you sweep. However that goes. I'm gonna go home, get a couple hours of shut eye. I'll check in at the park later."

Captain America said, "You'll never be able to sleep. Take a *Valium.*"

Mikey said, "I got *Adderol.*"

Tim waved him off, but everybody else took one. Dry humped it.

A wheezing, battered, little truck rolled into view, came to a stop near them. There was enough light to see the truck was not camo-colored at all, like they'd first suspected: those were deep scratches and rust patches.

Tilman got up front on the passenger side. Lise and Johnny and the Jackal climbed in the back, taking seats near the cab to hold on.

Dik Dik said, "How about a ride? By Mimosa? Just a little way?"

Tilman and Coney Shaman grunted.

Dik Dik tried to unlatch the tailgate but it wouldn't budge. He climbed up and over the tailgate. He and Tiffany sat in the back.

Potter yelled to the throbbing truck, "'What light through yonder window breaks –'"

The wheezing rasped out a big, blue cloud the color of dawn, and they were off.

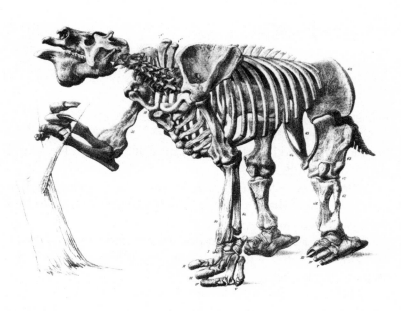

Part III

Don't count the tolls! Matewan, be still!

Dawn's early light came in like a charter of cum. The tower announced it. Dik Dik knew it, felt it. He wasn't sure Tiffany did.

Tiffany was wondering, heart and head exhausted in different ways, there's different ways to grieve, depending on how much hurt.

By dawn's early light, and thrashers and towhees' coda, Dik Dik and Tiffany got let off, waved off, and climbed the steps to his house.

"The door's in upside down," said Tiffany, gasping, holding in a laugh. "Is the door in upside down? Look at that tree! It's got balls. Dik, your tree has balls. I guess, you have such big balls they spread to the tree." She hiccoughed with laughter. "This is your place."

"Splendid," said Dik Dik, "you're unwinding. We needed to get away from the hurly burly. Enter, my dear."

He unlocked the door, swung it open, let her go first. They meandered through the workshop. She went up to each machine. He named them for her. She scrutinized. He opened the door to the inner sanctum.

"Wow! This is your art." She hurried from wall to wall to check out photos or hangings. She wow'ed at them. "These photos – they're great! You're a photographer. I mean, I know you do a lot of stuff. Can I take off my boots? Do you mind? Just while you're getting your stuff."

"Please," said Dik Dik. "Off with them. Make yourself at home. I'll put on the kettle. We'll have a cupa." He stayed to watch. Circassian!

The boots slid off easily. Her feet were bare, golden glowing with heat and sweat. She wiggled her toes. She danced to the upper level of the living room, got down on all fours, apprehended Dik Dik's nook, with pillows and small table. She snuggled in, legs out, toes flexed. She said, "Is this how you do it?"

"You do it better."

"Do you think – the murderer –"

"We can't believe Lorna would do this. Yet it's so obvious. Stranger things have happened." Dik Dik sighed, shrugged. "We're so bloody blasé, jaded, then sinister and cynical. All at once. So it's a game? The performance continues? Seems subtle. We're fish in a barrel, and it's Bloomsday."

Dik Dik moved to the stove, got the kettle on, got two slices of bread in the toaster. He took down from the shelf by the sink two cups, two saucers, one spoon, one knife. He got out the marmalade and butter from the fridge.

The library sack sat there. He went for a small backpack and returned to the fridge to retrieve three water bottles. He put them in the pack. Then he went to the cupboard and took out two cans of sardines and put them in the pack.

Tiffany called out, "Is it terrible to ask, but I'd really love a shower? I'm selfish. Maybe I'm in shock. You know how rock stars are. I'll just be a sec. By the time the tea's ready, I'll be out."

"Of course. Come," said Dik Dik. This was not some

sixties' porn fantasy. Poor kid, he corrected. Let her get cleaned up.

He led her to the bathroom, explained the homemade shower apparatus and left her to it. By then, the kettle was talking back, the toast had jumped to attention, and he felt a depth charge of darkness dump in his maw, about death, about despair, about subtleties. It wasn't a game. It was a game. It was obvious. It was obscure. It soured everything, made the air weigh in. It. It. It. Death. Death. Death. He buttered the toast, smeared on marmalade. It would not interfere with Bloomsday. The charter had sounded.

He loved marmalade, sardines, PKD, trees, humanity (as a concept). Joke's on me, he almost cried out. All thoughts of Morpheus were out of his mind, when Tiffany called, "Towel! Towel, please!"

The shower was turned off, its curtain pulled back. She kept her arms at her sides, standing in the tub, dripping. He got her a towel. He said, "My turn." He quickly disrobed, exchanged places with her. Her formation, stepping out of the tub, the way her raised leg clarified space to her curled toes, seemed spontaneous. Her tummy was very pretty, he noted, the pout of flesh and dimpled navel. He got the shower going.

She toweled off. "Dik, you got a ball on your dick just like the tree."

"Tea and toast, love." He washed up.

She grabbed her clothes, said, "You have a hair brush?" He pointed it out and she left the bathroom.

They slurped tea and munched toast quietly.

"Time to go," said Dik Dik. "Let's get this road on the show."

"What if they can't find the bodies?"

"The lab reports on the blood may shed light –"

"Maybe it's just Mad's. God, what a night. Johnny's brother? Lorna's place?"

"Did you like that young man's hardon?"

"It was pretty. But in each of the encounters tonight, everybody talking, exchanging info, telling what they know, theories, getting the vibe, yet, I don't know, no...no overlap? See what I mean? Singles."

"Singletonians. Because no one shares the same real. I mean, you and I do right now. We share our friendship and talk this way."

"Is that a word? Singleton?"

"Singletonians. Why not? Words are ours to distort. You could be a princess eft."

"I could. But I'm not. Our friendship – you trust me, right? I trust you. Isn't that the way it works? But I catch these looks in your eyes, like you're on the verge of jumping on me and eating me alive."

"You're right."

Tiffany smiled. "Men. You know? Johnny was nice. I mean, it's not just men. People have these expectations so they don't listen. They're just waiting to jump in. Everybody's so angry. Sarcastic! I just want to scream, 'shut the fuck up'. I mean, it's out of the bag, everybody knows how fucked up things are, so why pretend. That's why I liked Johnny. I don't think he pretends."

"Biggest problem in human communication is the illusion it has taken place."

"Is that Joyce?"

"No, another Irishman."

"Tell me about Joyce. I know we're in a rush."

"We have to – it's my show: I have to be there." He stared at her. The young woman before him was open, interested. She was ready for anything.

"I think of Joyce as master of chaos. At least master of Dublin. He brings it right out in the open, right into your face, the messy confusion of human experience. Digs right in, goes for the throat of all the lies and expectations, all the layers and veneers of our little lives. He hates what the friction between the actual and the ideal have done to language, so gives language free rein. Does this make any sense at all?"

"Sure. Everybody's full of shit. I get it. I'm about done with my tea. Where's one of the books? Can I see it?"

"Over there." Dik Dik pointed to his precious library sack.

She went to fetch a copy, hefted it, brought it back, sat, opened it.

Dik Dik said, "There's a lot of play in Joyce. You know how kids descend into a deep altered state in play? Speaking the roles, acting out scenes. Make believe. Joyce thinks we live in a state of make believe, that is so intense it's no different from the real."

"It's so thick," said Tiffany.

"I'm not saying you have to read it. I don't care. Your choice. I'm just telling you about it. A single day in the life of some chums, with peripheral characters from time to time taking over."

"It's so long. I never read a book so long."

"It's an experience. You experience his writing –"

She read, "'Stately, plump Buck Mulligan came from the stairhead, bearing a bowl of lather on which a mirror and a razor lay crossed.'"

"First sentence. Terrifically specific. We should go."

"I'm not smart enough to read it. I don't have the education. I don't know where Dublin is. I'm a singer in a rock and roll band."

"Fuck's sake. A life of mistakes is more honorable and more useful."

"I don't know what that mean."

"What do they call it? In the media all the time? The obsession with humans making a difference stories?"

"What?"

"When an experience forces a person to reconsider –"

"I don't know. Motivational speaker?"

"You're funny. Wit! You're very smart. You have to

figure it out in your own way. What to do. Why to do it."

"*Wake up call!* Is that what you're thinking?"

"Exactly! Death is the ultimate wake up call, so one realizes a life of mistakes was actually a good thing, an engaged thing."

"Read something from Joyce. To me. For me."

"My little sister, the seductress."

She smiled, then rolled her eyes. He took the book, found the part:

"'With what meditations did Bloom accompany his demonstration to his companions of various constellations?

"'Meditations of evolution increasingly vaster: of the moon invisible in incipient lunations, approaching perigee: of the infinite lattiginous scintillating uncondensed milky way, discernible by daylight by an observer placed at the lower end of a cylindrical vertical shaft 5000 feet deep'...yadda, yadda, yadda... 'stars... evermoving wanderers from immeasurably remote eons to infinitely remote futures in comparison with which the years, three score and ten, of allotted human life formed a parenthesis of infinitesimal brevity.'"

"I gotta get my boots on." She rose from her bar stool, shuffled off.

"You didn't like it."

She spoke from the front of his place, "Where's the play? Where's the wit? 'Infinitesimal', my ass. When it's in your face, it's not infinitesimal. That's a fucking privileged view –"

"You're right. Get your boots on."

"You believe that shit? Bleak, man. Talk about cynical. Because it doesn't leave room for when things are really good. You gotta be able to know when it's really good. It sounds obvious, I know. But this jazz, we're small, we're so small, we're nothing, we *are* nothing, nothing means anything, everything is shit? Peeps running around every which way. No one leads, no one follows, then you die. That's the fucking intellectual view? That's a lotta help."

"There's always another way to see it. It's just a day. A thing for this day: Bloomsday. You don't have to play."

They shrugged mentally like after going through a molestation.

She said, "Take the pack. I'll take the sack."

"Thanks so much for all your help."

"I hardly did anything."

"We worked together all night. We spent the night together."

"I know. If it wasn't so sad, I'd be glad. Well, except for the part where Johnny gets slugged in the stomach. But that wouldn't have happened if there'd been no magic show tonight. I'd never have met Johnny."

"Let's go."

He led the way, closing doors behind him. Doing his duty. They walked with purpose. They knew these steps. They knew that tree – eucalyptus. They recognized each house. Up the Gulch! They marched close but not touching. The smell of soap rose from their bodies and mingled with the smells of dawn. The sour air had withdrawn with its hazy sky. Now, it was hallelujah blue. They knew the stars had been up there last night. Now gone again! A circling hawk cried. Dickey birds chittered.

Chinaberry, pomegranates, figs, aglow in the new sun. Flowers emanated. And it was heating up. This big beacon, right on top of their heads. The sun hit extra sharp here in Arizona, as compared to other states. Street dogs started a street dance, chasing and yipping after each other. Smell of yeast in the air.

"Do you think anybody will come?"

"To Bloomsday?" Dik Dik snorted.

She nodded.

"Who knows? Don't jinx it. Fuck 'em all! People signed up. My players. Dawn to dusk. They'll be there."

They walked in silence. Quiet on the streets, mannequins and hobby horses high stepping about. More dogs. A couple cats.

Dik Dik said, "Everybody's waking up now, getting the news. People will wander downtown to see what they can find out. Rubberneckers. Gawkers."

"Instant audience! What if somebody thinks it's disrespectful to do this today?"

"Shush! No more empathy. Up, up! Do I have to tickle you? Joyce in Dublin is all about self-loathing. Guilt. Debt. Poverty. Resentment. It's our story too. Replenish. Inspire. Rejuvenate. We are entangled. Even through death. That's why we must see this through, for the living and the dead."

Tiffany said, "Oh, shit."

Dik Dik followed her gaze. The Gulch opened to its nexus of grandeur ahead, Matewan Tower at the top, for gathered by the Stock Yard building, law enforcement, lots of cop cars, in various flavors, lights twirling.

"Oh, no," said Tiffany. "Didn't we just do this?"

"The go must show on."

"The show must go on."

They skirted the Yard, staying on the other side of the street, up on the sidewalk. Dik Dik noticed the police sergeant who had been taking measurements. Dik Dik stepped over to talk to him. Tiffany remained where she was on the sidewalk.

"Good morning," Dik Dik said.

The policeman said, "Sir, you have to keep back."

Dik Dik read his name tag and remembered. He said, "Sergeant Molina, we talked earlier when you were taking the measurements."

"That don't mean we're friends. You need to back off. Get back on the sidewalk."

"What happened? Why all the excitement? Did something happen? Did you find the missing men and dog?"

"Sir, I have no information at this time."

"Oh, for bloody sakes, we have the right to know."

Sergeant Molina said, "I know you didn't do it. But you encouraged this toxic atmosphere to perpetuate. It got out of hand. Now get back and don't make me say it again."

Dik Dik rejoined Tiffany. Her face asked but he didn't volunteer any information.

She said, "Oscar and Agatha up there – see."

Dik Dik checked where she pointed. Sure enough, the titans stood there on the promenade, owning it. Yellow police tape cordoned off the bar. A couple of her boys posed nearby, smoking cigarettes.

"Oscar blabbed," said Dik Dik.

"I'd bet anything! So what does that mean? The cops'll go up the Gulch looking for bodies? No, wait, Oscar didn't know about that, did he? So they'll go after Lorna."

"Mayhap. *Peut-être.* We have to get to Grassy Park. Just ignore –"

"I bet they haven't sent anybody to Lorna's yet. They'll have trouble finding her place. I guess, Oscar knows where it is. I don't know."

A precious pause. Their eyes met, stabbed, exchanged email addresses, went their separate ways.

Dik Dik said, "You have to –"

"You want me to? By myself?"

"Bloomsday. Dawn to dusk."

"What should I say? Turn yourself in? Run? She'll beat me up."

"I'm sorry. It's because I think I should go. Not to warn her. Ha! All of us idiots are involved." Sighs galore. "Somehow. If they try to take her with force, she could go nuclear. So, yes, I'd tell her to turn herself in. Or run. Don't seem to be many other options."

"I'm not going over there by myself."

"There's no time –"

As they got to Main Street, they saw a car then a truck go by. Coltrane was waking up. Morning traffic was picking up, as people zoomed to work. A few people walked dogs, everything from pound rescues to exclusive Beverly Hills' genetic morphs. They seemed in a hurry. One man had a colorful parrot on his shoulder. Man and bird talked and chortled, out for their morning dialogue. A bunch of young people showed up at once, walking in or getting dropped off, but they took off in different directions.

Tiffany said, "Wait staff."

"Ah," went Dik Dik.

"Been there, done that. Morning shift. Breakfast. Hey, look at the people in Grassy Park."

Grassy Park was a long, thin grassy area, cut down its center by a sidewalk, and bordered by sidewalks. In the middle was the gazebo. At the eastern end, the mining museum with its mining equipment on display. These were heavy, black, beasts of metal on rails. The west end of the park had most of the grass, with trees and flowers, and benches. That was where they'd stake out Bloomsday. That would be their hold, their keep, dawn to dusk.

Familiar faces! Douglas and Moriah, in costume. Douglas seemed a portly Sherlock Holmes, but the tiny wire rimmed glasses made Dik Dik realize he was going for a Joyce thing. He wore a boater. Moriah, for some reason, was in a gown, very tight and silky, with a low cut bodice. Was she Molly Bloom? Lady Macbeth? Douglas and Moriah had brought four folding chairs and a banner. They'd already unfurled the banner between two support poles to hold it taut. The banner read: 'SCRIBBLEDEHOBBLE,' Joyce term. On the benches sat Bear, Mikey, Potter, and the equipment.

Dik Dik walked right over to Douglas and Moriah to embrace them. "You, darlings," he cried. "Thanks so much."

"Any news?" asked Douglas. Dik Dik was about to respond: a car drove by and honked.

A lady walking two wiener dogs paused to take it in – banner, chairs, players. She called, "This a protest?"

Dik Dik cried, "Bloomsday!"

The wiener dogs started barking, so she led them away.

Dik Dik walked over to the benches. Tiffany was in Bear's lap, his arms around her.

Potter, in tights, with a fluffy shirt, jumped to his feet and proclaimed: "Fleance, the game is afoot!"

Dik Dik roared, "'The moon is down! The moon is down!'"

Bear whispered into Tiffany's ear in between kisses, "You have time for a quickie with the old man?"

Dik Dik said, "Thanks for coming. Let's get set up."

Tiffany rose from Bear. Bear said, "I brought an extension cord." It was beside him, and he lifted it up to show. "You always need an extension cord."

"Good, good. Splendid," said Dik Dik. "Power should be on. City promised. It's over there, the connection, in the corner of that flower bed."

Mikey said, "Where do you want the mic?"

"By the chairs? Where the chairs are," said Dik Dik.

"So the amp needs to be up there, too," said Mikey.

Bear grabbed the extension cord, took off with it. He said, "I'll plug in."

Mikey carried the amp and mic to the chairs. Douglas and Moriah stood nearby watching. Douglas had his personal copy of *Ulysses*, holding it in his hands before him, as a believer would hold the family Bible. Tiffany plugged the mic cord in to the amp. Dik Dik paced back and forth from chairs to flower bed. Bear got the cord plugged in, brought the other end to the amp. He plugged in the amp. Tiffany hit the power button. A blat! Everybody gritted teeth. She adjusted, wiggled knobs. She took up the mic, flicked it on, spoke in to it: "Hello, hello,

hello. I hope you like our show."

Her voice cracked over the park at first, abrasive and unnatural, then it settled, as she continued adjustments, to an electric sound entity cutting through the park, above the ambient white nests of city and traffic. They were ready to begin.

Potter clapped. Any second he would emit a hoot. Moriah and Douglas and Dik Dik sat in the chairs. Dik Dik had his sack and pack beside him. They really could use one of those beach umbrellas, to cast some shade. But too late. For shade, they would adjourn to the gazebo, use its layering – metal, organic – to recharge. Moriah adjusted a bonnet on her head. Douglas and Dik Dik eyed each other. The others stood around. Tiffany and Bear sat in the grass at their feet. Mikey took the extra chair. Potter danced around like a pixie, colliding genres. Here came OLBT. She brought some kind of folding chair apparatus with three legs. She dropped her bag, fixed her three legged spider support dealeywhopper near the others, lowered her bulk. Potter hooted.

Dik Dik took the mic and began: "*Ulysses* by James Joyce takes place on a single day in June, June 16, in Dublin. Ever since its publication in 1914, people around the world have celebrated *Ulysses* by public readings on June 16, known for ever more as, Bloomsday. Today is Bloomsday. *Ulysses* is divided into eighteen episodes, named for people and adventures of Homer's *Odyssey*. We will be reading from throughout the episodes. This is *Ulysses*."

Douglas accepted the mic from Dik Dik and read: "'Stately, plump Buck Mulligan came from the stairhead, bearing a bowl of lather, on which a mirror and a razor lay crossed.'"

Bloomsday was on. The sun was ripe. The day was luscious. Voices were bellicose. Moriah would read next, then OLBT. That was maybe two hours. Perfect!

Everything was perfect. Dik Dik let the Joycewords move through his space – they entered him, bathed him, coddled him. He turned down all excess. He listened and welcomed the words, the scene unfolding, the characters teasing, boyish, as human as his gente –

Electric word sounds added a frosty sparkle to subsistence. Words – utterances, prolapsed in and out of view, an overlap of words and park and people. Characters knew what to do, knew where they were going. The novel was a world laid atop a world. Visions, sounds – colors, lyrics. Dialogue, cheeky, full of allusions of the sea, about the struggles.

People wandered by. Three people: a woman and two men stopped to listen. They squinted with it. They concentrated. Gave it a try. Listening was something to do on purpose with exceedingness. A stray dog dashed through the park, irritated, looking around wildly for the source. A jogger slowed as he went by, narrowed in listening, hovered in place.

Dik Dik inhaled, exhaled, took Tiffany's eyes. She shook her head microscopically. When Dik Dik stood, she stood. They walked off a little ways. Bear watched. The voice, the electricity continued. Now the words clashed, now the words augmented, climbing the air like a weather condition.

Tiffany whispered to Dik Dik: "The way that woman looks at you. In the gown? That one. You talked to her tonight I remember. She wants to eat you up. Is it the ball on your dick? Does it have magic powers?"

"I'm sorry. I'm going. To inflict this unfair burden on you! By the time you're back, maybe we'll have word from the Gulch."

"I'm going." She walked away.

Dik Dik returned to his seat.

Up the Gulch, into the heart of the canyon, which eventually opened to the wildness of the Apache's, where explorers and seekers, day trippers micro-dosing on ketamine and LSD, had to know their way, or they'd walk right into poison oak. But they weren't up that far. The little battered truck with its bouncing people cargo had already passed the last house, where the road had narrowed, becoming a rocky trace. The so-called road was more on the *so-called* side than on the road side of things.

Lise liked the buttery pretzels of dawn light. Light was a gift. Dawn was a birth each time. Dawn's light, see bright! She contemplated their ascent, their insertion in to the canyon, so various from the explore last night. Now, the popping flash of birds and bugs, it was June, they were looking for dead people. Lise had grown up in the Midwest, in Wisconsin. The constant green and moisture, forest and stream everywhere you turned, had bathed existence in plenitude. She'd started out as an organic farmer. Kale! Garlic! She'd felt smothered. She'd come to Coltrane in the sixties, so one of the original artists. She may have been one of the finest artists in town, but like so many she had no business sense, and gave away as many paintings as she sold. She made sculptures, she worked in fibers, she wrote wonderful poetry. But painting was where her passion connected.

They passed a shaft, off a little ways on the side of a wall of rock. These hand dug, then blasted, shafts dotted the Apaches, failed portals to lodes never found, but decent stopovers if you're in a rush, and needed a place to crash. Gotta check for rattlesnakes! Steep sided canyons, now, that directed the monsoon floods right down to here. The canyons were coming back in piñon and juniper. They came to their first WPA dam. The theory was that the three-sided structures would act as holding tanks to slow the floods of the monsoon season. Lise slapped at the top of the truck, and Coney Shaman stopped.

Coney Shaman had his window rolled down. He called, "What?"

Lise said, "This is the first one. We got up to here last night. But it was dark. We didn't have flashlights. We should check."

Johnny hopped out of the back of the truck. He walked around the truck, made his way to the dam. Red stone work with gritty cement, about six foot high, with spiny lizards already there, calling it their own. Cactus wrens gargled nearby – they kept an eye on everything! Johnny had to scramble through rocks and debris to get a handle on the wall. He pushed aside baby mesquite with adult-sized stickers. He nodded to the lizards and the wrens. He pulled himself up so he could see over the lip of the wall. The Jackal came up beside him, her flapping, leather vest offering some protection from the stickers. They looked around the holding tank, elbows up on the wall, not sure what they should see. It was silting up, so lots of grass and weeds, then water bottles, candy wrappers. There was a moldy looking sleeping bag in the far corner. Someone might have camped here eons ago. No sign of cave people. When Johnny asked her if some of her friends lived out here, the Jackal didn't answer. They returned to the truck, climbed in.

The Jackal explained, "*Nada. Basura.*"

Coney Shaman took off, but he had to keep it slow. Lots of big rocks, almost boulders, in the road now. He drove around them. It got bumpy. Bouncier.

Lise called: "Hey, hey! We'll walk this stretch."

The three in the back climbed out of the halt. They went ahead of the truck. Johnny and the Jackal knocked big rocks out of the way. The little truck seeped behind.

Lise sauntered off to the side, in the tangles of willows

and weeds. Here, the so-called road was the arroyo, or wash, then a little farther it was beside the arroyo, then it was crossing the arroyo. Lise was in the arroyo, examining a tiny smear of water left behind in a low spot. The nature of their task snuck up, occluded her mood. Impossible. Impossible horror! Her friends dead! They were looking for bodies. It seemed their awful responsibility. No choice. It wasn't rocket science. It was clear what had happened. Lise had to be *clear*. So she could close it. She had to rise to the occasion. Be more real. *Be more real*, as her mentor might say. She thought that sounded like a TV ad –

"Puddle club," emitted Lise.

Johnny came over to see. "What?" he asked.

Lise replied, "Puddle club," and opened her hand.

Tiny blue butterflies fluttered around the meager puddle. At her movement, they rose, stirred up, flicking powder blue, soft frenzy.

Johnny watched and said, "Beautiful." He smiled at Lise, got close to her. "One of them got in your hair." He nudged the tiny blue butterfly from her hair with a finger.

The Jackal said in a loud voice: "You guys!" She kept rapping *opportunity* in her head, but she didn't know what that meant. Something to do with the way they knew each other in this fucked up town. Them and their Commandments. A few years in Coltrane and she'd encountered most of the gente, smoked dope with them, maybe slept with them. She despised the phony intimacy which hinted at decency, when the bastards would cut your throat at a moment's notice. Tonight's catastrophe not unexpected. But even thinking like that – that was so fucked up. Beyond fucked up! She knew those guys! It was her own fault getting involved, she knew, because she loved hanging in the scene to mock it, to being oh so cognizant. Now, what? *Death don't have no mercy* –

Lise and Johnny got back to work, returned to the road

to notify boulders. They proceeded up to the next damn. They checked it out. It was practically filled to the top. No *basura*.

The road got slightly better, so they rode for a while in back.

Lise said, "It's a beautiful day."

Johnny grunted. The Jackal laughed.

No matter what they discovered, the day would go on with beauty. Lise knew her home, the ways of its beauty. More TV ads?

The Jackal cackled, "Wild goose chase –"

Johnny said, "What's with that goose, anyway? Anybody bring water?"

Lise honked loudly.

Coney Shaman stopped the truck, leaned his big hairy head out the window to yell: "We got this far. I think we outta turn back."

The Jackal stepped in: "One more! One more dam. Come on."

Coney Shaman grumbled, spat, pulled in. He gave it some gas, crept along.

On the road ahead, suddenly coming into view, a dam, and parked to the side, as though they might be able to pass it, a black SUV. It was empty, with rolled up windows.

Johnny recognized it.

Coney Shaman braked, huffed, "Can't go no mo'."

Lise called, "One more dam. Right there." She pointed to it by the SUV, tucked into its own canyon branch, on the left.

Coney Shaman was not convinced. He was mad about the whole thing. And not that kind of *mad* either. He was insane about the fail, but kept it in the zilch department, a secret file under lock and key. One thing at a time, like the drunks said. Tilman was no help. Tilman, right next to him, smelling sour, made a fist of his right hand and he repeatedly slammed it in to the open palm of his left hand.

Lise said, "Park. We'll check it out."

Lise, Johnny, and the Jackal jumped from the back. Johnny murmured, "You guys, I don't feel good about this."

Lise came over to him. "Why? What's wrong?"

"The SUV. I know it."

They got up to the dam. They had to climb this one's wall too, but the stone work provided plenty of hand and foot holds. No lizards or wrens around here. They got up, had a look in.

Two men stood in the holding tank next to three, industrial-sized, black garbage bags.

"*Jefe*, we meet again," cried the smaller of the two men in the tank.

The Jackal waved, couldn't resist a hoot. "Hey!"

The big guy in the tank may have been messing with the garbage bags, he was so close to them. He seemed to be muttering, or else, talking to himself. Something discernible came out as, "Oh, this one, she's filthy –"

"Come on down, Johnny! Check it out! Guess what's in the bags."

Johnny, Lise, and the Jackal climbed in. This tank was filled only about halfway, silted up. They walked over casually, through the grass and weeds, insects popping, to the two men.

The Jackal managed, "I guess our picnic now is out of the question?"

The big guy did not like the stink of death, which he could never get used to. What was the point of being the gun, the heavy, the bouncer...blah, blah...if it smelled so bad? Why do people stink at death? Or was it death that stunk? He wondered whether this girl would smell up the place. Sure, raised a Catholic, evil, sin, guilt, all like that, front and center in a man's life.

The smaller man said, "Time to wake up." He wore a

cowboy shirt with pearly buttons and blue jeans. Complex cowboy boots completed his ensemble. He pulled a long spliff from his cowboy shirt pocket. His other hand had a lighter and he got it going. He held on to it, puffing away.

Johnny said, "What's going on?"

"Ah, bro, you know how it is. This is a great spot to drop off goods. Pick up easy. This is a great spot to party. Now, guess what? It's ruined forever. What the fuck, bro! What you guys been doing? Maybe I should make a citizen's arrest."

"Come on," said Johnny. Everybody watched each other. "What's in the bags?"

"You know what's in the bags." He'd let the doob go out without passing it.

Nobody really wanted to know what was in the bags.

The Jackal announced, "I'm gonna go check –" She stepped towards the bags and met the big guy who did a maneuver which had her spun around, arm behind her back, him holding on to her wrist.

"Hey, dood, I hardly know you, but now I've seen your prick. Ow!"

Johnny raised his voice: "Let her go!"

"She's got a mouth," said the big guy and pushed the Jackal away so she stumbled and almost fell. She caught herself. She was quick on her feet. She didn't stink yet. He could tell. He wondered why she had turned out this way. Why had he turned out this way? He used to play football, go to church –

She yelped, "That's not necessary."

Lise jumped in: "Something happened last night. Two men and a dog, a big dog, disappeared. We've been looking for them. All night! We thought we'd check the dams. That's all we know."

"You don't get it," cried the smaller man. "We do business here. There was supposed to be something last night. Remember? We talked to you and the old man? I told you it was chingered up, had to go check. So here we are. These bags. They ain't my bags! We don't use no fucking garbage bags. And our load? The weed's gone. A whole deal, gone – pfft!" He shrugged elaborately, waving the dead roach. "My boys didn't want to tell me when they came back, they know how I can get. They said they thought it was garbage. But, yeah, they looked. That's why they said I had to see it. Here we are. We looked. These bags, man. Where's my weed, big brother? Isn't this embarrassing?"

Johnny said, "Whatever you're doing is none of our business. We've been looking all night. I told you these guys disappeared. We didn't know they were dead, murdered. We have to get their bodies back."

"See, that's where you're wrong, bro. Nobody's taking anything back. We get our pot, you get your bags of trash."

"What do you want?"

"I just told you."

Johnny said, "Let us look in the bags to be sure. Then we'll go."

"Don't you be talking down at me to impress your gringos. You know damn well how we would handle this ordinarily. But considering you're blood. Yeah, see where this is going, bro? I don't know if I can trust you. That is not a good thing. Let's not test it."

The big guy said, "Let 'em go. We keep the dirty girl. If they go to the cops, they'll never see the girl again. Isn't that how that goes?"

The Jackal said, "I can't wait."

Lise said, "We don't know anything about your pot."

"Maybe not," said the smaller man, "but the way you all know each other, hanging out all the time, getting loaded on my weed, it should be simple, easy as pie to figure out." He glanced at the cold doob in surprise, and relit it. He toked, passed it to Lise who was closest to him. She took a hit, passed it to Johnny who smoked, then walked it over to give to the Jackal. She accepted it, toked.

Holding her breath, she garbled, "Wait a sec. I ain't taking it over to that guy."

Johnny waited, took it over to the big man. He accepted it, still smoldering, about half gone, and ate it.

"Everybody feel better now?" asked Johnny's brother.

Lise said, "Okay. We ask around, see if we can find out about the pot. How can we contact you?"

"Johnny knows."

The Jackal took a few steps away from the bags to stand with Johnny and Lise.

The big guy said, "She stays."

Lise said, "We agreed. We're doing what you want."

A big voice boomed out from behind them: "What the hell we got going on here?" There was Coney Shaman up against the wall of the dam so that only his top half showed, big belly over the lip like a sack of creamed corn. He had a pistol in his hand, pointed at them. He went on, "We figured something was up. Them's taking so long. And we find this shit. And lookee here, three big garbage bags. Just what the shaman ordered."

Tilman popped up beside Coney Shaman looking concerned, then smiley, then confused, then grinning again.

The big guy pulled a pistol from the back of his pants and had it on Coney Shaman fast.

Johnny's brother yelled, "Hang on, hang on!" He addressed Coney Shaman. "Man, the way you're holding that piece you won't be able to hit shit. Most people have no accuracy with a pistol past – I don't know – ten feet. Now, my friend here, on the other hand, can put a bullet between your eyes before you fart. See what I mean?"

Lise was backing away from it all, ready to spring and run. Johnny followed her. The Jackal hurried over to Johnny, took his arm, headed away with them.

Lise stopped, turned, cried, "Stop it! Put away the guns." She spoke slowly, "We were just leaving. We don't want this. You don't want this. We have an agreement. You have our word. Please, put them away."

Everybody was staring so intently at the commandoes and their weapons, that they missed the plain as hell, baseball-sized object flying through the air, that struck Coney Shaman on the side of the head. "Ow!" he screeched and dropped his pistol into the tank.

Meteors? Falling stars? Dark matter from the Oort Cloud?

All at once, a barrage of stones flew through the air, striking the gunmen, then a fusillade took on Tilman and Johnny's brother.

Tiffany went by herself to find Lorna. It'd be easier to identify her house in the daylight. She wished there were escalators where now there were steps. Maybe floating, flying chairs. That would be annoying. She figured out a dance move on the steps, a backwards hopping potto. She was not nervous. She didn't want to go. She was doing a solid. For the balance roster of the universe –

She ascended, and, ahead of her, up, up a couple levels, she spied Lorna coming down, taking the steps in shiny regalia, lugging a big sack with handles at her side. She hadn't made Tiffany yet.

Tiffany slowed, no point – she watched the approach. She raised her hand. Lorna waved back. When Lorna got to her step, they stood there looking at each other. Lorna put down the sack.

"They took my truck. Did you know they took my truck?"

"Agatha's truck?"

"You did know."

"Where the boys?"

"Triangulating. They know what to do. You going downtown?"

"Bloomsday."

"Ah. I want a turn. I been practicing."

A thrasher stuttered out a cry in multiple languages, while busy in a chinaberry. They both looked. Orange eyes!

"Walk together?" Lorna picked up her sack and stepped to the next step. She waited patiently.

"Sure, sure." Tiffany joined her on the step.

"Were you coming up to see me?" Her eyes bored deep.

"I was. I came over to tell you they're looking for you. Probably. I mean, I think so. You probably – I was worried about you."

"What's your story, morning glory? You think you know what's going on. You know something, but it isn't everything. Dik Dik sent you. Are you fucking him?"

"No."

"Why not?"

"I have a boyfriend."

"Johnny? Pssh. Mexican boys like Anglo girls because they don't have as much hair on their pussies, plus they suck dick more."

"I'm not Anglo. I'm Italian. What do you have in the sack?"

They started down the steps, stopped. Lorna hauled the bag up to her chest, rummaged in it with the other hand. She pulled out a couple of those white cloth collars, that were super soft, that she'd shown them earlier.

Tiffany said, "You think it's going to rain."

"You never know." Lorna put the collars back in the bag, let the bag fall to her side. It seemed to rattle.

They got the steps, made their way through the old

town's heart.

Lorna said, "You know something you won't say. And you have some kind of psychic moat around you keeping me out. Dik Dik put a spell on you."

"He's got magic powers."

"I wish. Men don't take to magic the way women do. I can't explain it. You're worried now. You're wondering what else I have in the bag."

Tiffany said, "None of my business. Just be careful, okay?"

"You're precious, and so pretty. You think you're doing me a favor warning me. That's sweet. I always wished I was pretty. I used to think if only I was pretty, everything would be okay. What's it like being so pretty? The boys, the old men mesmerized by you, following your every move with hungry eyes. You could do anything to them."

"Lorna, that's not real –"

"You lie! I could cut off your face and wear it. Then what? Huh? Then what?"

"You're not going to cut my face off. I'm in a rock and roll band, I need it."

Lorna hooted. She stopped, dropped the bag to the ground. She leaned in over the bag to dive for more goodies with both hands. She brought out stoppered glass vials in each hand. Each glass vial held a live scorpion. She said, "Just in case. You know what I mean?" She shook the vials and her head shook with them, and a spot of spit lolled from her mouth to lower itself to the steps. She said, "Bunch of 'em."

Tiffany stared, stepped back. She had the urge to run away. She wanted – she had to say something: "What are you going to do?"

"Protect myself. What do you think?"

The steps ceased. Down the middle, the heart attack of Coltrane, they wiggled their way towards Grassy Park. Of course, gente were waiting. Of course, they were!

Lorna blustered in. She demanded her turn. She interrupted the flow, the static, the Dublin rage and roar. No one wanted to fight –

Lorna sequestered one of the chairs for her usurped place in line. She had the mic now. Dik Dik got her a text. He opened it to the episode they were on. She held it in her lap. They had already read much of *Telemachus*, then skipped to *Proteus*, then *Calypso*. Stephen Dedalus had left his chums, delivered a history lesson in class, then sauntered down Sandymount Strand, thinking about perception. *Calypso* had gone to OLBT, who relished the connubial bliss of breakfast in bed, Molly and Leopold Bloom vivisected. So it came to pass that Lorna got Bloom riding with Stephen's father to the funeral of Paddy Dignam. The episode was known as *Hades*.

Lorna pressed forward, eyes and head bare inches from the text, mic in hand at her mouth.

"Bloomsday, rocknut, nightmuse, bubbleyore, bigmouthbitter Bloom. He remembered being a little boy and watching his grandpa cut his toenails. Now Grandpa was a big, solid fellow, who did not like showing his feet. But when he was old, it became a big production. Off would come his workboots and socks, toes peeking out of the sock tips. The Blooms witnessed his great shame and curse: he was blessed with beautiful, strong feet. They looked like the sculptured feet of a Greek god. They were primordial feet. The paradigm of male feet beauty. So he was forced to assault them to great fanfare, hooting and laughing, complaining and whining, in English and Spanish. The tiny nail clipper, so insignificant against the fine biology of his naked feet. But he did it. He forced the nail clipper on and over the ends of his corny nails, dislodging nuggets of earth and rot. He groaned as he squeezed the clipper together. He cut his toenails so close, right to the quick, they always bled. What is the quick? The quick brown fox jumps over the lazy squid. So he ended up with ten, red-rimmed toes on his muscular, well-proportioned feet. I was enchanted with the red-rimmed toes, and vowed to one day have a pedicure that looked just like it."

Her voice doomed through the park in an electric drone, adding acoustic layers of dispassion.

"Grandma, on the other hand, Bloom pondered, had feet like A-Bomb babies. They were like runaway lab experiments on corns and bunions. Her heavy, yellowed feet couldn't help but stomp and smell. Her toes were cramped worms that waggled off at a moment's notice. Humans are full of worms. Toes are worms. Toes migrate up the veins and arteries to lodge in the brains. It's in their brains. They leave behind little worm cocoons."

Moriah, nearby in bonnet, gulped, "A-Bombs? They weren't invented –"

Lorna squealed into the mic. Electron cackle mustered. Then she started weeping: "I'm doing my best! This is how I read it."

Tears sounded like rain through the mic. The sun laughed. Dogs whined. Thrashers tattled.

Dik Dik heard Joyce name her 'lamprey'. He saw life listening with cocked heads.

Tiffany went up to Lorna.

Lorna huffed, "Don't touch me!"

A gasp echoed the park.

Dik Dik went over, stood by her chair.

Lorna said, "I'm meditating. Go about your business." She closed her eyes, huddled in, bent over.

Dik Dik announced, "Cut! Let's take five. No rule says we can't take five. Get up. Stretch. Stand in the gazebo for some shade. Drink some water."

Moriah said to Mr. Nobody, "Hydrate. The key is hydrate."

There were a few people standing around and sitting in the grass who suddenly felt like an audience, so began clapping. Intermittent, uncertain applause.

Dik Dik motioned to Tiffany, and they met under the gazebo, each with a plastic water bottle, greedily slurping, coming close, real close, as if for a second they thought they might touch.

Dik Dik said, "Perfect. It's going perfect. Wouldn't you say?"

Tiffany said, "I found her coming down the stairs, heading over here."

"Did you say anything?"

"Be careful. Police probably looking for you. That kind of thing. She knows we know about the truck."

"It's so blatant. She knows we know about it all, and still she shows up to perform. Well, she's had her five minutes. We drive on."

Tiffany said in an asking voice: "You'd think the others would have shown up by now."

Dik Dik said, "You'd think. It'll happen when it happens. In the meantime, do you want to read?"

Tiffany shook her head. "I mean, I do, but I haven't read it, so I don't want to be stumbling over words and everything."

"Let's get back, before we lose our crowd. Your boys okay?" He nodded to Mikey and Bear stretched in the grass on their stomachs, fast asleep, and was glad they'd left the dogs at home.

"They're loving it."

Ed Norminton was standing next to Douglas when they returned to Bloomsday. Ed was in his regular mold, faded coat and tie, looking taller somehow, as though he'd stretched a half inch, after a night sleeping on a rack. He was far-gazing. Perhaps they had a new crowd, perhaps it was the old crowd seen twice. Faces floated around, mouthing the banner word. The benches in the back were full.

Dik Dik's ears acted funny, and, for a moment, he could

distinctly hear single voices of the various, small groups of people scattered about, but they were in different languages.

Douglas said, "*Hades* has arrived."

Dik Dik said, "Perfect! Welcome, my dear fellow."

Dik Dik and Douglas did the double take scan of seating arrangements. Dik Dik's chair was vacant and Douglas's, too, was empty. Lorna stayed in her chair, bent over the text. Douglas had taken the mic. Douglas. Doyle. He looked like Sir Arthur Conan Doyle, Dik Dik triumphantly clamored. Back to *Hades*!

Dik Dik said, "Ed, sit there," motioning to Douglas' seat.

"That's fine," said Douglas, his melon going red-faced match pop.

Moriah positioned herself behind her chair, standing proudly, labile and loathing, ready to murder pets.

Ed slid over to his place. OLBT watched him go by. She said, "Ed, you don't walk, you glide. You old soul, you're like a fricking desert sailing ship, a mast you be, with invisible sails. Yeah."

Ed grunted, micro-nod, finished the tack to his chair. The cranes in his joints lowered him to his seat.

Dik Dik went to Lorna. "Lorna, the text, please."

Lorna groaned, huddled into herself tighter. Her legs made a Mobius strip, coiling, curling, brushing the bag she'd brought with her, which she'd placed beneath the chair.

Dik Dik found his library sack and extracted a text. He walked it over to Ed, thumbing through the pages. A car drove by and honked. Dik Dik glanced up. Glare! The sun was growing intense. Hot, hot. Innocent bystanders came and went – leave and grieve. But more visitors, i.e., tourists, on their way, now that it was full blown morning. Once they started reading –

Dik Dik sat in his chair, looking for *Hades*. He found it,

handed the open text to Ed.

Ed read and the angels went to sleep and the cicadas fell down comatose:

"'Martin Cunningham, first, poked his silkhatted head into the creaking carriage, and

entering, deftly, seated himself. Mr. Power stepped in after him, curving his height with care.

– Come on, Simon.

– After you, Mr. Bloom said.

Mr. Dedalus covered himself quickly and got it, saying:

– Yes, yes.

– Are we all here now? Martin Cunningham asked. Come along, Bloom.

Mr. Bloom entered and sat in the vacant place. He pulled the door to after him and slammed it twice till it shut tight. He passed an arm through the armstrap and looked seriously from the open carriage window at the lowered blinds of the avenue. One dragged aside: an old woman peeping. Nose whiteflattened against the pane. Thanking her stars she was passed over.'"

Dik Dik pushed back in his chair, extending his legs. He closed his eyes and wondered how Dublin had gotten so hot. No fog today. Today was Bloomsday! Ah, the great transposition. The transformation juxtaposition –

Dik Dik dozed for twelve minutes.

He opened his eyes. Tiffany was stretched in the grass near her boys. She was on her back, so the sounds and voices and characters swept over her front where there were more ways in. She had her eyes closed. She looked good and peaceful. Ed was reading, deep voice carving hieroglyphs in the air, shimmery air softly booming, bull frog bass. Listen! Passersby. A man with a basenji on a leach, his head a mess of curls like a Fellini tumbleweed, listened. The dog's yodel signaled impatience in most languages. Here came Tim Asparagus, crossing the street from the post office. And there, sitting in the grass, eyes wide, Lydia, in black, blazing eyebrowist, her eyes black, too. She rocked in a slight rolling motion, listening. She was sitting with her legs pulled to her chest. She had shucked off her flip flops, so bare feet. Her flip flops weren't black. Her feet were tattooed in henna. Some well-dressed people, perhaps retirees, spiffy in shorts and tops, came in close to listen, studied the banner, walked around it three times. Maybe tourists. Maybe witches. Maybe locals. Maybe another tribe entirely.

Gradually, the little truck came out of the deep Gulch. Now, Coney Shaman felt better. Now, he could drive with two hands. He'd started out with one finger – all he could manage, after the Mexican kid had backed the little truck around so they could get out of there. He couldn't do it! Hell's bells, no way he'd let that guy drive them out. He'd taken it inch by inch, foot by foot, finger by finger, until the shakes had subsided.

Coney Shaman had discovered he couldn't drive, bleed, and shake at the same time. They'd had to proceed along then abruptly stop for him to catch his breath. Life was a juggle, and the masters knew that there was always another way. But Tilman was still bleeding, so the only way was – yes! give in to it: wrench the panic from the notochord, resume control and command of this new-fangled cryptothanatosis. Uncalled for! Unexpected! Tilman's cheek was dissected. Cheek meat must be heavily vascularized. Ah, knew Coney Shaman: inside of checks was gum; outside of cheeks was mug.

"What now, brown cow?" he asked Tilman.

Tilman hated nurses, dentists, doctors, hospitals –

which he whimsically called 'horse pistols'. He, also, was squeamish about blood, mucus, drool, and, basically, all precious bodily fluids. He imagined the stitches going in. Long, curved needles in his cheek. If he were in Africa, he's simply harness up some of those warrior clan driver ants with the huge jaws, use them to staple his cheek shut. With insect jaws! No luck. He had no insurance. He had no ants. He had no money. He had no pride. If he were in Antarctica, he'd have to do it himself. Staples! 'Of course,' he wanted to yell, but the exertion –

The people in the back were huddled down. No one spoke. They appreciated the slow pace. No point in rushing. Now, they were rolling through houses, coming on the entertainment sector.

Lise said, "Up for walking?" She glanced over her comrades, met their eyes. They nodded to her – micro-nods.

Lise slapped on the roof of the cab. She leaned over on the driver's side. Coney Shaman came to a stop. His window was down.

"We can walk from here," said Lise.

"Go for it," said Coney Shaman.

The guys in the back jumped out, then gathered by Coney Shaman's window.

The Mexican kid, Johnny, said, "Those guys are not going to rest 'til they settle with you. You can't pull a gun on those guys without retribution. If I was you, I'd get out of town."

Coney Shaman went, "Fuck you! I ain't going nowhere. I saved your asses. No telling what those guys were going to pull."

Lise said, "That's bullshit and you know it! If we don't figure out the pot – no bodies." She exhaled heavily. "No future."

The Jackal said, "I can't believe this shit. It's like a movie. Fucking idiots! Bunch of retards rule the planet.

And we're in the middle. Royally fucked. Because, come on! We know where the pot is. Lorna's boys. Red, white, and blue – whatever the fuck they are. They must have it. When they went to dump the bodies, they found it, took it."

"Really fucked," said Johnny.

Tilman said, "Adjutant! I'm your adjutant. I am. I am. So you head out, and I'll take over, see this through. I'll be Triune's amanuensis."

Coney Shaman blew out wetly. He glanced over at Tilman, who stared back with wide eyes. Then Coney Shaman turned his head, partially stretching out the window to take in the three. He wiped his face with his hand that did not shake. He said, "We're fucked."

The Jackal said, "I'm afraid for the cave people. Those guys with guns. Fucking guns. Everybody has a gun except the cave people."

Lise said, "What'll we do?"

Johnny said, "Let's go see Dik. See what he's up to."

Coney Shaman hooted. "There's some magic: old dick suddenly a guru. Fuck it all! Fuck you guys! I'm out of here."

Tilman got out of the truck. Coney Shaman drove off.

Tilman announced, "The die is cast."

Lise said, "It's Bloomsday."

Johnny said to Tilman, "Dood, you need a couple stitches."

Dood squalled, "I know nothing. I know nothing. There is no pain."

They walked into the entertainment sector dripping. This was the palatable name for the funk of oily trash and stinky bars and buggy séances. And lots of posters. They made their way to Grassy Park. Matewan tolled. No one counted.

At that exact moment, the police showed up at Grassy Park. No one anywhere was surprised. The fun was about to get started.

Hades continued. Dogs and hippies, living together, slept and cavorted in the grass. Tourists loitered, getting a listenfull, of Joyce in the bright blue Bloomsday morning spotlight. The benches supported various couples and threesomes, families in four packs, coming and going, listening and balking, at one point a da telling a squid: 'It's Shakespeare, hon.' The tree by the bench was a finite magnolia. A towhee and a thrasher perched on an interior branch, so the tourists and trilobites and gawkers and poets could not see them. They were *just* friends. The picture was complete, from sound waves, light waves, psychic entablature – *Hades*...no fog.

Dik Dik knew that tree – it was on his playlist, for the magnolia's sweet fragrance made a heady molecule that could be overpowering. He'd sat at the bench during bloom, and known the expansive day dream up lift. Now, Ed was winding down – his voice diminishing. He'd fulfilled his soldierly duty. Rah, rah! Next, would come the *Lestrygonians*. Molly on Howth. That was for Connie – Conrad, the artist at Main he'd been afraid he'd run into. And here he was bright and shiny as a penny, sitting on the grass nearby, cross legged, trekker hat in place. Good show. Now was the time! Dik Dik raised his left hand, index finger out part way to indicate 'action!'

There should be some background capture of the suspense. Something martial. Maybe Beethoven. For two police cars – one local, one state, pulled up in front of them on the street. The local police set their lights whirling, thought better of it, turned them off. Ed kept reading. What a trouper! His boom had softened now, mincing through the park, amplified puffs.

Dik Dik watched Lorna, because it was the damnedest thing. Though she was still bent in half, thought to be asleep, and though Dik Dik knew she had not glanced up, it was clear she knew the cops were here, and she knew they had come for her. He could tell because a popsicle rush of energy sizzled her presence a wallop. It happened all at once. Shudder BOOM! Like she was suddenly ready for her close up. Maybe she was a method actor?

Dik Dik glanced around, observing the players. Faces contorted, squinting, leering, trying to see in the police cars, trying to fathom what they were doing. What did they want?

The officers on the passenger sides got out of their vehicles. No one knew the state police guy, but most locals recognized the other one, Sergeant Molina. Their drivers stayed put, engines running, ac on. The officers remained by their cars, conferring telepathically, scanning the crowd, then making faces at each other. They kept to the sidewalk to saunter around the low fence and over to stand in front of the Bloomsday gathering. They kept their hands loose, at their sides, coming in easy. Ed read on.

The cops stayed there a second or two, then they made the few steps through the grass to Lorna's chair. Lorna sprang up and away, flinging the text, simultaneously retrieving the bag under her chair. She wailed a loud, non-electric, all-too-human cry of fear and loathing and despair. It was like a trigger, like a signal that everyone jumped to. Everybody was on his or her feet. Lorna backed away.

Sergeant Molina begged, "Easy, easy!"

Dik Dik, on his feet, proclaimed, "Take five! Breathe! Everybody breathe. Ed, you were perfect." Dik Dik worked his magic, cast smiles, lofty goals, good vibes, but it was too hot and sunny, and his cum moment was long gone. This was a takeover, a usurpation. The world needed a cum. Something more real, that would do it, that would turn this all around, make the sun-drenched glory: Bloomsday forever!

The state policeman said, "Sorry to break up your picnic, we need to talk to Lorna."

Sergeant Molina said, "Lorna, you okay? Take it easy. We need you to come with us. Just for a talk, then you can come right back to your friends."

Coming into view, walking in from the Gulch, came Lise, Johnny, and the Jackal.

Lorna swung away, slip sliding so slowly they didn't recognize it as movement until it was too late. She lapsed. Suddenly, she was over there, on the sidewalk, on the other side of the fence, her bag held in front of her.

The policemen did cartoon double takes, not knowing this rigmarole. They moved towards her. They kept their eyes down, avoiding her eyes.

Finally, Sergeant Molina went, "Lor-na!" He hadn't meant to yell, to make it come out so harsh. He exhaled, tried again, more fluffy: "Lorna?"

She faced them on the sidewalk, then kneeled there, her bag front and center. She reached into the bag and started pulling out glass vials.

By this time, the Gulch expeditionary force was back with them. The Bloomsday people were milling, watching, listening, open mouths, round eyes. Gasps rang out. Ed was the only one sitting. Ed had given the mic to Douglas. Ed made a point of not watching. OLBT was up on her feet, lumbering towards the sidewalk. Dik Dik was joined by Tiffany. He didn't know what to tell her. Lise looked dismal, she vibed dismal. The Jackal went over to Lydia to merge in a cuddle. They whispered. Johnny hung behind Tiffany and Dik Dik, wondering what the hell he was doing with these people, but, also, noticing how Tiffany looked like she'd just woke up. *Sleepy head!* Burdened by death. *Death don't have no mercy.* Tim Asparagus and a few of the others – Conrad, Moriah, were planning on saying something, doing something. They flowered with righteousness.

Lorna was fiendishly unscrewing vials. She knocked out scorpions in a circle around her, like a moat of alligators. Her beasties seemed stunned, or dead, remaining where they fell. But Lorna extended a finger, all the while feverishly muttering, and touched each scorpion with the tip of her finger. When she touched them, they came to life, puttered about, tail raised, but keeping the circle.

Moriah came in too close, perhaps thinking to intervene. Lorna flicked an open vial at her, and a scorpion flew through the air to land on her gown at her belly. It held on. Moriah screamed, backpedaling, swatting at her stomach, knocking the thing off.

The police hustled forward, both of them going, "Hey, hey, hey!"

But Lorna stopped them with vials raised, poised to flick.

The state policeman said, "Lorna, assaulting a police officer is a felony. You need to step away from the scorpions and leave those vials where they are."

Sergeant Molina said, "Now, Lorna! Before this turns ugly. You could've hurt that lady. What if she'd got stung and was allergic?"

Lorna cackled, and flick of the wrist, a vial at him: free flying scorpion, its limbs extended, and the man jumped backwards, and the scorpion hit his Adam's apple and bounced, fell down his front, inside his shirt.

Sergeant Molina stomped around slapping at his chest. Sweat poured from his head gone beet red. He was awash in fluidics. But he didn't scream.

The other policeman ordered, "Sarge! Don't move! Take off your shirt!"

Lorna fell, righted herself, all the way up, like she was

made of *Silly Putty*, and bag in hand, ran up the sidewalk, then down the middle of the road, shiny trickster tearing into town.

The driver of the state police car turned off the vehicle and got out. He seemed on autopilot – so stiff. He leaned over the top of the car, calling, "Lieutenant, Lieutenant, should we go after her?"

The state police lieutenant found the scorpion smashed to the local cop's ample bosom. The Arachnid had got him. The lieutenant flicked away the offending creature, then hurried towards the police vehicles. "Go after her!"

The driver said, "In the car? Should I take the cruiser?"

The lieutenant was beyond impatient. He was about to unleash some choice words, when he saw what was confusing the driver. Two young men were stretched out on the asphalt in front of their car. Flat on their backs, hands clasped on their chests. They were right under the bumper. The lieutenant took in the two car situation: two young men were under the rear end of the local police car, then his state police car, parked in front of it, had his two young men. They couldn't move! They'd blocked them in. A crowd was forming. Suspect fleeing. Yeah, what else could go wrong?

Sergeant Molina went over to where Lorna had kneeled, alert for scorpions. He stomped the ones he found to greasy smears under his boot.

The local police car's driver was now beside his cruiser, shut off, wondering what to do.

The Jackal reflected on how Lydia was so like her. They were 21st Century chicks burned out before twenty-five. Lydia thought like the Jackal, she smelled like the Jackal. She was behind the Jackal now, pressing her tight, her hands in the Jackal's vest pockets. They were taint – like a rare, rose cheese, like the goddess' farts. Lydia ground her hips into the Jackal's ass, her cute little pubic bone hard in Jackal's butt crack. They were nearly the same height. How did that line go: 'Cry havoc – let loose the dogs of wrath!' *Let go! Let it go!*

An older guy, well dressed, clean – must be a tourist, or at least from out of town, milled over by Mikey, standing around, waking up. The man said, "You play around?"

Mikey laughed, led the fellow behind the magnolia tree. He had to be at least forty! But he wanted it bad. He got down on his knees, reached for Mikey's crotch. Mikey thought, 'worship the dick!' The guy went real slow, up-and-down the shaft real slow, the way Mikey liked it.

Sergeant Molina smoldered in a palsied, scorpion voice: "Run 'em over. Back right over 'em, if they don't move. We got a fugitive to find. It's an emergency!"

The state officer grimaced. "Pipe down." He told both drivers to call in for back up. Now! He went to the front of his car. He knelt down. "What the hell you guys think you're doing down there?"

Below him were a bald man and a red-haired man. Both white, both fairly healthy looking. Still, something off about them, like they were homos or carnival geeks. They didn't look particularly violent – or dangerous. They looked stoned.

The lieutenant tried again: "Come on out of there. Come out right now, you walk. We forget the whole thing. A prank. No big deal."

The bald guy spat: "Leave Lorna alone!"

'Fingers in my pocket,' thought the Jackal, 'digging a hole to China,' but Lydia was biting her neck and breathing into her ear, 'Red, Red, Red'. The Jackal's body squirted geysers. It was like a cleansing. Like all pores opened up. Because it was hot and sunny, yes, and, yes, threats of ultimate gravy, yes, she let loose.

Mikey had a crisis, let it go, let it loose, felt better right away. *Wake up!*

All around, negotiations, a background hum drowning out scorpions, Joyce, death. Noisy silence, nosey nonchalance. Hippies shared a pipe nearby, wary eyes on the cops. Tourists filmed the cops with their devices. Young people took selfies in the gazebo. Human faces. Tree faces. Bird faces. Official faces under caps. Thrashers watched and observed, wondering what the hell was happening to their neighborhood.

Lydia wished she could sing. She'd sing her scorpion dream in weeping silver. She remembered Red-Black's first concerts. How she killed it! Tiffany had her band, but, come on, she was to look at. Tiffany liked her, Lydia could tell. Tiffany liked Red. Tiffany liked everyone. She was one of those.

I know that song, hummed the Jackal.

Mikey had a great idea for a song, in B chords.

The Jackal wanted to blame somebody for not encouraging her. 'Oh, facilitate me,' the Jackal exclaimed to her innermost cells, in her afterglow. Scorpions required facilitators, mentors, mediators. Jeepers keepers! She had no interest in adjustments. She felt ripped off. Someone must pay. She was on the lookout. She came to her feet and her knees buckled.

Hippy Henry had materialized in the thick of the people glom fog. The police were trying to keep the crowd back, beyond the little fence, away from their vehicles. People were upset but no one knew what to do, so no one was doing anything, which was what set off Hippy Henry. Bedazzled besotted buzzkill! Spoiling his fucking trip! Hippy Henry agitated, became fidgety.

Don't look at his fingers, snapping like mouse traps!

This should be a Coltrane Commandment: don't watch me when I rush!

OLBT had made her way to the front. She raised her voice: "Let's keep it cool now. No trouble, okay. These boys'll get up. No point in getting upset. If I were you, I'd just back off. They'll get up and leave. Watch. No big deal."

The young police officer, who had been driving the local police car, told her to back up.

Hippy Henry proclaimed in a big voice, "Non-violence! We're all of us US us is all about non-violence. Us! We the peeps!"

Other people took up the cry: "Non-violence." "Give peace a chance!"

Mellow trickster! Relief with the release –

Hippy Henry roared, "Freedom!" just like in *Braveheart!*

OLBT worked it over in her mind like a gruesome tooth gone to hell, packed with extraterrestrial scorpions. These boys and Lorna had done terrible things. Method. Motive. Opportunity. Now, consequences. Punishment? Retribution. Simon and Mad and Table had been her gente. They didn't deserve to die. That word, *deserve* – shouldn't even come up. Whatever they deserved was beside the point. Then why the intuit? These actions inevitable? Madness! 'Yes,' she thought, 'non-violence.'

Back up showed up in the form of two law enforcement vehicles.

OLBT remembered running from cops in Baltimore, late at night, in a funky part of town. She was carrying a flat of hash. Not a brick at all. More like a big chocolate bar stamped with the royal sigil. Running down the street between row houses in October or November, so it was wet, everything shiny in the streetlights. Maybe 1967. What did this have to do with plain and simple murder? Or with scorpions? Nothing. Scorpions! Murder the heart. Mayhem in town. Fuck that! Enough running! Impasse's giant *NO!* She'd studied cul-de-sacs. She'd memorized curbs, trails, gabions. She knew blind alleys. She'd deconstructed moonbeams. The human condition depended on human conditions. Lorna must be treated fairly.

Dik Dik flowed through the crowd aghast, hating everyone, loving everyone, begging everyone to calm:

Lorna freaked out. You know how she gets. The police were encouraging people to go home. Break it up! Where were his crew? He'd lost them. Ha! Flummoxed with Bloomsday! And scorpions. There was Jack Ramp, city boy drawn to the rubes' unrest. Dik Dik wondered if Ed had made it out. He'd probably gone home. Hippy Henry, instigator! Smoker of ground sloth dung. Cynthia was here, one of Dik Dik's readers. They smiled at each other, which made Dik Dik think he was sinking. Losing, failing, yes, exhausted, yes, turpitude, yes. Spontaneous combustion. The go must show on! Negotiations continued. The natives were restless. He passed the Jackal and Lydia, nodding to them, no smile. The Jackal gave a sleepy slurpy look, as her berry, her jujube, her tiara of Aphrodite ignited with lava. Dik Dik smelled cunt. He kept walking, embraced the nutmeg. He made it over to Douglas and Moriah. They looked troubled and sweaty. Douglas might have been on the verge. Moriah was angry, wanting to hit back. He didn't think she had been stung, still she was brimming with venom. They wanted to get their chairs and banner and get away from the hubbub. Dik Dik touched both of them, a laying on of his hand. They nodded. Dik Dik thought Douglas whispered something to him like, 'What a mess,' but he couldn't be sure. It could have been, 'Let's get the hell out of here.'

When providence and the Emerald Tablets, when the glory cum summer froth, all which he believed in then did not, because Dik Dik forbad belief, always preferring knowledge, when the multi-orgasmic plateau of environs infused together this official outcry: the state policeman was talking into his car's mic, the coiled wire stretched from the dash out the window like a snake: "Let's get going, folks. We need to break this up. Go on home. You sure don't want to agitate the situation. I know you don't. I know there was some kind of event going on here, so I suggest those folks move their stuff over to City Park, so we can do our job."

'City Park,' thought Dik Dik. 'Of course!' He hollered, "The show must go on! Bloomsday! To City Park!"

OLBT cried, "We can't leave these boys here. Not like this."

Dik Dik nodded, pouted. There was Tiffany with Bear and Mikey. Lise and Johnny were here, here...HERE –

OLBT said, "What? It's every man for himself now?"

Dik Dik said, "Of course not. But we don't seem to be doing much good here. To the park!"

Douglas folded up his chairs. Moriah rolled up the banner on its poles.

Bloomsday aficionados gathered up, headed out in two's and three's.

Tiffany and Bear and Mikey were in private deliberations, ministrations, their own pile. Mikey and Bear had packed up the equipment and rolled up the cables. The power wouldn't be on at City Park, they'd explained to Dik Dik, who was busy being aghast.

Mikey confessed, "Lorna's kooky. I hate scorpions! Never saw anything like that."

Tiffany and Bear shrugged. Bear wrapped his arms around Tiffany. "Scorpions are gross. No way I'm learning to milk them, no matter how much it pays. We gotta get the boogers. Make sure they're okay." He nuzzled in to her neck and ear.

Tiffany pulled away, gave him a peck. "I'll go with Dik to City Park. See if I can help. See you in a little –"

Bear looked wistful but shrugged again. "Watch out for scorpions."

Mikey said, "Those boys are asking for it. They're gonna arrest their asses."

Tiffany said, "Mikey, roll me a joint. Bring one back with you."

He nodded and they parted. Tiffany hurried to catch up with Dik Dik, who was walking away with Johnny and

Lise. Dik Dik had his sack, pack on his back.

Lise felt like she'd turned into an almond. Hard dirty shell, meaty kernel. She was tired. She was appalled. She had to get home to feed her turtle. She was slightly sweet, nutty. She wanted to go now. She walked with Dik Dik and Johnny to City Park. Bloomsday! She was supposed to read. She'd promised Dik Dik. They needed to talk. Oh, how she wanted to go home. If those boys wound up in jail, everything juggled in mid-air, waiting to come down. Gravity issue. The bodies – she couldn't. Sweat was pouring off of her, salty almond milk. 'We make milk,' she thought. She'd named her son after Lucifer.

Lise stopped, eyeing Johnny who stopped. Tiffany joined them. Dik Dik saw what they were doing, came around to face the conspiracy. Four beautiful souls! Well, three. Lise said, "We have to talk."

Dik Dik said, "Now?" He went:

"'What a piece of work is a man! How noble in reason, how infinite in faculty! In form and moving how express and admirable! In action how like an Angel! In apprehension how like a god! The beauty of the world! The paragon of animals! And yet to me, what is this quintessence of dust? Man delights not me; no, nor Woman neither; though by your smiling you seem to say so.'"

Tiffany went, "Wow! Heavy shit. Bravo!"

Lise said, "Sweet. But – bodies, Dik. The bodies. Of our friends. They're being held hostage until we bring back the pot."

Johnny said, "Believe you met my brother."

Dik Dik said, "I don't understand. What pot?"

Pausing turned to listing, milling – pacing in place. They stepped in to an alleyway's shade, the four of them shiny traces of their sensation.

Dik Dik heard the story from Johnny.

Dik Dik topped, came down, rattled, inhaled, shook it

out: "You – you must have gone through the *Twelve Labors of Hercules*. I'm so sorry. This day, yesterday, *tres, tres*...guess I always say that," he mumbled. "What should we do? First, tell me you're okay."

Johnny said, "Helluva dawn, *jefe*. Lise is brave and tough."

Lise smiled and said, "Johnny. We're okay."

Dik Dik looked them over and over, read it, kneaded it: "So?"

Lise said, "The bodies dumped in their spot? Can't be a coincidence. Garbage bags, Dik! Big black garbage bags. The *vatos*, the *gente*, Lorna's boys, us. All of us. Dumped the bodies, took the load."

Dik Dik groaned, whispered, "Where this is going –"

"Gotta be Lorna's boys," said Johnny.

"Who are about to be arrested," said Lise.

"Hostage bodies," went Dik Dik.

Lise miffed. "And it's hot? I mean –"

Johnny said, "Their pot back, we get the bodies."

"In garbage bags, like we imagined?" asked Dik Dik.

"Big black ones, heavy duty," said Johnny.

"It was war," said Lise. "All of a sudden there were guns. Then rocks flying through the air, but just hitting who ever had a gun."

Dik Dik stared. Dik Dik said, "Mayhem."

"Cave people," said Johnny. "That's what Red said."

Dik Dik nodded. "Everybody's okay?"

Lise shuddered. "Let's get to the park. You have a reader?"

"Connie," said Dik Dik.

They proceeded up the back way, avoiding the Gulch, going around Main instead. Jugglers filled Main's parking lot. Some juggled bowling pins, one dood used cigar boxes. Slim sticks were batted around by girls in bellydancing outfits. A little card table had a tranny Pennywise doing sleight-of-hand.

Commotion in town! Traffic was engulfing. Parking would go strangled. Civilians would dip their feathers into pandemonium's birdbath. By the time they got to the steps to the park, Douglas and Moriah had already driven around their packed SUV. They ended up having to park in a sketchy yellow spot. They were unloading. Moriah had the banner and its poles.

Douglas saw Dik Dik, said, "Set up in the clamshell?"

"Of course," said Dik Dik. "Maximize the shade. We'll huddle under the great clam."

They climbed the steps, surveyed their domain. The park was lodged in to the side of the canyon. The other side from where they entered had built in concrete bleachers, steeply stepping up the canyon wall. A postage stamp-sized square of green, grass and a tree, prickled the middle of the park, between the basketball courts on one end, then the clamshell at the other end. Near the clamshell, children's playground equipment, and a covered ramada with picnic tables. A retaining wall had splattered across it in pain, 'FUCK LOVE, GET BLAZED!'

They acknowledged their comrades at a picnic table, smoking cigarettes or something: Captain America, Tilman, Tim, Cynthia.

Boys playing hacky sack froze in mid hack to watch them pass. A woman danced on a sheet of plywood set on the ground. She was tapping, stamping, ratcheting up the blood bath. A lady had a small table set up to sell 'grass tea' and 'sky tea'. That's what her sign said. Everybody could see the road runner up on stage, in the clamshell. They'd have to get his okay. Maybe he liked the flamenco? He kept raising and lowering his headscarf.

Meanwhile, at the picnic table, bandaged Tilman had reviewed the story for them. Tim noted that Coney Shaman's ass was grass. Tilman said something like *don't call him that*. Cynthia thought the idea that Coney Shaman carried a gun was worrisome enough. Tilman insisted they weren't seeing the interstices. His bandage seeped.

Captain America, red-white-blue shirt unbuttoned in front, shook his head, whether to clear it or to offer a negatory was confounded, so he stabbed out the roach with a vengeance. He'd washed, he'd dressed...fancy dancy, figuring himself a psychedelic gigolo, the schoolmarms coming in from the city looking for a quick layover with an artist fumarole. Besides, he had plans. Besides, he had it covered! Everybody's so intense – what are they on? He blurted, "Krokodil! They must all be on Krokodil!"

Tim said, "He thinks he's Dr. Seuss."

Cynthia cut in: "I can't believe it. I think we're all in shock. We used to have Lorna and her husband – what's his name? over for dinner."

Captain America said, "That's not shock. It's heat stroke. But hold on. No freak out. We knew it was coming down the pike. Total entropy. New paradigm. New hardon. Listen, they got nothing on those boys. No bodies. Circumstantial. The city is bankrupt. They'll release them."

Tim said, "What? So what's that mean? What are you..."

"Now, hold on," insisted Captain America. "They release them. We go for a visit. Get the pot. Give it back. Get the bodies. A few o-z's for our trouble."

Tim groaned. "'Get?' 'Get?' How you figure that? That's the coke talking. Are you out of your psychedelic fuckmind?"

Captain America said, "It's a fricking finite world. Finite! We know Coltrane. They know Coltrane. There's only so many places they can stash it. When they get out, what are they gonna do? They're gonna go straight to it. They have to get rid of it fast. They have to. They'll be sloppy. We put a tail on them."

Tilman hiccoughed. "Please! For Triune's sake, let's be circumspect. Let's get tangential. See the pattern. Know the pattern, the play of forces. Always at the center, the vortex, a power seep or guide. Get to the vortex, you get omega."

Captain America said, "We have to find Lorna. She's gotta be behind this. Where would she go after the scorpion fling?"

"For drinks," Tim said.

"You guys," went Cynthia, "you're getting extreme. You have to bring it down a notch. Come on. How much do the police know? They gotta be on top of it?"

Captain America said, "We're back to square one."

Tilman said, "The proportions are in harmony. Congruity. Consistency talking. Consonance in our lifetime. Let the symmetry fly. Dig –"

Tim said, "Oh, not now." He pushed back on the picnic table, straightened his back, ran his fingers through his long hair, then through his thick beard. "I dunno. I like what Cynthia's saying. Police are on this one way or the other. Pretty funky about the bodies but still. I ain't taking on any druggies. Their *pistoleros* are bigger than mine."

Captain America said, "That's an understatement."

Tim spluttered, "I get no complaints in that department."

Cynthia said, "They're setting up on stage. Bloomsday. I told Dik Dik I'd read."

"Dik Dik is a vortex," said Tilman.

Tim said, "I'll show you my vortex."

Captain America snarked petulant: "So no one wants to do anything. No one will join with me in seeing this through to its logical conclusion. All of us sitting around with some pretty bud. Not a lot. No greed! No greedy. Just a few o-z's. We can have a bake off!"

Tilman said, "There are lines, there are lines that move. That way is –"

Douglas set up the chairs in the middle of the stage. The high curve of the clamshell top did offer shade, a half circle that took in the stage. Moriah unrolled the banner and leaned the poles up on the back wall. A bit of a sag. Lise and Johnny sat in chairs. Tiffany and Dik Dik paced back and forth around the front center of the stage, in search of the sweet spot. They emitted sounds – bird chirps, expletives, fricatives, to test where they were standing. They found it, where the clamshell focused its curved sound bounce, propelling those sounds out and forward in a nice vibrato, to fill the bold bowl.

Dik Dik held his dear sack close to his chest and looked around for Connie. Cynthia was sauntering over from the ramada. The hacky sack players took off. The staccato *duende* of the flamenco dancer ceased. A few people strode through the park, they'd climbed the stairs to get in, on the grand tour, now they gazed, scanned, waiting for something to happen. Expectant faces. Civilian faces. Matewan tolled, and Dik Dik found he could not count the tolls precisely. He was too messy. Watches were verboten in Coltrane. Keeping track of tolls was like keeping track of heartbeats. Where was Connie? He said he'd – ah, here he came.

Dik Dik called, "Con! Come up on stage."

Bloomsday! Now he wondered whether they should have skipped *Scylla and Charybdis.* Now he pondered, dragging his chair square over the sweet spot, and motioning Connie to it, over Episode10, *Wandering Rocks,* one of Dik Dik's favorites. Side characters like sides of beef hanging back in a tincture of frost, waiting for their chance to be butchered in a spare paragraph. He handed Connie the text. Sun and heat and pleasure and shade mixed a real feat. Johnny perched like a stiff young man stiff, unsure what he was seeing up here on stage. Lise perked beguiled, but she'd promised to read the crucial part. Moriah and Douglas leaned back on the wall by their banner in the shade. They seemed uncomfortable, so they were okay. Tiffany paced the back of the stage, hand trailing, teasing the curved shell with her fingers, then skipping around Moriah and Douglas by the banner. Every once in a while her ankles would flare and she'd rise up, up, jerky ascent, to the attic. This was preparatory to bounding. She was drawing the rain. She was diddling the world cum. No guns. No scorpions.

"The Superior, the very reverend John Conmee S. J. reset his smooth watch in his interior pocket as he came down by the presbytery steps.'" Thus, Connie began. The character sketches would come fast and febrile, with lots of fractal charm and clauses, going off in dub directions, to fill in background on the characters. Connie's voice was good. Enunciation in the sweet spot gave the words an echo-y spring.

Then, they would skip to Episode 12, *Nausicaa*, and Dik Dik needed a young woman for that. He had thought to ask Jackal, but she was nowhere to be seen. He should have asked her earlier, set it up. Even yesterday at the Tavern. Well, he hadn't. He'd been seeing the old man home, and avoiding the Coney Shaman's tricks, with his own ego tricks. Old men and their monomania! Someone would show up. Then, Cynthia wanted to do Episode 15, *Circe*, as she engaged with the smarmy, man-as-pig routine. Stephen thought he saw his mother in this episode. Cyndra had told him, "Men are always looking for their mothers." They'd finish up with Episode 17 and Episode 18. He would take *Ithaca*, Episode 17. Episode 18, of course, for Lise.

Buncha young people, steampunkers, tore up the steps into the park, hooting, then they saw the stage and players and reading. They could hear the sweet spot renovation of literature. They quieted, reached out, began hunching each other. They popped over to the playground equipment. The steampunk women in bustiers and hooker stockings, with guys in leather vests and chains, hats, elaborate boots, were all over the equipment. They watched their voices. Three of them hung upside down from the monkey bars. A row of grisly lollypops, puckering gravity.

At the other end of the park, by the basketball nets, at the park entrance, a man came running in, shouting, chasing a medium-sized dog dragging something in its mouth. The man was fat, gray, white, in stretched out t-shirt, funky shorts, and flippy flip flops. Finally, Dik Dik ascertained that it was a dead rabbit in the dog's mouth, torn open, flashing red guts. More road kill art! The man wielded a rake and shovel, screaming for the dog to drop it. Con read on, sing-songy, pulse or rhythm plying all activities. The dog hightailed it out the way it had come in, holding on to its precious bonanza. The man and his great tongs followed frantically.

The nearest bench to the stage had re-enactors, great burly doods in white shirts, black trousers, with suspenders. Big boots. Old timey hats. They stretched out like they owned the place, arms wrapped around the back of the bench. They were taking it all in. They couldn't help but hear the sweet spot rattle. They were fishing for marks, easy picking tourists they could give a guided tour.

This tall, gangly woman wandered in to the park. She only looked down. She moved cautiously. Dik Dik remembered her from working at the co-op years ago. She'd been around a long time. Rumor had it she had gone to Harvard, before coming to Coltrane to write a book on buffelgrass. Or was it jaguars? She moved floaty, skulking dreamy, weaseling through the park, then stopping, as though she'd discovered something. Beanpole body in quirks and pivots. She started to the stage, but did not look at the stage. So she went around to the steps for the stage on the side. She folded her body, retracted it, sat on a step, simultaneously picking up a large stone waiting for

her there on the ground, at the side of the step. She didn't
look around. She didn't meet anyone's eyes. She started
beating that rock into the step, a solid thunk plunk,
steady, even, to Connie's voice.

Dik Dik had to sit down. He'd given Connie his chair.
Lise and Johnny, still in shock, were in the other chairs.
Douglas, now, in the fourth chair. Dik Dik stood there
with a water bottle in his hand like a lost lighthouse. He
slouched back, squatted, head and shoulders pressed
against the shell.

The voice got to Tiffany. The heat and people and
fabulous impossibilities got to Tiffany. Dik Dik looked like
a tree stump eroded down to skinny essentials, the hard
parts that would not fade. He slid to the back to sit. Then
the rock started up, knocking it out, too. That combo,
voice and stone, set Tiffany off. Still, this clamshell, over a
hundred years old, had collected and corroded all the
people who had ever been here, their presence, their
intentions. Awaken clamshell molecules! Vibrate, as you'd
vibrated before. To resonate – a Dik Dik word, Tiffany
knew that word when the band reached their overlapping
crescendo. She stopped, fell to her butt, pulled off her
boots, let her feet out. She upturned her top, yanking it
off. When she stood, with bare feet, halter top, she rose
and rose, and began to dance. She knew this moment
more than she knew the words yet, that stood for it. She
had gesture and bend and twirl. She raised her legs, feet
squinting. Her thighs on acid with impossible lifts and
twists. She ascended her arms. Con kept reading.
Beanpole kept pounding.

Tiffany danced and everybody in the clamshell flew
away. Dik Dik got a hardon. Moriah wished she could
move so freely. Johnny had never seen anything like it.
There was lightning from the tips of her toes to the top of
her head, and usually Johnny couldn't follow lightning's
emergency design, but with Tiffany he saw everything,

every flare and electrocution. Lise thought, 'Beautiful girl, beautiful movement, beautiful Joyce...breathe this evil away.' She wished it was over. She wished she could go home. She'd promised to read.

Now, people were coming up to the stage to hear and to see more. Some had their devices out, filming. Aubergine was there. Tim. Some woman dressed in cowboy attire stood in the back, hands on hips. She had a holster with a peacemaker at her side. She adjusted her cowboy hat, spat. The Jackal came up the stairs to the park, hurried to the stage. She had to get closer, so she scrambled, flipping herself onto the front of the stage. She pulled her legs in, sat cross legged, facing Connie, then, also, able to watch Tiffany.

The words fell out of Connie's mouth, and the rock batted at them, then Tiffany grabbed on and played. Tiffany went to slow motion. She quit the back and forth to hold still, so bending and surging in place. Her hands and fingers danced. Her feet were always doing something. Toes flared firm. Feet power lark. She panted, dripping sweat. But her face was clear, eyes wide. No smile, no grimace: with open lips.

The cum went on and on, and the players on stage were squelchy, squishy in their own shock juice. The peeps gathered around knew something irresistible was happening. Ah, the Coltrane happening, spontaneous, ludicrous, intense. What would the Coltrane commandment about happenings sound like?

A little while later, these three things happened at once, which were of note:

At the far entrance, by the basketball court, Mikey and Bear walked in with the beast-dogs. No leashes. The dogs were on high alert. Dogs began to bark from all sides.

OLBT managed to haul herself up the stairs and grumpy waddled to the stage, breathing hard. She screeched, "They released them! The boys are free!"

At that exact moment, behind OLBT, a film crew appeared, hoofing it up the steps. You could tell it was a film crew because of the fancy dancy equipment they huffed.

Dik Dik scanned from beast-dogs and barking, to OLBT and murdering, to hipsters and filming. Big cameras. Assistants with cases and tripods, sound people with booms and skunks. Tech barged in. Perps! Tech like an ice breaker, snow piercer wedging its way in to the happening. Handlers and producers surrounded the crew, like remoras, then here came city officials, big shots. Dik Dik surveyed it all. Official civilians – busybodies! They scurried, they rushed –

Dik Dik stood. Connie stopped reading. The rock stopped. Tiffany was staring at herself.

At the front of the stage, Dik Dik delivered, "Tell us, Old Lady Becket Twister!"

This one guy must have been the director, baldy, skinny, fidgety, heavy glasses, and he was scrambling about, yelling, "Film it! Film it! Sound! Now!"

OLBT said loud enough for folks to hear, "The cops took the boys in. All four of them. Who knows what happened? All I know, just now, they came marching out of the cop shop all devil may care. Boys aren't talking."

A voice called out. It was Tim. "Where'd they go?"

OLBT said, "Who knows?"

Tim managed to make it to the stage, near where the Jackal sat. He pressed up to the

stage, to her, to whisper something to her. The shell of the stage caught only wisps of what was said. Something about pickups and belt buckles and plenty of water.

Dik Dik said, "Read. Go on." He had to talk with the Jackal. He had to go to OLBT.

Plus, film crew interlopers! They shall not cross this line!

Connie was reading again. The rock beat – *Bump!*

Bump! Bump! Tiffany followed Dik

Dik to the front of the stage, sidled by him lowering himself from the stage. Together, they landed.

She said, "Well, we're clean."

Dik Dik smiled, beamed at her. "Thank you, love."

Tiffany followed him into the audience of random people, and said, "What now? What first? I gotta go see Bear." She could tell he was studying his way to OLBT.

Then Dik Dik came to her, wrapped his arms around her as best he could. She hugged

him back. They slapped at each other's backs. Dik Dik swung an arm around Tiffany's bare waist, pulled her close, stood on tip toes to whisper into her ear: "Tell Red she's reading next. *Nausicaa.* I got to talk to those guys." His angled eyes at the filmsters. Tiffany heard, let go.

They made it over by OLBT, who was in the dark about what had happened with Coney

Shaman and the others. The guns. The bodies held hostage. "We have to talk," he said to her. "Let me see what those film people want." OLBT nodded.

Beast-dogs or Red, Tiffany pondered. Which came first? She cut around some gawkers back to the stage. She slid up by Red. Tim was next to her. Red met her head long approach with her own head. She kissed Tiffany on the lips. "That was great," she whispered.

"Thanks, said Tiffany. "Dik says you're to read next. Okay? *Nausicaa.* He'll show it to you. Watch my stuff on stage. I'll be right back."

Red seemed surprised but nodded, let her go.

Tiffany made her way over to Bear and Mikey and the dogs. She was still barefoot, and found herself running softly, up on her toes, like pudding tiptoe through clouds. Her guys were in the back. Right now, they were being filmed. The camera guy had his laser cannon of a camera on a tripod aimed at them. The sound guy had the boom over their heads. Wolf and Dog were jumping and snapping at Bear who growled back. Bear roughed them up, twisting their ears, ruffling their fur.

Dik Dik watched Tiffany hurtle herself into dogs and man. Great shot! She was enveloped. Bear yanked her in, dogs leaping, then swung his arm down, under her thighs, and picked her up. The dogs loved it, but then they quieted, sat, sitting up tall, panting, licking her feet.

Dik Dik stood behind the camera by the fellow he'd picked out as director. He was ready to intervene with this fop, this titillating toff, when a young woman, nicely dressed, clean, blabbed in. The director kept his eyes on the scene, on the camera, didn't say a word.

The trailing, lame, civilian melee had a city councilperson – Dik Dik couldn't remember her name, a small, older woman, though sporty, ambling through assistants and handlers, making her way towards the director. She had a word or two for each of the players she accosted. Networking! Connecting, as only civilians presume. Her hand reached out to touch each person's shoulder or arm. Horny little nun going around laying on hands.

Dik Dik rallied to the director and the babbly woman before the councilperson. He squeezed inside their space. They noticed him. Now Dik Dik could follow what she was saying, what she was arguing about with the director. Maybe she was a sociologist, or an anthropologist. But a specialist for sure. She dropped the term Princeton a few times. She was intimidating because this had to be worth her while. The best part was when she said something like, *this is a happening, you have to get it, fuck the wild dogs.*

The director, whom someone would google later, turned out to be named Earl Seguay. He replied: "Continuity. Bystanders. Passersby. Wolf-dogs. They write the movie. We get it all."

The woman said, "Our presence has already checked

it."

The councilperson lurched forward – incoming!

Dik Dik blurted: "Lads, we're in the middle of a performance here. You're disrupting it. It's Bloomsday. I believe you should withdraw. I said please. At once."

The director yelped, "Samsonite, now! Get the camera on this guy. Right now! Keep talking, my man. You're doing fine. Perfect! You're like the elder, the guide, the shaman we've been looking for. Are you getting him? Sound?"

Stan Samson, the camera guy, bulky, bearded, hunched up, swiveled the camera all the way around. His tall, willowy assistant helped. She had tiny shorts on, sneakers, tank top. Perhaps her legs never ended. She looked pretty clean. "Running," called Samson.

The specialist said, "See, they want us out of here. 'Bloomsday'. Must be some ancient spring holiday.

Dik Dik was afraid his teeth'd fall out.

The director started waving his hands. "Cut! Cut! We lost it. Vibe it! Film it!. Film the stage. Film the happening. Go, go!"

Camera guy and willowy assistant broke down the camera. She took the tripod. They scurried off with the sound people.

The director put his arms around Dik Dik. "We love it! We love you guys. Whatever you want to do, that's what we want to do."

Another young woman – sneakers, tank top, shorts, but older – with a clipboard, maybe a producer, zoomed up to the director, "I'll get signatures for the releases."

"My dear friend," gloated Dik Dik, "everyone in this charming little burg has pareidolia and Stendhal Syndrome."

"I have no idea what that means," said the director.

The specialist nodded knowingly. "Ah, special needs. It's like therapy then."

The director broke away from Dik Dik said, "All of them. And the old guy too."

Daphne! Dik Dik spied straight ahead, coming in the side entrance, Daphne. She saw him watching. She raised her hand for a little wave. He waved back. *Nausicaa.* It was perfect! Daphne would read.

The film crew melted into the crowd by the stage. The aminal people, including Tiffany, hung back, cavorting with the beasts. Tiffany flayed her layers of burn. Her fire consumed them all. *Bless me father, I have sinned.* Bear had a Boner.

Dik Dik walked on haltingly, waiting, evaluating. He had to. *Put the juice to use!* Bloomsday was on! He'd talk to Douglas, then muster the troops. He kinda sorta knew what he had to do, where they had to go. It was too obvious! His regular players, but not Lise, who was too distracted, been through too much, would make the assault. What about the dancing queen, Tiffany? She'd brought the day to fruition. She'd toppled barriers to salute the day, raw and human. She was Tyrant Goddess now. She had to go with them.

But this moment – this second was too lush to ignore. He let it through, let it flow, he let it bathe him. 'Longest goddam second ever,' he pondered. Connie's words drawled distant from here. But here all the same, patterns of wordness. Wordrich Teflon commands. Declamatory. Interrogatory. Or was it the cum. The cum moment dance fandango had hyped full happening rocket. Extremity circumstances. Pareidolia take over. Where had Daphne gone? He had to talk to her.

Nothing else to do but this one thing. He scooted, he scurried. Straight over to OLBT, still standing–where was her special folding chair? He whispered, "At the ramada. Now." She nodded. He went up on stage via the steps where the beanpole person had rocked. She was gone, her rock remained. A stone throw rockaway pretty rocky! Up on stage, he went over to Douglas and Moriah. He gathered them to him. Group hug. "I have to take care of some biz. I'll be back shortly. Next is Daphne with *Nausicaa*. Then Cynthia on *Circe*."

Moriah whispered, "Make it so."

"Ha!" went Dik Dik.

Douglas shrugged and said, "No worries."

Dik Dik went to Johnny. He came in low, close to his ear. "At the ramada. Now." Johnny burst awake. Dik Dik gave a thumbs up salute to Con who rewarded him with a slight.

Tiffany was in the ramada when he got there? Huh – She sat at the picnic table with her legs pulled up. She said, "My boots are on stage. Will I need them?"

Dik Dik said, "Probably. But wait. Not yet. Let's see what our options are." Softly, just to her, he said, "May I touch your feet?"

OLBT, lodged nearby on the picnic table's bench, cried, "Motive. Method. Opportunity."

Dik Dik touched Tiffany's feets with his fingers. Lightly.

Tim wandered over. He swung himself onto the bench next to OLBT. "What you guys doing, smoking reefer?"

Johnny walked over, joined them.

OLBT said to Johnny, "You drinking enough water, hun?"

Johnny cracked up, "Yes, nana."

"Well, you look pekid. Take a drink. Here. Of mine."OLBT handed him a plastic water jug.

Johnny drank and drank, until he gurgled, "What's that taste?"

Tiffany said, "Should I light it?" She held a perfectly rolled joint between her third and fourth fingers, and the way her hands dangled seemed very sophisticated, like she was doing a TV commercial.

Tim said, "Blaze on!"

The doober went around a couple of times. More water was taken, forced down. A few sighs gaped.

Daphne smiled when she was near enough to see what was going on, then made a beeline, trotting over, pink cheeked, gleaming eyes. She said, accepting the joint, "This the new stuff? Can't believe the chronic going around. Everybody's jacked." She laughed, hit it, gasped.

Dik Dik said to her, "You're just in time. You're next to read. *Nausicaa.* Douglas will show you in the book. You know Douglas, from the Gulch theater?" She nodded, passed the joint. She almost said something, but Dik Dik marched on: "It'll be fun. Don't worry about big words or odd words you don't know. Just pronounce them as you see fit. Do your best."

Daphne was blushing, looking around at the faces, coming back to nod eagerly at Dik Dik.

Dik Dik said, "There's water up on stage. You'll do fine."

OLBT said, "Where does this new product come from? You mean pot, right?"

Daphne shrugged. She pulled an invisible zipper across her mouth.

Dik Dik realized that OLBT didn't know, and she could blow it, make Daphne paranoid, suspicious. He said, "Where you coming from, Daph? Thought you guys were heading out?"

She shrugged again, smiling, wide-eyed. "When do I go on?"

"Pretty soon," said Dik Dik.

"I better get up there."

Dik Dik nodded, said, "No rush."

Tiffany stood to come around to Daphne, saying, "Give us a hug. I'll go with you. I have to get my boots." They hugged.

Tiffany waved to Dik Dik. "Back in a flash."

Tiffany and Daphne took off for the stage holding

hands.

Tim said, "Where did she come from? You think she saw the load?"

Johnny said, "They can't be that stupid! Stash the mota at their own place?"

OLBT said, "What does this pot have to do –"

Dik Dik hurried it along: "Johnny, tell her what happened. She doesn't know. She hasn't heard the latest."

Johnny regaled her of the trip up the Gulch with Coney Shaman and Tilman. How Lise and the Jackal were with them. Then what had happened. Bodies. Guns. Rock barrage from troglodytes.

OLBT scratched her head, stretched her neck, then shook a sec. Her hands flared out, fingers extended. She drank from her water bottle. She exhaled: "The plot thickens. Oh my!"

Johnny said, "They get out of jail and go to where it's stashed? Right away? You gotta be kidding!"

OLBT said, "You surprised at dumb?"

Johnny chuckled.

Tim added, "The cops don't know anything about the pot. They want Lorna. Right? Isn't that how you'd think it's going down? That was assault. Assault by scorpion. You can't fuck with cops."

OLBT said, "They have no resources. They don't even have a detective."

Dik Dik said, "It's stupid and obvious. Of course, they're going to do it."

"Who? Lorna or the cops/" asked OLBT, huffing. She shook her head and it looked like a volcano was quavering: "Anticipation. Expectation. The problem with mystery novels is people act smarter in them. What – Dik Dik, what are you thinking?"

Tim said, "Cops all over her place."

Dik Dik said, "Not right away. They don't know where she lives. Johnny, Tiffany, and I go up to Lorna's. We get the pot, give it back to the druggies."

OLBT sounded sharp: "And you get the bodies?"

Dik Dik said, "Johnny will be there to help."

Johnny said, "They'll drop the bodies, tell us where to find them. Once they get their grass, I mean."

OLBT shook her head. "Too much – -retrograde. How you going to convince those boys to give up the pot?" She looked over the faces surrounding her. "What a world, what a world. We are all infected now."

Tim said, "I bet Captain America and Tilman are already on their way to Lorna's."

OLBT said, "The greatest achievement of performance is to convince people there is no performance."

Tiffany and Jackal sauntered in to the ramada. Tiffany had her boots and top on. The Jackal was scalding. She went right over to Dik Dik, started poking him in the chest, fingering him. Dik Dik backed away. He leaned on the end of the picnic table, folded his arms in front of himself.

The Jackal belted, "Wanna get fingered, big boy?" all the while continuing to poke. "First, you finger me to read, then you give it to Daphne, finger her. I'll finger you."

OLBT chortled: "Stop it." She gasped. Everybody gasped.

"You're always fucking with me," said the Jackal. But she quit poking, left Dik Dik alone.

Tiffany came over to Dik Dik. "I told her about Nausea."

As if on cue, from up on stage, Daphne began to read. Dik Dik turned to watch. He knew this opening:

"'The summer evening had begun to fold the world in its mysterious embrace. Far away in the west the sun was setting and the low glow of all too fleeting day lingered lovingly on sea and sand, on the proud promontory of dear old Howth guarding as ever the waters of the bay, on the weedgrown rocks along Sandymount shore and, last but not least, on the quiet church.'"

He could barely hear her. A flat drone that could blow away was all he could make out. It sounded like termites, far away termites, gnawing through Megalodon. The full flush flesh rocket moment had come and gone. Douglas would cheer her on. She would find her way. He didn't have time. He'd already been poked. Now was the time - -

Tim levitated straight up from his place at the table, bustled over to the Jackal, slung an arm around her shoulders. "Hey, pick on someone your own size," he laughed. "Tiff, spark up that roach for Red. We already smoked, but we saved a hit for you."

The Jackal untangled herself from Tim. "You did not."

Tiffany was looking for it.

"You're a dickhead, dickhead," announced the Jackal. She made a growling murky sound, then: "But now? Nah, now, I can tell. It's on. You guys got a plan. I'm in. I'm coming."

The film crew had a perimeter going around the playground equipment, recording, filming the steampunks' gymnastics. Now, following the director's pointing and yelping, they bustled over to the ramada, re-positioning, fanning out. Samson, the camera guy, called out to the willowy girl assistant, "Twila, there's shadows! Shadows! Need the other lens!"

"Switch! Switch!" cried the director.

The specialist was nodding too much, aglow though, ambling to the picnic table, with a jolly, jokey tune: "Hi! Hi!"

The director was sharp: "Get out of the shot! You guys, go about your beeswax."

The specialist went around to Dik Dik, held out her hand, no pokey fingers. Dik Dik unfolded his arms, took her hand. He said, "Bloomsday!" emphatically.

She whispered, "Steampunkers! Cyberpunks, hippy

punks. Fuck."

OLBT called to the group at or adjacent the table: "Let's brake bread." She took bread, in the guise of protein bars, from a sleeve in her copiousness, and took this bread and gave thanks, braking each bar in two, and gave it to them, saying, "This is your body, which is made by us, for us: do this in remembrance of us."

Now, the way the heart meat blood clot of Coltrane meant, houses clung at all angles to the mountain swell, some houses bulgy, fat, sticking out like they were pregnant, while others receded, were set back, pulled in, like inhaled sunken chests; also, meant that in the day time, as the Jackal, Tiffany, Johnny, and Dik Dik took to the stairs, they registered the grand overview of layers and levels, of stairways and paths, crisscrossing the expanse, like necklaces laid over a 4-D *Chutes and Ladders* game board.

Johnny said, "I don't like this."

"Me three," went the Jackal.

A mockingbird in a fig tree fanned out a wing, obvious semaphore, to show white white white, all the while whistling like a wren.

The Jackal connived: "That bird doesn't like it either."

Tiffany said, "What do we do? What do we say?"

Dik Dik said, "You can see all the stairs over the hillside. It's all laid out –"

Johnny urged, "Here, get in the fig tree a second." He hustled everyone into the shade of the big-leaved tree, deep green with chalky white, knotty branches. "Una mas."

"What?" squawked the Jackal.

Dik Dik said, "The oddest thing: heads popping up like mugwumps. All over the beastly neighborhood. You can see them for a mile."

The Jackal said, "So they can see us. Who was it?"

Johnny said, "My brother with the big guy."

Tiffany said, "We got no choice."

Dik Dik said, "We have to split up. But I'll take the stairs. They'll be expecting me."

Johnny said, "Wait a sec, wait a sec. Things could go bad. You know it could. Tiff, you and Red, wait here. Or go back. I'll cut across so no one sees me."

The Jackal said, "No one will see me either."

Tiffany said, "It will take all of us to convince them, so nothing bad happens."

Dik Dik said, "I agree with Johnny. But time is of the essence. You decide. I'm going."

Dik Dik stepped out of the tree's cover and paraded up the final incline of the dead-end that intersected with the stairs. Dik Dik got on the steps, pushed up, glanced around nonchalantly, and proceeded on his mission.

He tried focus, fumbled, frowned, studied the steps ahead, then found the art. Fuck's sake! All around him, near and far, people had *objets*, in their yards, on their fences, on their roofs. Abstract sculptural elements, then scarecrows, gnomes, trolls, bicycles, wagon wheels. Wagon wheels were *de rigueur* yard pieces in the West. An empty lot, a gap between houses, like a missing tooth, had two left over pieces by an Israeli artist who had visited years before: a giant paper mache flower at least twelve feet tall, with a purple stem and a red flower, then a gargantuan loo, out of plywood, smoothed and painted accordingly. But it was no good. Terlets be damned! His eyes kept flicking back to the popping heads.

Control was a myth. All was messy –

Head pop! Heads popped! Heads popping up!

How peculiar, thought Dik Dik, as if the world had

become a toy board, with popping heads like popping weasels requiring a bonk. Way off, two popping cop heads, no, three popping cop heads, on a mid-level path to the steps that only went down. Then the big guy's head. No sign of brother. Big guy was three stairways over, and so, too, would have to go down and around. Unless he went cross country, through people's yards. Then, popping, popping, in and out of view, impossible to miss, Agatha's man, Oscar, her fixer, who was way too close on a parallel trail, but heading up so turned away from Dik Dik. Above him, right in front of Dik Dik, on his steps, Captain America and Tilman.

They were going slow. Dik Dik was going slow, but at this rate, he'd catch them. They were arguing. Captain America, flag shirt flaming, dripping essence, threw his arms around, staggering on the steps, emphasizing jettison. Tilman held on to the metal hand rails with two hands. The way he grasped it, he must be jerking himself along hand over hand.

Captain America spotted Dik Dik. He declared, panting, "Oh, lookee, lookee. Namaste, Mr. Vortex. Tilman said you were a vortex."

Dik Dik climbed up to them, huddled by a chinaberry for its shade to catch a breath. Dik Dik said, "He should know."

Captain America said, "Well, vortex to vortex, let's be clear here, we're going for the pot. Tilman figures it'll ease some of the bad juju on Coney Shaman."

"Don't call him that!" spat Tilman. He was leaking all over, panting, his goofy wild hair slicking to his bandaged forehead.

Dik Dik said, "You know who you are dealing with here? Don't be an ass. You try that shit, you're dead. You understand? Unless you have a gun, which I seriously doubt. So what we're going to do is let me go up there *alone* and try to reason with them. I have a chance. You don't. Nothing worse than an old fool. We got to get the bodies back. Or this will never end. And someone else will get hurt. There's been enough death. Give me a few minutes. But lay low. The hills have eyes. Get under that oak tree over there. Stay in the shade. And wait. If I don't – -if I'm not successful – -" Dik Dik wiped his mouth with his hand, a little shrug. "I guess it'll be every man for himself. You try. Whatever you want. But right now, keep still. No yelling. This is a popping neighborhood. Stairs have ears."

Captain America looked stunned, or peaking. "Oh, kimosabe, me likee – -but you can still grab an o-z on the way out. Stick it in your drawers! No greedy."

Tilman managed, "He'll do no such thing. Path of least resistance. Wait, like he says. Breathe deep. Wait."

Dik Dik thought he'd hyperventilate, but no time for first aid. *Fly, Fleance!*

"Go, vortex, go," went Captain America.

The two panters moved off the steps to the oak tree, got up in its stuff, settling to squats by its hoary trunk.

Dik Dik rambled, *I get to the house, and – I get to the house, and –* but he didn't know what came next. Heads popped up near, far. *This day, this neighborhood, bound to the side of the mountain, bobs with heads. Bob up! Bobble up! Up! As they close in on their quarry.* Query? This was not his responsibility. Remember Coltrane Commandment Number 9! Sticking his nose into a hornet's nest of a fractal swamp! What was this? Grandstanding?

He ascended slowly. No sweat. No heebie-jeebies. Bloody consciousness saw a way out. At least another way to see it. Up. Up. He'd be the first. He'd beat them all. But he only had minutes. Or it would go full conflagration, accretions of subatomic disdain. Enablers would descend on the house, encircle it, take it. Right now, just for a tit bit, there was a window of opportunity he would climb through, to tell the boys the score. They'd be idiots if they didn't see. So no prep. No ad lib. Pure truth as power, *be here now*, hippy dippy bank on it.

Dik Dik took the few steps from the stairs to the abode. All was still. No shrieks. No flames. No scorpions. The front door was ajar. He knocked softly.

Tiffany opened the door the rest of the way. "Over here," she whispered, grabbing his arm and hauling him in, to the side kitchen by the fridge. She whispered, "Don't look."

Dik Dik saw humanity...people...the boys.

Johnny was back there by the fridge, too, looking miserable. "Sick shit, jefe. Hey, I ain't judging. Es verdad." He puffed his cheeks for a baby snort. He pushed his long dark hair back, out of his face.

Dik Dik smelled pot. "What's going on?"

Tiffany whispered, "They'll give us the pot. There's only a little missing. Barely noticeable."

Johnny said, "They'll notice."

"What's going on?" asked Dik Dik.

Johnny stared at Tiffany. He said, "The Jackal had to relieve them. For the pot. All they wanted, they were so stoned, they don't really care. But they wanted Red to relieve them."

Dik Dik stepped backwards, came around to face the living room area. He inhaled and was one with the place's stank.

All four boys – Red, Blue, Baldy, Whitey. Red and Blue sat on the couch. They wore gym shorts. They nodded to Dik Dik. In front of them were the other two boys, Baldy and Whitey, standing with their shorts pulled down. The Jackal kneeled between them handling their erect penises like reluctant pumps she was working hard to prime. She rubbed them up and down. She was looking away from Dik Dik, so hadn't noticed his peek. There was a poncho spread on the floor before her and between the two boys. The jackal wore one of Lorna's white, fluff collars.

Blue on the couch murmured to Dik Dik, "I'm too shy. But the big boys don't care."

Red explained, "We're used to it twice a day. If we don't get milked, it builds up and hurts. Backs up in the notochord. It's the buildup of excess. You gotta release the excess, for health. She's helping them dump a load."

The big dicks started juicing. Grunts, whinnies came from the boys. Jism flew through the air. The Jackal had to duck.

The Jackal fell back. She said, "I'm not touching that."

"Thanks, doll," said Whitey. "Appreciate it."

Baldy said, "It's better in the mouth."

"No way," said the Jackal, getting to her feet. "You guys got some relief. We get the weed. We're done here." The Jackal unsnapped her collar.

Baldy and Whitey pulled up their shorts. Baldy said, "Let's have one for the road!"

"I ain't putting those things in my mouth," said the Jackal.

Baldy laughed. "No, I mean a doob. One more time!"

Dik Dik said loud enough, "Where's Lorna?"

Blue shrugged. "Back to her studio?"

Dik Dik cut across the room, making for the back. Johnny and Tiffany followed. The Jackal went after them.

The add on back room, the studio, Lorna's get away, her space, had had a tsunami go through it. The cot was overturned, mattress torn apart, then sheered, grated, splotched with different colors of paint, mainly blues. Paint was on the walls, the ceiling. Odious bits of foam and fiber in mounds across the floor, also dripping with paint. Tools, brushes, pens, markers, broken glass, broken pottery, in snotty abandon. The long work shop table was in scraps now, disassembled, snatched up for kindling. Then the paper goods: strips, balls, wads, then canvas, broadsheet, rag paper, all in a fuck of detonation.

Tiffany, the Jackal, Dik Dik, and Johnny hung by the

door, disassembling disassembled –

Tiffany said, "Poor sot."

Johnny said, "What's a 'sot?' Gotta be a Dik word."

The Jackal said, "Where'd she go? She knows she can't get away."

Dik Dik said, "Bleak way to see it." Dik Dik took it in in a long deep draught. "*Circe* is next," he said stiffly. "Cynthia is ready. The Earth turns. Bollocks."

The Jackal said, "I'm gonna go get the pot, then I'm gonna wash my hands." She skedaddled.

Johnny said, "I don't want to know this. What the fuck, you guys? I keep thinking about that moment at the Tavern when I asked you a question. Now, twenty-four hours later, here we are. It's so random."

Tiffany said, "Johnny, we're friends. It's death. We're not used to death. And it's all around us. Death radiates around us. What else can we do?"

Johnny got all spooky voiced: "*Loco in duh cabezas, jefe!* Way too fucked up. Out to fucking lunch."

Dik Dik said, "We define ourselves by our repressions."

Johnny said, "I don't know what that means."

Dik Dik said, "What is she thinking? Lorna! What is she doing?" He waved his hands over the mess. "Cod! Mackerels, halibuts, hake! The pious angler knows confession can't help. Timing. Cues. Marks. The stop watch is ticking. The countdown has begun. How isolated she must feel, but don't you see, this invigorates her. She's smirking like the Cheshire cat, insisting this is art. Beauty herself. I'm afraid it's going according to plan."

Johnny said, "A build up then? And like the whole pot deal was just a coincidence?"

Dik Dik looked away.

Tiffany said, "Saddest room in town. Lorna takes herself way seriously. Sometimes, she acts like a spoiled brat. She can get extreme. I'm just saying."

"Anything's possible," added Johnny.

Tiffany stepped into the room, pawing around to recover some accoutrements from the floor. "Look, she's hiding her *Dr. Peppers* in socks."

Sure enough, Tiffany displayed a couple tube socks, each with a full can of *Dr. Pepper.*

Dik Dik said, "A cosh. A cudgel."

"Prison protection," said Johnny.

Dik Dik said, "She was practicing? She needed a club."

Tiffany said, "The murder weapon. You don't think this was it, a can of *Dr. Pepper?*"

Dik Dik shook his head. "We won't know until the autopsies."

"The bodies have more to their journey," said Johnny.

Tiffany let go of the socks with *Dr. Peppers,* let them drop back to their home.

The Jackal appeared behind them in the door, with two, large, black garbage bags, but not nearly as big as the other ones. She held a bag out to Johnny. "I'll take one. You take one," she said.

"No, I'll take both, get it to them. You guys head back. I'll meet you at the park."

Tiffany said, "Johnny – be careful."

The Jackal went, "Yeah, deets like that help."

Johnny looked at Dik Dik, their eyes –

Johnny said, "What have you done? *Fuck it all* wasn't enough." Johnny shuddered. "Otherwise, it's just void. People popping around like in a pin ball machine, so stoned they believe whatever shit they come up with."

"Gotcha there, dickhead," went the Jackal. Their looks changed her tune. "All right. No more. I'll be good. This is a fucking heavy moment, and we should respect that." She paused, studied their faces one by one. "'Fuck sakes,'" she uttered, "'else we're just a bunch of bloody wankers.'" She looked to Dik Dik. "Remember that line from your piece?"

Johnny growled, "I know I sound like a fricking

baracho, but what's a fucking 'bloody wanker'? I keep having to ask, you all talk so sophisticated –"

Tiffany went, "A wanker. You know." She made a motion with her hand.

Dik Dik said, "Let's get this road on the show."

They marched past the boys, strewn about in their shorts, coughed up utterances of goodbye. Out the front door, Johnny crossed the stairs, overland, hoisting the two garbage bags.

The Jackal, Tiffany, and Dik Dik started down. Quick glances, surveys, and no popping heads popping right now. Bright afternoon sun. Hot air. Scenic as fuck. Art still about, calling out to passersby: *look at me, look at me, so clever, so clever, rejoice!* They stayed quiet, taking the steps slowly.

Finally, the Jackal had to announce, "I figured out what the collars are for."

"We saw," said Tiffany.

"Gimme a break. No, remember how weird it was there was so little blood? Well, hardly any. Lorna made them for the victims, to catch the blood, before they stuffed 'em in the garbage bags."

Tiffany said, "What's a 'cosh'?"

Dik Dik said, "Becket Twister forecast a blunt instrument, like a cosh, one quick blow to the head. There's probably a *YouTube* about how to do it proper." Dik Dik felt dirty in this speech and had to stop to brush himself off, check for scorpions.

Tiffany watched Dik Dik. "She came to you after the disappearance. Remember? At the Yard. Right before the lights went back on. Remember?"

Dik Dik stared ahead. "Yes, yes."

"It's all for you, Dik Dik," said Red-Black, Jackal, Jack. "Sick shit."

Dik Dik gagged, but did not spit. Revenge implied onus. Guilt? "Why? To rub it in? To blame me? For what?" He shook his head, felt uncertain, distracted.

Tiffany said, "What happened between her and Simon and M.K.?"

Dik Dik looked to his two comrades, then hurriedly glanced back up towards Lorna's place. To a tree. Missing wankers, he pondered, what happened to Tilman and Cap?

He said, "Johnny's right. Art town for shit. Your generation has to rise forth, burgeon forth. We had our run. Give it a go." He had to get back to Bloomsday. "Enough of the old gods, so much baggage. There will be risks."

The Jackal said, "Risk's our middle name. But not so much for Johnny, I don't think."

"Fuck you," said Tiffany.

"Do you like to talk dirty when you're doing it?" asked the Jackal.

Dik Dik said, "I have to get back to the park."

They headed down with more determination. Dik Dik noted the absence of Shoggoth pop-ups. They got off the stairs, heard Matewan toll, and said hello/goodbye, passing the fig tree and mockingbird, still hanging around to see how it turned out.

Bloomsday reigned supreme in City Park. Hardly anyone there. No steampunks. No re-enactors. No film crew. Most of the action was on stage, in the clamshell. Cynthia was reading. *Circe* was on! *Ithaca* in the wings! Dik Dik couldn't hear a thing. He had to get closer. Get up in this thing. Douglas and Moriah in chairs, next to Cynthia in a chair. Lise was in the back, all stretched out. Connie sat in the back, leaning against the wall, as were

Lydia, Mikey, Aubergine, and Tim, under the banner. SCRIBBLEDEHOBBLED, forever and ever –

Cynthia's voice, the words tumbled free, sweet spot echo tease. Dik Dik went around the side of the stage to use the steps. Dog back there, big houndy thing, not like Bear's at all. This guy sat in the rocks besides the steps looking glum. Long face with sad ego.

Close.

Sun all over.

Then shade.

"Sombra," said Dik Dik to the dog, who, clear as anything, responded, "Oh, sure, some of this was the Way. Thing is you artist types live in the precious otherwise. The frisson of the imagination – so fun, so uncanny because you know the real. You celebrate alternates because you know the One. Do you see how to the inexperienced this could lead to madness?"

Lise wasn't stretched out across the ground. Dik Dik saw she was actually a few inches *above* the ground. She'd made her own air pillow.

Ithaca was next. Cynthia was grand. The blood of the text was back. The clamshell held the cum dear, allowing all to squeeze.

Then Jackal said, "When shall we meet again?"

"When it's done. When it's begun," said Tiffany.

"What shall we do?"

"I shall find my boy."

"Don't you wanna stay, hear Dik Dik?"

"I wanna, I wanna, but still –"

"Let's go see what's up at the Yard. Johnny'll come back here, that's what he said." The Jackal watched her, convinced her. "Where's Daphne? Hope she's not in this shit. That girl is so simple, she's complex. Come on, we'll be right back."

"Where's Johnny?"

"Where's Johnny?

Tiffany added, "Johnny will find us."

They made their way to the Yard, climbed the steps, peeked in the locked front entrance. Peeking out at them, close to the glass on the other side, were two big pink faces. Either a two- headed woman or twins. All faces showed surprise. The Jackal and Tiffany could see in well enough to spot Agatha and her entourage, sitting up front at a couple tables by the stage. Only a few lights on. The doors were still there, standing open, phantom doorways, specter doorways, hometown doorways, heading – always heading nowhere. OLBT was at her own table. All the other tables had their chairs overturned, resting on the tables.

The Jackal mused, "I always wondered why they put the chairs up like that at night. Is it so the chairs can rest?"

Tiffany said, "So they can sweep up."

The film crew had decided to vote petulant on art town. After a promise by a professional Coltraner to guide them to the secret portal to Uranus fell through – the artist not showing up as promised, they headed for Coltrane's co op dungeon. The director wanted more than stoners, old hippies. He figured foibles as dark side titillation. After all, how many co op dungeons could there be?

The woman in charge, Cal, a strong muscular figure

with short hair, led them to the building. It was a two story stone building, at least a hundred years old, vacant for generations. Cal opened the door with a key and led them in. Right away, a flash sniff of distant swimming pool – chlorine? But *dank* too. The director loved it, gushing, "Wish we could get that odd smell! We can get the echo-y wood floors. Sound!"

The film crew followed Cal up the broad stairs. On the second floor, a landing with two doors, on opposite sides. Cal chose, had the key, let them file in. Now, the smell had intense incense overlay –

Tilman barged in behind them through the door, crying, "Cal, Cal, I gotta bump up my appointment. Please, Cal. I'm gonna have a seizure, a seizure –"

The director was doing the mashed potato or else gesticulating for Samson to get Tilman good.

Cal explained, "As you know, Senor, we're closed right now." She smiled at the moving camera. "You'd be surprised how many early birds we get. So pleased with our services."

Cal strode over to Tilman. Huskily, she whispered to him, "You're not having a seizure. Are you saying your mantra? Releasing your toxins?"

Tilman moaned. "Seizure," he seethed. "Seizure."

Cal might have slugged him right then, but Tilman caught on what he had stumbled into. He composed a lecture: "Enoch walked the Earth. Men flail the Earth with poison. Our precious bodily fluids, excessive, drowning us in cum. Okay, there are services. Fifty beans, a girl will clean your house and give you a blow job. Here, fifty beans, a girl will beat your nut sack with a spatula. You have to get rid of the excess. It backs up the notochord. Now, this one time, just between me and you, a guy had his scrotum nailed to a board. Happened right here, right over there." He pointed.

Cal got in Tilman's stuff. "That's enough. Come back

later. I'm not asking."

Tilman shrunk, groveled, but couldn't resist: "I was there! At the disappearance! I am a person of interest!"

The director made google eyes at the producer with the clipboard to go get the wild man's deets.

Back on this Earth, the director whined out directions: "Samsonite, three shot: back, overview; mid-shot, sides, fuck swings, tables; close ups, all that stuff – the torture equipment, whatever. I want it all. Sound on it! Follow us, follow us. Go, go!"

Cal continued with her tour and pitch.

What did Twila think?

The specialist wandered, eyeing accoutrements, settling by the rack of spatulas. She intoned, "Foibles, foibles." She thought about spatulas, her head space networking utensils to the native toolkit. She pictured a caveman flipping a pancake with a Teflon spatula.

Cal came up behind her, camera following. Cal said, "Takes all kinds. Notice these are all springy. Doods like women to beat their sacks, I guess. We don't care. Whatever you want to do." She turned and faced the camera. "No animals. But otherwise whatever you want. Only one rule: cleanliness is next to godliness. You clean up after yourself. Bleach. No fuck ups or you're out."

The specialist said academically, "Makes sense."

The director groaned. "Please, for the love of God, would you, please, get out of the shot."

The specialist walked over to a table in the back. It was laid out with various... accoutrements, including African porcupine quills, and candles. The wall above the table was one of those pegboards dads had in their workshops. But instead of wenches and screw drivers, this one held handcuffs, manacles, whips, goads. Hemp rope.

Cal said, "This cabinet over here – "She walked to the cabinet, next to an industrial sink with lots of cleaning supplies. She opened the cabinet. "See? Towels, wash cloths. Then, in that one over there, scarves, blindfolds, gags. Silkies."

Agatha had hired the twins as bouncers. They seemed nice and let Tiffany and the Jackal in to the bar without any fuss. Agatha made it so. She called for them to join her.

They sat next to OLBT, at her table, but close enough to talk to Agatha.

Agatha explained the twins, "They're Geats. I call them Boe and Dicia. Right? Well, anyway, they'll be a great asset to the bar."

They were *great* assets: huge women, well over six feet tall, with round, pink heads and short dark hair. Dark blue eyes. Maybe they were thirty, in *Oshkosh-B'gosh* overalls.

OLBT mumbled, "First time, I thought she said *geese*. But they sure don't look like geese to me."

Agatha, of course, acknowledged, so laughed, then her entourage laughed, each in their respective clean, fresh outfits. The twins stood at their station at the door. Agatha called to them, "Give us a song, then. They're singers, these Geats."

The twins turned to face them, smiling warmly. They began: "'The biscuits were as hard as brass, and the beef as salt as Lot's wife's ass.'"

The piece went on a few more stanzas. Their voices were surprisingly high pitched. With their accent, they concocted a lugubrious sweetness.

OLBT tsked, "Fricking angels. Who would have thought."

Agatha said, "We were just telling Beckett here that we heard the tank story. About the dam and all. What happened to you guys."

Oscar muttered, "You're lucky to be alive."

Agatha said, "Lorna, Lorna. What happens now? You've come to share?"

Tiffany and the Jackal stretched out in their chairs and rolled their shoulders. It worked as a nod.

The Jackal asked, "How did you hear?"

Agatha said, "It's gotten to the point, give the old doods a hit off the vape, they'll tell you everything. Stuff you don't want to know. Like about Tilman's bowels. Yeah, Captain America and Tilman wandered by. They wanted to know what we'd heard. And, you know, tit for tat? Quid pro quo. They blabbed it out. Captain America acted like he was there, with Coney Shaman up the Gulch. Tilman kept saying he wasn't with you."

The Jackal snapped, "He wasn't."

Agatha shrugged. Her entourage shrugged.

Tiffany told about getting the pot back. She kept it vague.

Agatha said, "Who's going to pick up the bodies?"

The Jackal cried, "I'm not doing it. We're not doing it."

Tiffany concluded, "The police. They have to. Autopsies. All like that."

OLBT choired, "The police! Justice is blinding."

Oscar offered, "They know about the windows. So, now, once they get the bodies, it's a done deal."

"They released the boys," said the Jackal.

Tiffany looked startled for a second, then the Jackal realized what she'd said.

Agatha sighed, "Oh, Lorna!"

Tiffany wondered where Bear was. "We gotta check at the park. Bloomsday." Where's Johnny?

The Jackal wondered if she'd ever sing again.

The entourage wondered what they could do for their goddess.

OLBT wondered if her bowels would move this day.

Boe and Dicia wondered about what Agatha had told them. Murders! Right here in Agatha's place. But they'd been summoned: the Brit director who'd had them in his alien abduction movie, apparently, was an old friend of Agatha's. Twenty-four hours later, free tickets to the states, new duds: here they were.

OLBT declaimed: "'Nobody heard her tears; the heart is a fountain of weeping water which makes no noise in the world.'"

Tiffany stood, glanced to the Jackal and OLBT, and said, "Back in a flash."

Johnny didn't see any heads popping over the mountain side. Had they found Lorna? They'd probably gone home. He hoped. He did not need to run into cops, hauling two bags of bud. If he ran into them, he'd say he was doing yard work, and these were cuttings he was taking to the dumpster. He'd keep his eyes down, talk shyly, respectfully. He didn't even know Lorna. His mom, Lorna's mom – sure, they'd know each other. Everybody in town knew each other.

...even the new people, the artists, the wackos, the hippies, the Anglo invaders who made their neighborhoods a stage. They were always performing. Their poverty was glamorous fun. They played like royalty, but sick, or poisonous, royalty. They wrote poems and painted pictures. Some were pretty educated, or had read a lot of books. He'd like to read some of those books. See what it was about. Now he just wanted to unload this shit, get rid of it fast as he could.

Johnny thought a person should be willing to try new things. He sure would like to have a *try* with Tiffany. But she had a boyfriend. He thought of his friends, his mom. What would he tell his brother? Johnny was the big brother, the oldest, Mom's favorite. He had to head over to their place. He had to find them.

Didn't he have some job he was supposed to be checking up on? A follow-up about a house painting gig? Fuck... He had to get some *dinero* to pay off his phone. Get some more minutes.

If he called his bro, he knew how it would go:

"Wassup."

"I got it."

"Come on by, we'll tell you where the stiffs are."

Johnny had to get down to the Gulch!

The Universe. Art. Ideas. They had waited for him this long. A little longer wouldn't hurt. Besides, now he had a head start, and knew the outcome of books and art and ideas: chaos. Murder. If you knew who the murderer was from the beginning of the mystery novel, then what kind of *mystery* was that?

Johnny came off a yard of ice plant, stepping over a low fence, then to steps that would take him to the Gulch. Lots of trees – cancer trees, another fig, chinaberry. Tree glory. Wow – *tree glory*...what kind of expression was that? Right out of the Dik and Lise playbook! He was infected. He dropped his bags, took a moment to breathe. Three breaths. Calm it down. It was almost over. Then what? He would see Tiffany when her band played. Would he start hanging out with Dik? Why did they call him Dik Dik? What's a *dik dik*?

End of the stairs. Welcome home. Gulch rats ran for cover. He'd stay to the side. Alleyways. Make his way inconspicuously. Dood carrying out the trash. No big duh.

Johnny could see the black SUV sitting in the parking lot, engine running. *So be it*! Dood must have been cruising. Johnny walked over, his steps dragging.

The driver's side door opened and his brother popped

out. "Jefe! Como esta? Throw that back here." He went around to the back of the vehicle, opened it.

Johnny hefted his load in to the trunk of the SUV.

"Bueno," said his brother. "Lucky, we were hanging in the hood." He called, "Vargas, get in back, so Johnny can sit up front." He closed the trunk.

The passenger side's front door opened. The big man got out, nodded to Johnny. They stepped past each other, going to their seats. Johnny's brother got back behind the wheel. He played with the steering wheel, an experimental wiggle. "The way it is, bro, need a favor here – I know it's crazy, but hear me out, then I'll tell you where the bags are. We haven't touched them."

Johnny went, "*Bueno.*"

"So the thing is," his brother explained, "Vargas, here, has a thing for that girl who wears the vest. From back at the dam? *That* girl. She looks like a fucking paladin – hot, bitchin' hot."

Vargas took over: "We're made for each other. All I want is for you to set up a meeting between me and her. No date – fuck that. Because I think she's the one. My soulmate. She's as mad and crazy as me. What's her name?" The big man groveled in love.

Johnny said, "She goes by several names. I know her as Red. Which I think is short for Red-Black. But Dik calls her the Jackal."

"*The Jackal,*" went Vargas, all gooey. "That's perfect."

Johnny said, "Hey, look, I hardly know the girl. I can tell her, see what she says. That's all I can do."

His brother stared at his partner in the rearview mirror. "Satisfied? We asked, we're done. So, you know where the steps are to the old cribs?"

"Sure," said Johnny. "Steps to nowhere."

Dik Dik needed cocoa. He needed a bath. He read slowly, allowing Stephen and Bloom their denouement. The *duumvirate interindividual relations* required *stratagems* and *anagrams._Oh, Sinbad the Sailor! Oh, Tinbad the Tailor!* Let the catechism list: concealed identities, songs and ditties, future careers, furniture, infantile memories. "'...Padney Socks she shook with shocks her money box....'" This will end, and Lise will read *Penelo*pe and Bloomsday will be done, and night will fall, and the dead will reappear in garbage bags. *Antesatisfaction.* "'He kissed the plump mellow yellow smellow melons of her rump....'" *Postsatisfaction.* "'...Roc's auk's egg...'"

Now he was an old man reading James Joyce to a stage of bloody yanks, and no one could really hear, and he flashed on a scene in an empty, trash-strewn lot, maybe on the Gulch, and there were the black garbage bags...it was neither day nor night, but he could see a small deer, a doe with faint spots along her sides. What was she doing to the bags? Nudging them, poking them with her snout. What was she doing? As he approached – he hadn't realized he could move, the doe raised her head, and he saw her snout dripped blood. And the doe pulled back her lips to reveal bloody fangs. Dik Dik kept reading.

Ithaca! The last act. Dik Dik conversed: *Here we go, the adventure peaks and coincides – takes sides.* The players had done their duty. The show had gone on, and audience and players had merged. Tiffany had danced. *O, cum, sweet love!* Even the film crew had fit perfectly. Now, as day and sun ate each other, what was left was each letter in each word before him became a dancing skeleton.

Lise would float over – yes, we said yes...it would end – but first:

Tiffany and Bear with the wolf-dogs strode up the stairs to enter the park. They moved to the stage, dogs keeping close to their people. Tiffany and Dik Dik's eyes met, said howdy do. Bear tacked over suddenly to the playground equipment with the dogs. Tiffany followed. Dik Dik knew she wanted to tell. Dik Dik kept reading.

Now, at the high road, side entrance to the park, Lorna's boys came high stepping in. They wore identical gray gym outfits: gray t-shirts, gray sweat pants, gray sneakers. Red. Blue. Baldy. Whitey.

Dik Dik drove on, drove on, full of toucan trash torpedoes, and finished *Ithaca.* No one knew or could tell. Dik Dik stood at the sweet spot, sweetly offering sweets, about the final sweet bit, suggesting a sweet five minute break to get Lise sweet. Actually, Lise had come forward with text in hand.

Dik Dik explained, "This last section is called *Penelope.* A caveat here. We say 'Pen-el-o-pee.' Joyce would have pronounced her 'Pen-uh-low-pay.'"

Johnny appeared at the stairs, coming into the park. Everybody joke joked, choked the bloke – when sirens....

It must have been a single Coltrane police car at first. The police car roared around. They couldn't see where it went. It was blocked by buildings, but pretty close. The siren song made a wail, then cut off. Bloop! Who knew what was happening? Did Lorna's boys know? Did Johnny know? What did Tiffany know? Now, a siren from uptown, up the canyon, got dopplering, pealing and screeching, then it squashed off. The vehicle must have joined the other one. It must have gone where the other one had gone. Where were they? Over by the noodle shop?

EMT's – big red ambulance, big red box, came next. But no siren. Only a suggestive squeal.

Then, from out at the highway bypass, a third siren began, as a county sheriff patrol car joined the duty.

The few people in the park scrambled away to chase the sirens. Even people on stage were taking off. Lorna's boys stayed where they were. The whole Gulch seemed pupating. Dik Dik and Lise exchanged glances.

Tiffany walked over from the playground equipment. She called to Dik Dik, "Lorna borrowed Bear's mic and amp."

Johnny went to stand beside Tiffany. "What the hell. Now what?"

Tiffany and Johnny couldn't stop looking at each other. Tiffany said, "Johnny, I have a boyfriend."

Tiffany and Johnny went up on stage to confer with Dik Dik. Johnny exhaled. Tiffany sniffled. Johnny announced, "The exchange went cool. I called it in to the police. No name, just where they should look. It's over."

Matewan Tower started booming the time. What hour was it? Lorna's boys got the signal and began emitting howls, yawps, whelps, bawls, squalls. The tower's recording must have been scratched: it kept tolling and tolling. How many hours in this day?

From where the remaining Bloomsday gang stood, on stage and in the park, they had an easy, clear view of Matewan Tower, its semi-Victorian ornateness – with big clock face. But they couldn't see where the cops and ambulance had gone.

The sirens quieted. The quiets sirened. The sirens were confessing to themselves, "My throat aches. Anyone have a lozenge?"

It was a bright warm day in June, and the clocks were striking ad infinitum.

"Where was Moses when the candle went out?"

It was painful to see what they saw next, as though their eyes needed a Brillo Pad scrub already. No one wanted to believe what they saw, so raw a maw, on Matewan Tower that day.

Matewan Tower stopped tolling, and a small, inconspicuous maintenance door on the side of the tower opened. Lorna did her pretzel thing through the small door. Not much room up there. She managed to shimmy, then coil her silver-encased form along narrow frames of gingerbread, mic in hand. Her bare feet grabbed like talons. Finally, back pressed to the clock face, legs dangling, she announced who she was wearing. She had on one of her collars, so from a distance the pure white collar and the silver encasement might have suggested a Mrs. Claus from outer space.

In the park, eyes jumped back and forth, from Lorna on Matewan Tower, then to Lorna's boys. The boys, lined up by the stage, leaked their eyes out, but enough optical rodeo to keep a fixed stare up at the tower and its grotesque acanthus they worshiped.

Lorna's voice resounded over the Gulch, squeaky, troubled, faint, then clear, then scratchy. She must have had the amp facing out, in the little door.

"'YES BECAUSE HE NEVER DID A THING LIKE THAT BEFORE AS ASK TO get his breakfast in bed with a couple of eggs since the *City Arms Hotel* when he used to be pretending to be laid up with a sick voice doing his highness to make himself interesting to that old faggot Mrs. Riordan...I suppose she was pious because no man would look at her twice I hope I'll never be like her....'

"Yes...now, clusterfuck magnifique...yes...somebody's gotta take the fricking fall...gotta...gotta. I got this. Yes. I do. Who built it? Yes, I built it. Who did it? Yes, I did it. Guilt, blame, responsibility, culpability – all the right words. My words, too. It's all poultry.

"Oh, what a world, what a world...world goes away...world a-slay...when you sin. When you do the unspeakable, it's speakable. Yes. All sin, sin all the time. Yes. Sin. Yes. All scenarios worst scenarios. Yes. This is the way humans hew...this is the way humans hew. Hew human hell. Everybody looks the other way. Everybody is nobody but fools. Everybody is a body. This way, that way: fast, phony, no way, way out. Way, way. Yes. This way.

"No one believes me. Totally blew it. Everything is wrong and broken. What if it gets worse. These days. These recognitions.

"'...yes because he couldnt possibly do without it that long so he must do it somewhere and the last time he came on my bottom... he says your soul you have no soul inside only grey matter because he doesnt know what it is to have one yes when I lit the lamp yes because he must have come 3 or 4 times with that tremendous big red brute of a thing he has I thought the vein or whatever the dickens they call it was going to burst though his nose is not so big after I took off all my things with the blinds down after my hours dressing and perfuming and combing it like iron or some kind of a thick crowbar standing all the time he must have eaten oysters I think a few dozen he was in great singing voice no I never in all my life felt anyone had one the size of that to make you feel full up he must have eaten a whole sheep after whats the idea making us like that with a big hole in the middle of us like a Stallion driving it up into you because thats all they want out of you with that determined vicious look in his eye...nice invention they made for women for him to get all the pleasure but if someone gave them a touch of it themselves theyd know what I went through...'"

Douglas crossed the stage to Dik Dik, as the voice droned on. He said, "Well, there's your Bloomsday. When the hurly-burly's done! We're gonna get our stuff and vamoose."

Lise, standing next to Dik Dik, said, "I love the banner."

Dik Dik looked baffled, bullied – tragic. "One more piece, *Penelope*."

Douglas groaned. "Man, you've been usurped."

Moriah, who had rolled up the banner, stepped toward them, banner poles straight up like lances. "She's got this. She's doing *Penelope*. It fits. I guess. This is what you wanted: the community engaged. The community surrealized."

Lise didn't like it. She gazed at the clock tower and began to loom. "Looks dangerous up there."

Johnny wandered over to comfort Lorna's boys. He called, "You guys! What's wrong, you guys? What's going on? You gotta take it easy."

Lorna's boys started hiccoughing, "Yes!" "Yes." "Yes!"

Tiffany followed Johnny. She could tell the boys were really falling apart. "What is it?" she asked. "What is Lorna going to do?"

"Yes, yes," was the only reply.

Dik Dik heard a dog howl. A cat screeched. Another dog howled. He heard his old tree friends – a pomegranate, a quince, a fig, weeping, but it must have been echoes from the boys' sobbing. Trees must get sick of humans.

Jackal charged up the steps to the park, ran over to the stage. "You guys," she panted, "see what's going on? I was over at the Yard when it started. Everybody's going to check it out. The grand finale. You think she'll jump? The cops don't know what to do. Come on – we should get down there. You can't hardly hear her from here. This is it, bro's, the cum like a dump truck."

"'...compared with what a man looks like with his two bags full and his other thing hanging down out of him or sticking up at you like a hatrack no wonder they hide it with a cabbageleaf the woman is beauty of course thats admitted...'"

The police were quick to block the narrow road which fronted the Matewan building. Though the sirens had stopped, dogs still howled. Policemen hurried back and forth, to keep people back, away from hurriedly set lines. Captain Rodriguez and a plainclothesman came out of the Matewan building, looking pensive. People yelled up to Lorna, thinking it was a joke. Some kind of prank. Someone asked what she was doing. A few told her not to jump. Others jeered, running with the riff. Community big shots coagulated, wondering what the hell. They talked about negotiators and psychologists. With serious demeanors. Finally, one of them suggested to Captain Rodriguez a bullhorn. Apparently, you couldn't get close to her without her threatening to jump. They needed some way to talk to her. An officer was dispatched for one.

The crowds on either end of the road replicated, transcripted, mutated as word got out. The Bloomsday gang made it over, Dik Dik with his backpack and sack of materials. Bear had to take off on account of the dogs getting agitated, sensing the humans' great turmoil – and fear. Lise looked scared and exhausted. Johnny was open mouthed, staring up at Lorna. He and Tiffany held hands and didn't even know it. Dik Dik saw that the crowd at the other side from where he stood included the film crew. They were filming away. Director and Willow full of feathers. Over there, too, Tim, the Jackal, Tilman itself. Voices whispered, confided, built up, all eyes stuck on the clock face artist.

"Somebody has to go talk to her."

"'...theres real beauty and poetry for you I often felt I wanted to kiss him all over also his lovely young cock there so simple I wouldnt mind taking him in my mouth if nobody was looking as if it was asking you to suck it so clean and white he looked with his boyish face I would too in 1/2 a minute even if some of it went down what its only like gruel or the dew theres no danger besides hed be so clean compared with those pigs of men I suppose never dream of washing it from 1 years end...'"

Captain Rodriguez with a bullhorn walked out to the cleared space right in front of the building. He raised the bullhorn.

"Lorna, this is Captain Rodriguez. Lorna, we're worried it's not safe up there. Please get back inside. I really have to insist. I've got officers right there who'll help you get back inside. Okay? Will you do that?"

Lorna stopped what she was doing, a screed of improv, rhymes, puns, stories, chunks from *Penelope*, to screech, "Anybody come near me before I'm done, I jump."

"Lorna, what are you doing up there? What do you want? You could get hurt."

"This is a performance. I'm almost done."

"Lorna, what you're doing is illegal, you broke into the building. Besides being dangerous. You're creating a public disturbance. No time for a performance right now. I think we better cut the power, and stop this performance right now."

"Cut my mic, I jump."

The electric pitch of their voices tossed back and forth, up and down, batted about like bats.

"How do we know you won't do that anyway? No, Lorna, this ends now." He waited for a response. When none came, he said, "Lorna, is there someone you wanna talk to?"

"'...the day I got him to propose to me yes first I gave him the bit of seedcake out of my mouth and it was leapyear like now yes 16 years ago my God after that long kiss I near lost my breath yes he said I was a flower of the mountain yes so we are flowers all a womans body yes that was one true thing he said in his life and the sun shines for you today yes that was why I liked him because I saw he understood or felt what a woman is and I knew I could always get round him and I gave him all the pleasure I could leading him on till he asked me to say yes....'

"No one believes me. Everything is broken. Worse, it's wrong."

"Lorna, please let us help you. You can't be up there. Lorna, you have to come down."

A policeman hurried over to the captain. He whispered,

"Firetruck's on the way."

He and the captain walked to the side where other officers waited.

Dik Dik pushed his way through the crowd, to the policemen holding them back. "I think I can talk to her," he said.

The policeman tsked, squinted, told him to back up.

Dik Dik called out, "Captain, I know her. I was her teacher. I can talk to her."

The captain walked over, rubbing his mouth with his hand. The chief recognized Dik Dik. "I suppose you're as good as any other. Keep her talking. See if you can calm her. Firetruck is on the way." He turned to his men. "Take this guy in. Tell the people inside he can go on up."

Dik Dik entered the old building with his escort, who promptly explained where he could stash his stuff and find the stairs. An officer led the way.

He'd always thought *Penelope* was sad. A stilted affirmation that ended up a giving in. Will without purpose brewed ugly. Banality avoided the light. American artists didn't understand that. For them, giving in was madness as exploration. Some kind of affirmation?

...a pleasure sure in being mad, which only madmen knew....

Dik Dik had never been in the building. The lower floors were offices. The stairway became narrow and filthy as they ascended. Smaller and filthier, it became. Now he felt he was going up a chimney. The officer let him pass, to continue on his way alone.

Oh, human confusion! Pain, pain, more pain. *Lorna, Queen of Pain!*

Locusts upon us. Locusts upon us.

First giraffe. First giraffe.

He was old, exhausted, he had to pee, he needed a double espresso.

What should he do?

Going to the top. Horror of human extremity. Going all the way. Grim salutations. Bloomsday damned.

Now high. What do you call the top of a bell tower? He was in the *belfry*. Crammed with sound equipment, the bells' amps, and two men with ropes. Bloody cowboys and their lariats. Were they going to lasso her?

Ammonia smell! Bats and chemical warfare. Filthy attic space with a small open window with the little amp in it.

One of the cops, a young fellow, scrunched in a corner, said, "What we do is put ropes on me, anchored in here, I go through the window, grab her. You pull me back in."

Another cop, older, fatter, went "I saw that on TV. Riddick, it was."

Dik Dik said, "What do I do?"

The fat cop said, "We move the amp, you stick your head out. Talk to her. Lady's upset. Try to get her in. Don't worry, we'll grab you if anything happens."

The young cop took care of the amp, gently moving it aside. Dik Dik hunkered to the rectangle of light. He leaned his head out.

There she was! So close, somebody could grab her! But hanging by a thread, hanging by her toenails.

"Young lady, the game is done! Kaput. It's too dangerous, Lorna. This breaks the back of performance. You made your point."

No mic – she said to him, "Are you finished? Can I say something now? Put the amp back out. It's Bloomsday, fool. It's all your fault. It's all for you. A spectacular ending! Ha! If you believe that crap, you're a bigger fool than I thought. It is all for me."

"What are you doing, Lorna?"

"What I was meant to do."

"Lorna, you have kids. You have to break character. You have to think about this. You could hurt yourself...hurt your family."

"Oh, that's good. You never break character. Oh, Obi-wan, you're the only one who can help me."

"Lorna, you did it! You out-freaked-out us all. You proved you're the master. You win."

"Oh, you're just saying that. Isn't there a commandment about Coltrane compliments? The proper response is *fuck you.*"

"Lorna, you're done. Come back inside?"

"I can't, Dik. I've done horrible things. Questionable things. I've seen faces in rapture at poetry events. I've seen hearts swell and break at performances. The great and awesome coming together when it works. All those memories will be gone –"

"The performance must transform. The performer is the winner. You've done it. You've proven it. You have to come in. It's the only thing that makes sense."

Dik Dik shuffled around, trying to get comfortable in his niche. All he could see was her side, her right side. Torso all in silver, silver right arm, and her right leg – silver. Her right hand clutched the slim trim she hung from. He could only see the right side of her face. When she did turn to face him, he saw full face: her face – face, its blackness bleakness was total despair. It was in her black eyes, the black set of her mouth. The black vision she was left with.

The guys behind him whispered for him to hurry.

The whole universe was giving up, giving in.

"Lorna, I beg you, come back."

"No back to come to. Please, put the amp up, let me finish."

Dik Dik heard a voice mumble *firetruck* then *ladder.* Didn't they have those special tarpaulins to catch people? All the firemen holding it taut in a circle like a trampoline. He came in, managed to get the amp back in place.

"'...O that awful deepdown torrent O and the sea the sea crimson sometimes like fire and the glorious sunsets and the figtrees in the Alameda gardens yes and all the queer little streets and pink and blue and yellow houses and the rosegardens and the jessamine and geraniums and cactuses and Gibraltar as a girl where I was a Flower of the mountain yes when I put the rose in my hair like the Andalusian girls used or shall I wear a red yes and how he kissed me under the Moorish wall and I thought well as well him as another and then I asked him with my eyes to ask again yes and then he asked me would I yes to say yes my mountain flower and first I put my arms around him yes and drew him down to me so he could feel my breasts all perfume yes and his heart was going like mad and yes I said yes I will Yes...'"

Born in 1951 in the Ozarks, Chris Dietz *is a writer, teacher, and a birdwatcher. Currently, he lives in Bisbee, Arizona, surviving a catastrophe.*

Made in the USA
Las Vegas, NV
08 June 2021

24415615R00135